Police Wit
Stop!

by

David Ryan

Dog Secrets Publishing

www.dog-secrets.co.uk

United Kingdom 2017

i

First published in Great Britain by Dog Secrets Publishing, 2017

www.dog-secrets.co.uk

Copyright © 2017 by David Ryan

ISBN 978-0-244-31939-7

Dedicated to every dog that has had to put up with a human. You all have my utmost sympathy. It can't have been easy.

Police With a Dog Stop!

Introduction by David Ryan

This isn't my story but the background is mine, so I'd better fill it in for you. In 1981 I was one of the youngest Cumbrian policemen to be accepted onto the Dog Section. I was twenty five years old, had six years of police service under my belt and was considered a stripling.

I'd walked the beat in Barrow-in-Furness, witnessing first-hand the decline of the UK ship-building industry with the knock-on effect on the local economy and crime. The reports of burglaries where the only money taken was from the electricity meter rose in direct proportion to the lay-offs at the shipyard. Often a window was broken to add to the authenticity. Frequently the broken glass was to be found on the ground *outside* the window... times were hard.

When I married a pretty young nurse they moved me the length of the county to the small market town of Wigton, predominantly the hub of a farming community but with one plastics-making factory that gave the whole area its characteristic chemical aroma. Wigton too had its share of what we now consider to be the socially disadvantaged, but who we knew then to be layabouts, scroungers, drunks and thieves.

It wasn't unique, just another small town where the weekend's entertainment was twelve pints and a punch-up in the street, with the prospect of a spot of domestic violence and a chip-pan fire at home later. And that was just the ladies. Petty thievery was rife, with the only honour being that they would screw each other's houses and nick each other's cars, as well as those of complete strangers - true social egalitarianism.

The country houses on the outskirts were targets for more serious criminals from Carlisle in the wee small hours. Scroats who weren't

1

averse to resorting to violence and travelled in small gangs, usually in stolen cars they would later burn out. The night shift at Wigton consisted of one officer after 1am, and the nearest help was at least fifteen minutes away and sometimes more. Fortunately your average scroat is a creature that is more frightened of us than we are of them... unless cornered and about to lose their liberty.

When the alarm was raised by a householder we would call for whatever assistance was available on our way there, and quite often a dog handler would arrive in a slightly battered unmarked van that was rocking to the sound of deep bass barking. He would have a quick look around to make sure they were gone (which they inevitably were), and then shoot off to his next job, looking for richer pickings to enhance his prisoner-count for the month. 'Elite' had not yet become a dirty word in the police.

Having already applied for the Dog Section several times and been knocked back to, 'gain more experience of working alone', I bagged myself a country beat at Ireby, which is just past the back of beyond in the picturesque northern fells, and had settled into the police station there with Sue and our young family, occasionally digging ourselves out of the snow, resigned to wait my turn to fill a dead dog-handler's shoes, when the call came... they were clearly desperate.

It was a time of recession, with the highest unemployment in the UK since the depression of the 1930s and rampant inflation; a time of industrial strikes, of civil unrest with riots in every major city and much copycatting in minor ones too.

Welsh Nationalists were burning holiday homes, the IRA bombing campaign was approaching its height, and the UK was soon to fight Argentina over the Falklands. St Pauls, Toxteth, Brixton, Handsworth and Chapeltown had literally burned through deprivation, resentment and racial tension. Combat seemed to be in the air, and we fought our own battles inside and outside pubs and clubs most nights.

If you think that the army is under-equipped you should try wading into a rumble of thirty steaming drunk Young Farmers, on your own, armed with a bit of stick in your trouser pocket and a radio that worked less often than British Leyland... and now they call them 'the good old days'.

But in moving from Ireby to Carlisle Dog Section I went from being the sheriff of my own patch - the only law for miles around - to being a sprog again. Most dog handlers had done ten or more years before joining the elite - it was considered an appointment for very experienced officers. Many came from the Traffic Department to be rehabilitated and integrated back into society. And a sprog must prove himself...

I've done a bit since I started out hunting thieves and burglars in the back streets, and battling with fighters and hard men on the front streets. Twenty six years handling, with the latter fifteen instructing others as well. I passed my Home Office accredited instructing courses and worked with general purpose, public disorder, firearms support, cash, drugs, firearms detection and explosives search dogs. After eleven years at the pointy end, being elevated to the dizzy heights of explaining to others how to do it was a relief to get off night-shifts, quick turn-arounds and call-outs.

But, back to 1981. Of course, I could never betray the confidences of the giants upon whose shoulders I stood; legendary handlers and dogs; hard dogs and harder men*; so nothing in this tale can be regarded as anything other than fiction. And as I said, this isn't my story, just a story of my time...

---

* Sorry girls, they were all men in those days - feminism had not yet struck dog handling - although we weren't too sexist not to work with some very nasty bitches.

The dry ditch is dampened by the heavy morning dew and each outer hair on my coat sports its own tiny droplet of water, giving me a ghostly sheen in the lamplight. Noddy, the lump of a human lying next to me in full waterproofs, endures the stiffness in his joints that comes from lying in one place for too long and passes wind, he thinks, silently.

Waterproof the trousers may be, but scent-proof they are not. I groan in sensitive disapproval. Dawn's not yet broken but we know the place well. We've been here every night for the past week. It's a great hide. We can scan the whole of the school field, which on three sides leads onto the back gardens of a large portion of the estate. An estate that has suffered over thirty break-ins since last summer.

We know our prey well, too. He enters by drilling a hole with a small hand awl below the catch in the window and flicks the latch up before climbing through. He works alone and takes only cash and small jewellery. I've tracked him through the grounds of the school before, but always the morning after, when he was long gone. He wears size seven Adidas trainers, from the prints we've seen, and cotton shirts, jeans and an army surplus camo jacket, from the smell they leave. He doesn't smoke and although he sometimes goes to thieve soon after a curry, he is never drunk. I can't quite pick up his job, but it's not something obvious, like a butcher or a baker; more of an office job involving paper. Smell can tell me a lot about prey. It also tells me that he's afraid whilst he breaks in, but not too much to stop. That's why we know he'll be back, and why we've lain in a ditch for a week of nights.

I hear the flick of the window latch and sit up to get my ears aligned for the next noise. I give a low growl to tell Noddy and he peers over the rim of the ditch, following my gaze. I can feel his heartbeat quicken and his need to ask, 'Where is he?' We both wait in silence for fully ten minutes staring at the back of two possible houses about seventy-five yards away, directly opposite us. Seventy-five yards is five seconds

4

from a standing start. Please the gods, let him come out the back. Adrenalin builds; we both know it's him and we're having him this time.

Noddy talks into his radio, sending cars to the edge of the estate, but not so close that some thick Plod will drive past and spook him. I can hear them arriving, but the prey won't. I'd like us to be closer, but as soon as we stand up we'll be silhouetted against the streetlights. I start to quiver in anticipation. Come on!

Another soft click as the back door shuts behind him and a creak as he climbs the garden fence into our field. Noddy rolls onto his stomach and slips one cold but sweaty hand through my collar.

Under his breath he's chanting, 'Police with a dog! Stop! Stop or I'll send the dog! Police with a dog! Stop! Stop or I'll send the dog!' over and over. But it's more for his benefit than mine. I don't need any priming. I'm having this one.

In the murky light I can see the slight figure start away from the fence to cut the diagonal across towards the back of the school. He'll have cash and jewellery on him. Bang to rights. Still the whispered chant, 'Police with a dog! Stop! Stop or I'll send the dog!'

I pull into the collar against his hand. Now! I'm ready! Come on! Noddy bursts upright and stumbles forwards, finding his feet with 'Hold him, son!' whispered in my ear before he straightens up, and I'm flying across the field with him lumbering behind. Time stands still. I'm an arrow zeroing in, eyes slits, ears flat, feet hardly touching the ground. He's dead meat. Halfway there and he looks up, but it's too late as Noddy at last lets rip,

'POLICE WITH A DOG! STOP! STOP OR I'LL SEND THE DOG!'

Gerr-off! What? Oh, it's you. Sorry, I was dreaming about the good old days. No need to prod me awake though. Back then you'd have been lucky to get within six feet of me, and if you'd reached to touch me you'd be trying to dial for an ambulance with the stumps of bloody fingers by now.

Yeah, yeah, yeah, I know. You want to find out about being a police dog. Well, let me tell you, you've come to the right canine cop. Just let me make myself comfortable. Not so easy these days with my arthritic hips... my old Mum's fault apparently, her hip score* was 8:12 but she was a bit of a looker and the Kennel Club says it's okay if you're below the breed average. Don't know what the Kennel Club know about it though, they haven't got the constant agony.

Anyway Dad's Teutonic ancestry made it a heavenly match and Bob's your uncle. Except in my case, when Axelrod-vom-Getwildersteinburger-The-Third is your uncle – it says so on my pedigree.

Hang on a bit, while I edge closer to the fire, they don't seem as warm as they used to be. Ahh, that's better. Just give that shoulder a rub would you? Bit dodgy, that right shoulder. Every time you grab a right arm and swing round it stretches the joint. Do that several times a week over your working lifetime and no wonder it aches. Don't talk to me about repetitive strain injuries. I reckon it's going to rain. Ooo, that's nice, just down a bit... don't mind me leaning on you, do you?

It's about time someone wrote this down; there's not many of us old-timers left and the youngsters these days don't know the first thing about doing a proper dog job. They pose around with cameras on their heads... In my day if you wanted an armed criminal confronting, it was teeth that got the job done, not taking pictures then hiding behind some numpty with a baseball cap and an automatic rifle.

Mind you, it's not just the dogs that have gone to the dogs, the whole job has. Health and Safety, proportionate use of force, Human Rights...What about Canine Rights? What about Sub-human Rights for

---

* German Shepherd Dogs suffer from hip dysplasia, an inherited tendency for the ball of the femur not to fit the socket of the pelvis. We can be X-rayed and scored out for each hip 0:0 up to 53:53 (who can't stand up). Mum's score was above the GSD average – gods only know what mine is, I haven't been scored.

Dog Handlers? I've heard in America they have a right to bare arms. Now that's what I call proper consideration. There's nothing worse than a mouthful of puffa jacket when you were hoping to taste blood.

And the paperwork! Any police dog lucky enough to get a bite has to sit around in the back of the van for the next four hours whilst their handler fills in report after report. I know that's only two reports, but handlers aren't exactly the sharpest tooth in the jaw. I thought things would improve when they went from joined-up writing to typing on a computer, but they're just as bad at that. If only keyboards were big enough for paws we'd be done in half the time.

We'd still need handlers, though. How would we get to jobs? We can't exactly drive ourselves; the minimum driving age is seventeen for all the gods' sake! Mind you, you can't call what most handlers do 'driving', it's more 'pressing the accelerator and avoiding things that come at you'.

Ah, for the days when dogs can type and drive, eh? We'd rule the world. Still, that's all in the future, and it's the past that you want to hear about. Got plenty of pencils?

🐾🐾🐾🐾

Where shall I start...? Born in the under-stairs cupboard, third son of Belle of the Ball Whilpington-Smythe and, along with Magnum, Magna, Magic, Macbeth, Maestro, Mable and Marcie, the proud progeny of Aaron vom Getwildersteinburger, Schutzhund 1 (failed), grandson of Zilda vom Getwildersteinburger, Schutzhund 3, Sieger.

'Sieger' is German for 'champion', and my granddaddy was one of the best. Dad would have made it too, but for his duelling scars. Had a bit of a mean streak, my dad. Got into a lot of bother as a youngster. His real downfall was biting the judge in his first qualifying test. As Dad used to say, '*NOBODY touches me there without warming his hands!*' Some say blood's thicker than water. It's tastier, too.

7

It was the time when British breeders of German Shepherds realised what a schweineohr they had made and were importing continental stock to get back to the proper working strains, but they didn't quite yet know what they were doing. Old Ma Whilpington-Smythe thought she had a nice looking bitch in our Mum and used a reject with a good line as her swain, hoping to get the best from both.

Dad had blown his chance of stud fees at home in Germany by failing to qualify in his Schutzhund - a requirement to be allowed to breed there - but was snapped up at a bargain price to be brought to the UK where, because of his heritage, he was much sought after.

Ma Whilpington-Smythe reeked like a tweedy old mothball that no amount of liberally-sprinkled lavender-water could disguise but, in that upper-class English slightly-befuddled-but-rabidly-financially-astute way, she was a shrewd cookie. She recouped Dad's cost many times through stud fees in Blighty.

Dad had a pretty good time too.

My litter was therefore a dodgy mixture of English beauty and Teutonic vigour, but it would be wrong of me not to say that I was, and still am, a fine example of both.

At eight weeks old I adopted a young couple, just married. To be fair, Mum was sick of the lot of us and I was fed up of winning the King of the Castle contests. Several people had come to see us and if I didn't like the look of them I'd hang back, or bite their fingers if they came close enough, so they'd choose one of the others. I picked Don and Marie because they looked soft, all coo-ing and simpering, and boy, was I right. Wetter 'n a bloodhound's nostrils.

Life at their place was a doddle. Didn't matter what I did, so long as I followed it with my 'cute puppy' look. I tried out a few things, like ripping up the sofa, chewing the legs of the antique dresser bequeathed to them by great aunt Christine, and pooping in Don's shoes. If I looked cute when they came back in, they thought I'd done it because I was missing them, and if I widdled on the floor they got really upset and blamed themselves. Great fun.

They picked up the basics very quickly, but I was a good teacher. Like on the first day when they gave me dog food and I refused to eat it until they put fresh chicken on top. I soon had a protection racket going where I would grab hold of electric cables or shoes and refuse to let go until they paid me off with something really tasty, and I made the postman give me bits of sausage to stop me tearing lumps out of him.

Both Don and Marie worked, so they felt really guilty about leaving me on my own, and provided lots of doggie toys for me to play with. Obviously I played with them all day, but then put them back in their exact places and shredded the curtains, or chewed the skirting boards. I wasn't actually bothered about being on my own, truth is I've always been comfortable with my own company, but I liked to work their guilt trip something rotten. It was my own way of getting them back for all the cuddling. I was their baby and I could get away with murder, quite literally in the case of three of Marie's treasured collection of teddy bears, a doll left behind the sofa by their niece, and their pet rabbit, Mr Benjamin Bunny-Wunny, who lived in a pen in the garden.

Mr Bunny-Wunny didn't actually have a checked waistcoat and a pocket watch, but you'd have thought he did, the way they talked to him. I mean, how stupid can you get, talking to a rabbit like it cares what you say? Anyway, turns out the dumb bunny couldn't run very fast either and what started as an innocent game of 'Run Rabbit Run' came to an abrupt end as he keeled over when I caught him.

I'd played the game a thousand times with my brothers and sisters and this had never happened before. How was I to know Benji had a dicky ticker? I tried mouth to mouth resuscitation. I tried chest compressions. I tried throwing him up in the air and pouncing on him.

Nothing worked. He was a dead rabbit. What could I do to make it up to Marie? I ate him, trashed his pen and blamed a passing fox.

Every night that week I barked ferociously at the back door, as though I had sensed something in the garden, and Don ran out with a torch, shouting, 'Get away, pesky fox!' then gave me a biscuit. Don was the kind of person who thought 'pesky' was a swear word.

This taught me a valuable lesson that came in very useful later, as a police dog. If you are in trouble, cover it up the best you can, and then blame someone else. If you are convincing enough you can get away with anything.

Outdoors was great once I'd trained them to throw a ball for as long as I wanted. All I had to do was drop it at their feet and they'd throw it again! If I thought they needed a bit more exercise, I'd keep hold of it and tease them until they chased me.

Whining at the door got me a walk and, if they were reluctant to take me, I'd go behind the sofa and widdle. Next time I whined at the door they moved pretty quickly!

They were loath to let me off the lead at first in the park, but I refused to, 'Go pee-pees' on the lead and again, to give them their due, they were quick to pick up the rules when I gushed forth as soon as we got home. From that sprang an arrangement where I let them shout and whistle as much as they liked, and I came back when I felt like it.

As I grew stronger I spent most of my time off the lead because they couldn't hold me, so I always had the opportunity for seeing off other dogs. Dogs can be a bit pushy, especially the ones that have been around a patch for a while. They think they own the place so if you're ever going to amount to anything you can't let them take advantage. A little tip for the youngsters reading: never take the first bite. Always incite them into attacking you, then you can batter them in self-defence.

I had this mean look that could be relied upon to provoke them. I would stand as tall as I could, ears proud, hair like a Mohican, tail stiff as a board and one lip curled Elvis-style. Every inch of me said, 'Come and have a go if you think you're hard enough.' It was a slap in the face to every self-respecting mutt I ever met. They would start with, 'Who you lookin' at?' and I would stand impassive, daring them to make a play. Eventually they would either bottle it and walk away, followed by my low grumble of, 'Loooseeeer', or they would build themselves up into a berserk frenzy. That was a bigger mistake, because they didn't have the benefit of my ancestry.

Duelling runs in my family like blood from a spaniel's ears. 'Red in tooth and claw' could have been our motto. If I say so myself, I was big, I was fast and I was prepared to go the distance. It also helped that I was as black as the coalhouse door (although with handsome gold markings). They were psychologically on the road to defeat before I'd even started. We'd practised all the moves back at Mum's place. Shoulder barges, ruff grabs and ear rips were usually enough to sort out the pretenders, but if things got really dirty I could pull out the joint-ringing, throat rips and eviscerating tactics of proper fighters.

At fourteen weeks old I bloodied my first Staffy (too slow) with not a mark on me, and in the next six months took over the neighbourhood in a bloodless coup. Well, it was bloodless for me.

For most of them, all I had to do was cock my leg and they'd wet themselves, but my final amateur bout was against a Labrador-Boxer cross. He liked to think he had a bit of the fighting dog about him, and he was a big brute who'd seen off some smaller dogs.

We'd been eyeing each other up for some time, but he wasn't off the lead very often and always got dragged away before I could introduce myself.

This particular day Don was early to work so I was taken out for a run sooner than usual. I used to like that because it meant that I got to

11

meet the so called hard cases that people couldn't control in public, so they walked them on their leads in the middle of the night. The Midnight Cowboys always thought they were special and would make a great play of roaring challenges at each other, safe in the knowledge that their owners would haul them away.

The morning sun was behind me just breaking the horizon through the trees on the edge of the park, and the gentle westerly breeze was in my favour, so I scented him first.

As I sauntered across, blacker than my silhouette and casting a long shadow in front of me, I could smell his testosterone mingling with the fear in his little old lady walker, because she'd seen what he was trying to make out: his nemesis. He was standing stock still, peering towards me, seeing the movement but not the form, straining his nose against the wind trying to collect some information about the black hole gliding his way.

His little old lady turned to go, heaving on the lead with all her tiny might, but Samson stood his ground, dug his paws in, then flipped backwards so his collar plopped over his head. His little old lady fell undignified on her derriere, just as I came into Sammy's focus.

I could just faintly hear a panicky Don in the distance, 'Major, No!' and 'Come here now!' But I was already in the zone. I chose my ground in open field, just to the left of the penalty box, keeping my advantage of sun and wind. I stretched tall, hackles like a razor and all canines gleaming; tail a feathered mast quivering stiffly. Little-old-lady was wailing like a trodden-on kitten as Sam came on.

No preliminaries, no pretending to sniff the bottom or standing with his head over my shoulders. He was straight in with a shoulder charge, using his superior weight to best advantage. Although I half side-stepped because the sun was in his eyes, it still knocked the wind out of me. I spun round to see him at the height of his turn, coming back for a second charge. But I knew the tactic this time. He was trying to get me down and stay on his own feet, so a nanosecond before he hit me I went to the ground, and saw the delight in his eyes before he realised his momentum had toppled him over me, and as he rolled I was on him, straight for his throat.

Neither of us had a secure footing and teeth clashed as he fended me away, still rolling out of control. Being the lummox he was, I was on my feet first, but he grabbed at my foreleg and I went down on top of him, dropping my shoulder into his ribs. He wildly slashed the air and split my left ear. I still carry the scar today, but to make it he lifted his head and I caught his bottom jaw in a good grip, shaking it terrier-fashion. It wasn't a killing hold, but it hurt him and kept him on his back until he raked at me with his back legs and I had to pull away, jumping lightly to one side.

He scrambled to his feet and stood there, panting with exertion and adrenaline, bleeding from the face. We circled slowly, staring each other out, looking for a weakness. This probably wasn't a good time to notice that I was still a kid and he was a good three inches taller and twenty pounds heavier than me but, even so, I knew I could take him.

I could hear Don lumbering up behind me and I needed this finished once and for all. This wasn't going to be a stalemate. I went over the top for the back of his neck and got a solid mouthful, puncturing with all four canines and ripping backwards to drop him on his side, but he wasn't done yet and turned inside his skin for a slash at my shoulder, gouging a line down the muscle with a fang as he went down. But now he was on his back, and his throat was mine.

I was on him like a stoat, full mouth bite and shake, pinning him to the floor. All he could do was try to wrestle his way out of it, but each time he moved I moved with him, standing over, still shaking him, now growling uncontrollably as I could feel his struggles becoming feebler and feebler.

The whole fight had taken about six seconds and I was surging with anger and youthful testosterone. Is it any wonder I snapped when I felt a hand on my collar? It could have been anybody!

It wasn't of course, it was Don.

That's how I came to join the police... and Don came to have puncture wounds through his hand and spend four hours in casualty.

Nowadays, the politicians that run the police like to think of it as a 'service'. That was never the case for me. I joined the police <u>force</u> not some namby-pamby wishy-washy lovey-dovey, 'It's not their fault they just need a cuddle' service. If I'd wanted to make the world a better place by offering tea and sympathy I'd have joined the Women's Institute. I enlisted to stop bad people taking advantage of good people. To lock them up and teach them that stealing, robbing people, breaking into their houses or battering them, is naughty.

If you want to take a social worker view of it, think of prison as a naughty step for big people. With a concrete floor. And a toilet with no lid over in the corner. Shared with a large bearded biker who likes to call you 'Shirley'. For a very long time. But I didn't know about all that the day the Plod knocked on Don and Marie's door.

You could tell it was Plod by the knock. It's not a, 'Hello...? Is there anybody in...?' inquisitive tap. They have an authoritative pounding that says, 'I want to speak to you and this bloody door is in my way. Open it up.'

I, of course, responded with my best deep throated bellow that made him hesitate for just a split second, framed in the open doorway beyond Marie as she opened it.

'Let him go,' he told Don, who I was slowly but surely dragging along the hallway, his grip on my collar loosening in his clammy hands. The tension released me like a giant rubber band, propelling me into Plod's chest with a thud.

14

'Ho-Ho-Ho!' he laughed like some fairground caricature, which cheesed me off a bit, because my friendly greetings usually resulted in shrieks and yells of 'Get 'im orf!' I was about to re-launch from floor level when a meaty hand thumped down twice on the top of my head with a 'Good, lad. That's better!' Strangely, I quite liked that. This could be a bloke I could get on with. As I leapt up again to register my approval by nutting him on the jaw, the big hand came down on my head again, stopping me short and leaving me in a heap on the floor.

'Gooood lad!' and he ruffled my ears.

I followed him to the sofa and when he sat down I climbed onto his knee. He immediately stood up and I found myself on the floor again. I tried again. He stood up again. He didn't look at me or speak to me, chatting all the time to Don and Marie. Five times I tried to climb on his knee and five times he ignored me and stood up. This was getting us nowhere.

He seemed to be a particularly slow learner, so I stopped for a minute to consider how best to teach him how he could get on with me, and the big hand came down to my head and ruffled behind my ears ever so gently. He still wasn't looking at me, so I gave the big hand a nudge with my nose and it immediately disappeared, but came back fondling my neck when I stopped the nudging.

Now he was getting it. I'd inadvertently trained him to stroke me when I sat still. Lucky for him he wasn't very quick on the uptake.

Most of what Don was saying was rubbish, just, 'Blah-blah blood everywhere...blah-blah eleven stitches...blah-blah nearly lost the use of my thumb...blah-blah can't handle him any more...' when he was interrupted by Plod.

'Does he retrieve?'

Don and Marie looked nervously at each other, then a tentative, 'Well, he sometimes doesn't bring it back.'

'Has he got a favourite toy?' and three minutes later we were all in

15

the back garden with Winnie the Pooh, a solid rubber ball, a screwdriver and a lump of sacking.

Okay, so my favourite toy was Winnie the Pooh. D'you wanna make something of it? Plod threw Winnie down the garden and I rushed after it, grabbed it and turned to look at him. He was on his hands and knees, clapping, whistling and trilling, 'Major' in a silly voice. Completely forgetting about Winnie in my mouth, I galloped back to see what he was doing.

'Goooood laaad.'

Winnie was whipped out of my teeth before I could say 'Hundred Acre Wood' and a red rubber ball waved in my face. The next five minutes was more fun than treeing a cat. The ball careered around the garden, bouncing off plant-pots and under bushes, closely followed by me bounding after it.

Every time I brought it back, he would throw it again, but not just toss it over my head like Don did. It would spin past or under my legs, or whiz off the garage wall. I never knew where it would be next.

I'd never been so excited in a chase game before. I was reaching fever pitch when the ball went into his pocket and Plod held my collar. He whizzed a nine-inch screwdriver down the garden. As it skidded to a halt he let me go and I pounded after it. It smelled strange, so I gave it the once-over before tentatively gripping it by the handle. It hung out of my mouth at a peculiar angle and I wasn't really happy with it, but I could tell this meant a lot to him, and he'd been so much fun I didn't want to let him down.

If I thought he'd been giddy before, this time he really went overboard, whooping and hollering encouragement as I tottered in a half circle back towards him, with this encumbrance dangling from my teeth.

He grabbed at the metal end and corkscrewed the ball past me. I gave chase and proudly carried it back. I knew I'd done well. I'd passed a test. I didn't know why, but it seemed important.

As he took the ball this time - I'd decided to give it to him to make my life a bit easier - he held my collar again.

'Just hold him for a mo,' he told Don, and strode off down the garden. When he was halfway down he tossed the ball up in the air several times, calling, 'Major, what's this?' He was quite excitable for a big bloke.

Then he dived under a bush and hid the ball there, or at least he thought he had. Actually he still had it when he reappeared and hid it under the next bush. By the time he'd not hidden it under four or five bushes, I hadn't a clue where it was. But I knew how to find out.

He came rushing up the garden and took my collar from Don.

'Where is it, son?' he urged and let me go.

In three seconds flat I'd scented it out. How difficult did they think it was? A rubber ball in the garden? Piece of cake. No, really. A rubber ball in the garden smells as strong as a warm cake in the kitchen. As I dropped it back into his hand he was whooping and laughing, but it went into the pocket again.

'I probably needn't bother with this, but just for the sake of putting the result on the form, I'll give him a go.'

At that he produced a piece of sacking from inside his jacket and waved it in my face. Cheeky arsch! I turned the other cheek, but he waved it again. There's only so much lip I'll take, so I grabbed the rag and pulled it off him, except he didn't let go. I pulled harder and he came with me. I dug in and tugged with all my might, but he was a heavyweight and I could only budge him a few inches at a time.

Eventually we reached a stalemate with neither of us shifting, but I wasn't letting go first. He laughed and released his end. Winning is a great buzz, and I trotted triumphantly round the garden with my trophy. He bounced the ball and I got so excited I dropped the rag and rushed over. He plopped it into my mouth and uttered the phrase that secured my future, 'Sold to the man in the black jacket!'

What is it with humans and paperwork? Papers were produced and signatures added. My pedigree was stuffed in an envelope with them, and my lead handed to the Plod. He gave Don the lead back and went out the front door for a minute, before returning with a proper lead; one that smelled of leather and saddle soap. It was six feet long with two brass clips, and folded over on itself. The other end clipped to my collar.

'We'll be in touch, but I don't envisage any problems,' the Plod told Don as they shook hands.

'Off you go with the nice policeman,' Marie said.

I didn't need any encouragement. This was the most fun bloke I'd ever met.

We strode out of the door and in one swift movement, without me knowing how it happened, I was in the back of a waiting van and unclipped from the lead as the door slammed shut. My eyes were adjusting to the darkness and my nose to the stench of masculine dog when I heard, *'Who are you, then?'* in a low growl from the next cage.

I don't like to be sneaked up on and roared in a combination of surprise and defiance, a guttural, *'Don't mess with me!'* threat.

'Qui-et!' from the Plod, who was now in the driver's seat.

It wasn't loud, but it was intense. Nobody had ever spoken to me like that before. I decided to sulk and 'huffed' to demonstrate that I wasn't being quiet because he had told me to, but because I was in a strop. I contemptuously ignored a snigger from the next cage.

I've already alluded to the driving skills of dog handlers, but this was to be the first time I experienced them at first hand. Most dog vans are a standard design of two side-by-side cages running from a bulkhead behind the driver to the back of the van, where we are confined by internal cage doors before the van's rear doors. There are variations on this theme, but most consist of raising the cages or shortening them to provide storage space for essentials like leads, harnesses, wellies and water bowls, and places for the tumbleweeds of shed hair to fester.

This set-up literally allows only for tunnel vision. You can see out of the mesh front of the cage through the windscreen over the driver's shoulder or through the window in the back door. Things are either rapidly advancing toward you or, if you turn around, equally rapidly receding. You have no comprehension of what is to either side, and turns at junctions or even bends in the road come as a complete surprise as you head for a hedge or worse, a wall, then veer to one side or the other at the last moment.

Police dogs develop various ways of coping with this. There are the Spinners, who whirl round and round in a tight ball, alternately seeing front and back views, *'Have we crashed? No we haven't. Have we crashed? No we haven't...'*.

There are the Barkers, constantly shouting, *'Look out! A tree! Swerve! Stop! Mind that car! Red light! Slow down!..'* Some combine these two strategies into, *'Look out! A tree! Have we crashed? No we haven't. Swerve! Stop! Have we crashed? No we haven't...'*

Bracers, generally older, wiser dogs, wedge their backs against one wall and their legs against the other. You can tell the degree of interest they have by whether they choose to face forwards or backwards. The Bracers looking out the back are either depressed or have seen it all before. Or both.

Whiners attain the greatest stability by spreading their legs one to each corner. They're not whining from fear, it just hurts a lot to spread your legs that far apart.

And then there are the Jumpers, who try to maintain the equilibrium of the swaying van by bouncing up and down. Like someone who jumps a foot into the air to correct the momentum of a falling lift as it hits the bottom of the shaft, they are convinced this works.

It doesn't.

I tried various methods over the years, but on my first ride in a dog van, I didn't know what had hit me. Which was why my co-passenger was sniggering from the other cage. Old Kaiser was a Bracer, developed early because of the particular driving skills of the Plod at the wheel, his handler. Or rather the particular lack of driving skills. As we shot off I hit the back door and stayed in that heap, or variations of it, as I was buffeted back and forth, side to side, rolling and swaying as we lurched through the traffic. This Plod had a seriously heavy right foot. It was so heavy it was permanently on either the accelerator or the brake. I didn't see the view from the front or the back, but I saw the floor, the wall, the ceiling, the floor, the wall, the ceiling. I swear my own backside passed me at one point.

After what seemed like an eternity the van thudded to a halt and I hit the front mesh like a bag of mashed spuds. I may have been down, but I was by no means out of it. As the back doors opened I made a dash for freedom, streaking past the dark figure silhouetted in the doorway. Unfortunately I wasn't as quick as I thought and choked to a stop as that meaty hand slipped inside my collar.

'Come on sunshine, let's find you a bed for the night.'

Bed? More like Bed-lam. I was dragged by the collar through a double doorway into a corridor that stank of dogs and disinfectant. I was assailed by the scent of dogs and bitches, young and old, German Shepherds, Spaniels, Labradors and even a mongrel. There was sharp pine, bleach, leather, woollen clothing, rubber boots, wet Hessian sack, food, pee, poop and some vomited bile. And the noise was something else. There must have been at least a dozen voices raised in the common dog rendition of, *'Who's there?'*

Didn't you know that? That's what dogs shout when you come to the door. *'Who's there?'* Granted, some, especially the smaller ones, sound more like, *'Who's there? Who's there? Who's there? Who's there? Who's there? Who's there? Who's there? Who's there? Who's there?'* But that's just small-dog-syndrome. They try to make more noise to bump up their self-esteem. What they lack in volume, they make up for in effort.

Confused by the mass assault on my senses I put up no resistance to being thrown into a cell. But as the metal lattice door clanged shut behind me I thought I'd fallen into an episode of Porridge. I spun on my heels and launched myself at the door, spitting and snarling fury at my captor. As my teeth clashed on the mesh I heard that same fairground 'Ho, ho, ho,' and saw his back disappear down the corridor.

Kidnapped and chucked in the slammer! I had only one thought, *'I hope I'm not sharing with a large bearded collie who wants to call me Shirley.'*

🐾🐾🐾🐾

Of course we didn't share kennels, and there weren't any bearded collies for that matter, but that first night in an alien environment played havoc with my imagination.

In the morning I'd had chance to have a good sniff round and things started to become clearer. I was in a four-foot by six-foot concrete kennel with a pop-hole to a four-foot by eight-foot outside run. There were identical kennels on either side of me and more after them. The inside faced onto a corridor wall and the outside onto an open grassed compound. I had a wooden bed, on which I'd huddled but hardly slept a wink, and a bucket of fresh water.

As usual, we dogs were up and about long before any humans and I took the opportunity to acquaint myself with my neighbours. On my right was a Labrador who told me he was a drug dog called Spliff and his handler was on holiday. He seemed a happy if simple sort and mostly wanted to tell me about how much gear he'd sniffed out. After listening to him for ten minutes I figured he should inhale less.

21

On my left was a terrified Shepherd called Maxie, who'd been kidnapped the previous week and was scared stiff. He babbled incoherently about spook tests, shotgun and stick-man coming to get him. His fear drenched the air. I had no idea what he was talking about.

People arrived and many of the dogs started barking. Some, like the Lab, were doing it for fun in a, *'Here we go, here we go, here we gooooo...'* kind of way. Others were shouting, *'Hurry up, I'm bursting!'* I was biding my time. I could hear Maxie trembling under his bed.

There was a stomping of wellies, a clanking of buckets and a grinding of pop-hole covers as dogs were shut in or out. Some hammered at the closed pop-holes or jumped at the metal gates, adding to the din.

I was inside watching down the corridor when a figure appeared crouching at the outside gate. 'Hello pal,' he said quietly, on his haunches, leaning his shoulder on the gate and looking sideways at me.

He was talking dog. Not with words, but in the way that most people don't. His body language was pure canine, or at least as canine as a human can get. He kept himself my height, turned sideways on and looked out of the corner of his eye at me. In words it says, 'Come and see me, I'm a mate.' Most people can't or won't bother to learn how to talk dog; they stand up, bend over, face on, stare straight at you and then reach out to touch you on the top of your head.

This is extremely bad manners and can appear seriously threatening to less confident dogs. That's why people often get snapped at when they greet a strange dog like that. We really don't like bad manners. How would you like it if a bloke came up to you, dropped his trousers, said, 'Have a sniff of that mate!' and stuck his bum in your face? Species-ism works both ways.

But this guy could talk my language and I went closer for a sniff. He offered the back of his hand to the gate and I wandered up. He smelled alright so I gave him a cautious wag. I didn't want to be rude on my first day.

'Okay son, let's go for a walk shall we? Walkies? What do you know?'

He was searching for words to communicate with me; words that he thought I might know from my previous home. What kind of idiot stands at a kennel gate with his coat and wellies on and a lead in his hand, and has to search for words to communicate 'walk'? Where did he think I thought we might be going? Finger-painting?

Anyway, I'd like to take this opportunity to scotch the 'dogs-don't-understand-language-they-only-understand-words' myth. Of course dogs understand human language. You can't hang around a species for this long and not pick up at least a smattering of it.

Oh, sorry, I forgot, you lot don't bother learning other animals' lingo do you? Too stupid or just too arrogant? Never mind, the reason you think we don't understand yours is that we don't always respond. Not responding doesn't equal not understanding. Much of the time you have nothing to say anyway.

Do you really think, 'Does ickle-wickle Sugar-Plum love his mummy-wummy?' is conversation?

Especially when Sugar-Plum hates his name and in his own head is called 'Terroriser of Cats and Mighty Destroyer of Small Fluffy Things'. Even Yorkshire Terriers have self-respect.

And when you do manage to communicate something sensible we have to shout for you to understand the reply. The answer to, 'Would you like to go to the park?' is an affirmative glance at the cupboard you keep my lead in. Any dog would understand that, but do people? No. You need us to do somersaults and leap up and down woofing before you get the message.

To tell another dog that there's someone at the door, I only need to

23

nod in the right direction. People don't listen unless you bark like a possessed banshee.

Actually, I not only understand human language, but also human non-verbal communication and human scents. I know cat, sheep, cattle, horse and dialects of them such as goat and donkey, some bird, although the accents can get a bit thick at times, and a smattering of rabbit, rat and even mouse (but they're mostly just saying 'Help!').

The new bloke opened the gate and as the bolt slid back I made another dash for freedom. For the first time I began to realise that I was dealing with professionals. Don couldn't have stopped me, but this Plod had his knee against the gate, allowing it to open just about my width, and as I barged through the gap his left hand slid into my collar whilst his right clipped the lead onto it. My momentum spun us full circle, pivoting on his left leg until I ended back at the gate.

As he clicked it shut he said, 'Right, shall we go then?' and walked down the line of kennels.

I had unwittingly stumbled upon a new kind of Plod. In fact, not just a Plod, not even just a Dog-Handler like the one last night, but an

Instructor

Dog-handling legend has it that Instructors are a breed apart from ordinary mortals. They don't bleed, they are never knocked over by even the most tenacious dog, they <u>always</u> know where the track goes, they instinctively know when you are telling the truth (or a little fib), they never hurry, never rush, but they're always there before you; they can out-walk, out-run and out-drink mortal men; they strike fear into the hearts of dog handlers with phrases like, 'Could I just have a word?', or 'Do you want to give that another go?' or, the worst thing any dog handler can hear, 'Put your dog away and step into my office for a minute'. Of course I soon learned to run rings around them, they're only human, but this was my first day and I didn't know diddly squat.

Still not knowing what diddly-squat was, I was more concerned with the rabid loonies throwing themselves at the kennel gates as I walked past. Maxie didn't come out from under his bed, but every other dog went bananas. Barking, snarling - the language would've made a Rottweiler blush! I bristled, but kept my cool, haughtily stalking past, giving them my, you're-not-worth-it complete disdain. I wish I'd had sunglasses to take off so I could've given them a hard stare.

We turned away from the kennels across the footpath in the grass and Instructor gave me a pat on the ribs, 'Good lad, well done.' Ha! It takes more than a few hard-cases rattling their tin mugs against the bars to scare me.

Through the exercise gate we went somewhere I came to know as Down The Field, or 'Dee-Tee-Eff' to the cognoscenti*. It was a football pitch sized field with a set of wooden jumps in one corner. You could tell it was football pitch sized because of the goalposts at either end.

On the way down fairy steps through a little wood I took the opportunity to mark my scent on numerous trees that were a distinct rancid yellow up to eighteen inches from the floor. I was going where generations of dogs had gone before, in every sense of the phrase.

DTF the Instructor produced stuff from a kitbag he'd been carrying, starting with a thirty foot line he clipped to my collar and to a goalpost. Then a rubber ball appeared and spun past me a few yards. Brilliant! This I could do all day! I brought it back and gave it to him to throw again. Soon I had the Instructor throwing the ball further and further.

He obviously didn't trust himself to keep up with me, because when he untied the end of the line from the goalpost, he kept hold of it in his hand, running with me to catch the ball. He started off with his dog-talk, kneeling down, play-bowing and making a big fuss when I brought it back, but I soon showed him I understood human and he didn't need to bother with the pidgin-dog.

---

* Literally 'those of us who know about scent', meaning of course, dogs. From the Latin 'cogno' = knowledge and 'scenti' = scent. Obviously.

Of course I messed him about a bit to test him. I kept hold of the ball when he tried to take it from me (that always wound Marie up - she used to beg after a while) but, what do you know, when I wouldn't let go, it made him produce another ball from his pocket and when I opened my mouth in surprise, he threw that one! Within minutes I'd trained this super-human to produce balls for me on demand.

I figured it was time we lost the long line, and I'd noticed that he often stepped over it if I ran round him when bringing the ball back. The next time I gave him the ball I nipped round behind encircling both his feet with the line, but I knew he'd step out of that so, immediately after he chucked it, I nipped round again and took off like a scalded moggy.

The double loop tightened around both his legs and tugged as I hit my end of the line. As his feet whipped from under him he went down like a sack of whoopee cushions and was dragged five feet before I choked out.

I'd heard the wind leave him and turned to watch. Then the swearing started. Non-stop without repeating himself, or moving, for a full minute. Actually, if it wasn't for the swearing I'd have though he was dead. Just lying there, but quietly turning the air blue. Then I thought that this could be the build up to my own death, or at least some horrible punishment, as his body started to shake, face down in the damp grass.

Until I realised that the shaking was caused by the chortling that was starting to punctuate the swear words. Transfixed, I watched him slowly sit up and unwind the line from his wellies, the chortles turning to laughs to guffaws and hoots, still cursing every bone in my body but grinning from ear to ear.

It crossed my mind it may be some sort of mania brought on by a blow to the head as he fell, so I kept my distance, then as he got to his knees I cautiously crept towards him wagging my tail. After all, it was only a joke! Then he put his arm around me and I licked his face to show him I hadn't taken the swearing personally. He hugged me and used the motion to lean on me, pushing himself upright. I owed him that I suppose. And then he unclipped the line from my collar.

We went through the screwdriver and hessian sack games from the night before once again, only this time the sack was more of a tube and he pulled it onto his arm to get better purchase. This was my first bite on a padded sleeve - the sleeve they use for our practice bites so it doesn't hurt them. It was like coming home... on your birthday... with best raw steak for tea.

Dormant endorphins soared through my veins. I growled and tugged backwards, shaking my head like a fighting marlin to dislodge his grip. I won the sleeve that day, and carried it back through the wood to the kennels. Okay, I was a bit of a show-off, but I needed to establish myself with the old lags. I needed the cred to shut them up.

Or so I thought. I was trotting straight through the gate back at them, of course. The biggest challenge a dog can face: another dog coming head on into their personal space. And boy, did they rise to the occasion. All except Maxie, who was still under the bed, wetting himself. The din increased as I jumped onto the concrete apron and into the kennel, the Instructor expertly flicking the lead's spring-clip off my collar and whipping the sleeve from my teeth at the last minute.

The next few days lazed by without much happening as I learned the rules. Slopping-out was every morning at eight as handlers came to take out their own dogs and clean the kennels with a vile concoction of synthetic pine-smelling disinfectant in hot water. Whoever made that stuff had never been in a pine forest, but it certainly competed with the dog smells, however much we marked over it.

Most dogs marked up one side of the gate or wall, some as a challenge, some to boost their confidence with the familiar smell, some just to establish their ownership of the property. I learned later that some dogs' handlers were lazy schafsköpfe who couldn't be bothered to take them for proper walks. These dogs were on the dirty protest, soiling their kennels every morning as a mark of scorn, and to make sure their idle handlers had just a little bit more work to do. I didn't need any of that and decided I hadn't gone through all that house-training of Don and Marie to let my standards slip now.

All of the dogs got a walk in the woods but I was one of the lucky ones because the Instructor took me out for a quick poop-break in the woods then DTF for fun and games.

By half-nine the kennels would all be spick and span and the dogs that were going out would have left us boarders to while away the day. The multiple clanking of buckets, swishing of mops and swilling of water down drains subsided as the heavy-booted handlers whistled and joshed into the distance, leaving us with the radio to keep us company through the morning.

We worked as a team on Pop-Quiz. Spliff was quite good on anything Indie, (house, garage or kennel), and I had a pretty good all-round knowledge. Maxie quivered a lot, but occasionally surprised us with his knowledge of late 50's skiffle. Apparently he'd had an owner who was a Lonnie Donegan fan.

In between quizzes we were serenaded by this thing I came to know and love as TheKennelMan. TheKennelMan was a strange creature that smelled more like us than we did. He gave life to the word 'unkempt'. I doubt he'd ever been kempt, but every day he seemed more in need of a good grooming than we were. Like a grubby Dorian Gray, as his kennels became cleaner, he became more dishevelled.

His grey matted hair stuck out at all angles like a massive dandelion that had been attacked with a machete. Occasionally a suspiciously stained bobble-hat nested in it. He always had a week's worth of stubble, in which dried egg-yolk and fluff were trapped, and his nose, ears and eyebrows sprouted luxurious tufts of what appeared to be the remnants of a horsehair mattress.

His beady eyes, wonky teeth and prodigious nose gave him the appearance of a ferret trying to hide in a bush. Obviously he was at the back of the line when good looks were being handed out and unfortunately this had made him late for the physique queue as well. He thought himself wiry, but was actually more stringy. If he was a bone, you wouldn't bother burying him.

TheKennelMan didn't so much wear clothes as just happen to be standing inside them. In the summer his tee-shirt slapped against his ribs in the breeze and in winter his ancient gabardine was tied at the waist with twine to stop it sailing him away. The wellies, folded over at the top in a jaunty buccaneer style, were welded on. Rumour had it that Mrs TheKennelMan had never seen his bare feet, and when chortling handlers asked, 'Do you take them off in the bath?' he would reply, 'What's a bath?'

Nobody could tell if he was joking or not.

He moved with a sloth-like grace and the overall impression was that if he'd dropped a bucket of water on his foot the pain would have to stop several times to ask directions before registering in his brain.

But, as is the way with these things, dame nature had compensated for her dubious gifts by endowing him with prodigious strength. He could stand his ground against the strongest dog and carried four buckets of water at a time. His might was so well known that people would come from miles around with stubborn pickle jars for him to take the lid off.

And, boy, could he sing. Not in tune, obviously, but what he lacked in melody, he more than made up for in volume and output. He sang all the time, from operatic arias to ditties from TV commercials, at the top of his voice. It drowned out the barking.

A master of his craft, TheKennelMan occasionally took us out to the top end of the wood and back, crooning away as we marked trees, clumps of grass and his leg. He never said a bad word to us. Most human talk to dogs consists of, 'Don't do that', in some form or another, but with the TheKennelMan it was always, 'Good boy', and 'There's a clever lad', especially when he sat down at the grooming bench and idly ran a brush over us, teasing five minutes of haute couture into an hour and a half of bliss.

Other than that we were pretty much left to our own devices until afternoon-walk and then scoff-time. Some of the inmates used to run up and down barking at their own tails, some would shout threats at the bunnies who taunted us from the wood. I relaxed in the sunshine and watched the world go by. If I'd had a ball I'd have slumped in a corner and repeatedly thrown it at the far wall, with a baseball cap pulled down over my eyes.

Maxie was by now a basket-case. Every click of a door frazzled his nerves and he gibbered, *'Spook, BANG!' 'NO! please....home'*. The smell of fear in his piss hung in the air like lily-of-the-valley around an incontinent pensioner. In his more lucid moments I tried to ask him what had happened, but although he started with, *'They took me into the woods...'* it dissolved into single words, always 'Spook' and 'Bang' punctuating the sobbing.

And then they came for me. Halfway through Pop-Quiz another Instructor came to the gate. I'd just got The Bonzo Dog Doo-dah Band from the first six notes of I'm the Urban Spaceman when the latch clicked and I rushed out.

Maxie was crying *'Oooooh, nooooo'* and dribbling from under his bed and, as I was clipped on, Spliff shouted, *'Good luck, man – have a cool one!'* All around the kennels dogs were going ape. TheKennelMan paused to watch us leave, leaning on a brush and grinning inanely, algae quietly colonising his coat.

Everybody but me seemed to know what was going on, so we

headed through the compound gate, this other Instructor strangely quiet. I gave his hand a nuzzle to try to cheer him up, but he withdrew and stuck it in his pocket.

I marked a few trees from habit, but I didn't really have my heart in it because I'd only been out an hour earlier. I'd had a particularly tough workout with the ball this morning. I'd run so hard I thought, *'It's a good job I don't have dodgy hips, they wouldn't have stood up to this!'*

At the top of the wood we didn't turn DTF but went left, deeper into the thicker trees, where the light was more dappled and solid shapes were difficult to make out. We walked about fifty yards and then just stood.

I could see a solid wooden scale jump, about six feet high, maybe thirty yards ahead of me, but the sun was in my eyes and I didn't have the wind direction either, although the scent of Instructor (assertive, confident, tall, rugged, light splash of soap, dry underpants, wet jacket, slight trace of lingering fungal infection in the boots) was all around us. The guy next to me dropped his shoulders and leaned onto one hip, so I relaxed and waited.

Then, from behind the scale jump came the *THING*. It was a huge amorphous fiend, featureless, the height of a man but black as the pits of hell, billowing and crackling as it lurched towards me.

Instinctively I went front end up and back end down, hackles up and teeth out, baying at the devil and forward into the attack. Until the end of the lead brought me to an abrupt halt, as the demon too halted. I glanced at the Instructor but he was no help, just standing impassively.

I just couldn't make out what it was, this animate ink-blot from the apocalypse. I stood my ground and strained towards it, trying to catch the breeze or make out shadow from silhouette, as it backed away and shrank. As my anger turned to curiosity it came at me again!

It grew massive and loomed terrifyingly only yards away. No retreat, I went for it again, jerking the Instructor on the lead, up on my

31

back legs baying furiously. It worked. It backed down again. Three more times it came at me, closer and closer, and each time I faced it down.

Okay, I know now it was my Instructor in a huge plastic body-bag, but the gut-wrenching terror at the time wasn't appreciated. Today, if I see a black bag fluttering in the hedge, it brings a little smile, tinged with the memory of the most fear I have ever felt.

You humans don't get it about black bags because your worst fears are social – zombies, vampires, aliens, goblins, demons – all in your image but with horns, terrible teeth or bits falling off. You most fear things that are like yourselves, but with an evil tinge. A psychiatrist might be able to make something about a reflection of your deepest inner selves, but all your fears have shape and form.

The black bag, until you know it is a bin-liner, is a shapeless, nebulous, nothing. It has no smell, no form, no identity. It moves, but not in a rational way. It scares because it is completely unfathomable, unknowable and unresponsive to communication. Wait until a black hole threatens your universe – then you might have some inkling of the terror of the black plastic bag.

I did what most dogs do at the reveal, when the Instructor takes off the bag and shows that it was him underneath, I looked sheepish and pretended that I had known all the time, and was just playing along with the joke. The Instructors laughed and patted me on the shoulders in that matey way reserved for those who know you know they know and, although they don't share your embarrassment, they understand you need a lift.

What jokers! Ha, ha, ha. What arsch-fällt.

Having laughed it off together, my Instructor companion and I wandered further down the path, not paying much attention to anything in general, and trying to look nonchalant. Then BOOM ...BOOM!! as a masked black-clad figure stepped out from behind a tree and blasted two rounds from a shotgun into the leafy floor.

I went straight into 'scared cat'. Vertical four-leg take-off three feet into the air, legs splayed and claws outstretched for extra grip on an equally vertical landing. As I hit the deck in slow motion, seeing the leaf litter spraying up around me, hearing the click as the shotgun broke and watching the two ejected cartridges pirouette through the pall of smoke, I knew I had about two seconds before the balaclava-ed stranger dug two more from his pocket and we were dead meat. The time Don and I spent watching all those cowboy films hadn't been wasted.

Still in slow-mo I bunched my legs under me and went for the spring that would close the ten yards between us in one. And hit the end of the lead in six feet.

What was it with this numpty holding me back? Back in real time I roared my defiance and flung myself forward again, as the gunman plucked off his balaclava to reveal another laughing Instructor.

Seething, I turned on the trottel on the other end of my lead and bit him on the thigh.

One bite. Hard.

By all the gods, but that felt good. And tasted sweet. By the time he had registered the pain I was standing off, bristling with, '*Come on then if you think you're hard enough...*' But all he came with was more laughing.

I'd bitten him with all I had; left him with four deep canine marks in the flesh of his thigh and blood running down his leg, and all he did was laugh. The two of them, laughing like ducks!

I didn't get it at the time, but being bitten was an occupational hazard to these guys. They didn't look for it, they tried to avoid it, but they weren't going to let it spoil their day. Nice attitude. And being laughed at by someone you've just maimed really takes the oomph out of your annoyance as well.

33

After a couple of minutes the Instructor on the end of my lead and the ex-gunman turned to walk back the way we'd come, back up to my Instructor, now with his plastic shroud bundled up under one arm.

'Well, no bother with the spook. How was he with the shotgun? Looked alright from here…'

'Aye, no bother. Bit of re-directed – did Pete in the leg.'

'Really? A good one?'

Pete looked pained, 'From the puddle in my boot, it'll bloody hurt tomorrow. Here, you put him away, I'm going to have to get this dressed.' He handed my lead to my Instructor.

'Get away, you need some Dettol on that!' as Pete disappeared through the trees.

'You can f…' his voice tailed away into the distance.

First aid was taken very seriously by Instructors. The first aid kit carried in all police dog vans consisted of a pack of World War One bandages and a bottle of Dettol. Dettol is a viscous amber liquid antiseptic disinfectant that kills 99% of bacteria on contact and, when diluted at a ratio of one part to twenty parts water, is recommended for cleaning cuts and wounds.

On the basis that more-concentrated equals more-effective, handlers encouraged each other to pour neat Dettol on any bite wounds. This hurt like being cauterised with a hot poker and actually damaged the skin surrounding the cut, making it more difficult to heal. Although macho handlers didn't scream in agony when bitten by a dog, they often did when neat Dettol was poured into the wound.

This caused much hilarity amongst Instructors, who knew the effects and didn't do it to themselves. Often when a new handler was bitten there would be shouts of, 'Send for Barry and the Dettol!'

'Why, is Barry the first aider?'

'No he just likes to hear people scream.'

My report card was written up in spidery Instructor-ese:

Hips and elbows - *Sound. Increased exercise daily to point of exhaustion on final test. No sign of strain under pressure. No lameness.*

Spook Test – *Recognised the threat early and responded with forward aggression. Focussed on the spook and refused to back down, held ground under extreme provocation and would have bitten. Calmed down quickly when threat terminated.*

Gun Test – *Initial reaction was extreme, suggesting lack of experience, however response was proactive aggression towards gunman with all-out attack. When prevented, redirected aggression to handler with single bite and release to leg. Not as quick to calm probably due to second arousal state in succession.*

Retrieve – *Will retrieve all tested objects, although metal with reluctance. Will retrieve ball until exhausted.*

Ragging – *Persistent. Will take full mouth bite on sleeve and rag. Will currently leave for ball, but will need to be watched to maintain this balance. Could develop a liking for it.*

Overall assessment – *Strong willed and needs firm handling. Very reactive and uses aggression naturally. Will take liberties if allowed. Given the right handler will make an excellent police dog.*

I'd passed all the tests and I was in, but when I got back to the kennels Maxie was gone.

🐾🐾🐾🐾

I asked Spliff what had happened to Maxie and got a hushed conspiratorial, *'Gone Home'* reply. It wasn't done to talk about the

35

failures, especially when an Initial Course was coming up.

The Initial Course is where every police dog and every handler starts serious training. The aim is for everyone that starts to finish, but it isn't always so. Sometimes dog or handler will break down in training, fail in some crucial aspect to live up to the highest standards.

These are the failures that are, 'Gone Home', but I had just passed the first hurdle of actually being accepted onto the course. I had been through the selection procedure that had terrified Maxie. It was as well he had failed really, because he would have never made a police dog as long as he had a hole in his Jacobson's organ*.

The selection procedures for dogs and handlers were designed to weed out the incompetent, lazy, cowardly or just plain feckless, so it was a miracle they had any handlers at all, as most police officers fall into at least one of those categories.

Dog selection was done on the basis of assessing our qualities and measuring our reactions in response to specific stimuli over a period of time. Handlers were selected on the basis of what was un-affectionately known as a 'shit-shovelling course'.

An interesting psychological experiment, the S-S course consisted of taking experienced police officers, used to making decisions affecting the liberty of the Great British Public and, by giving them the most demeaning of tasks, humiliating them for two weeks. Tasks like cleaning the kennels until they were spotless and then making them to do it again because they had been too quick.

Handlers were encouraged to join in by giving them as many trivial jobs as possible. They were expected to have a constant supply of tea and coffee should anyone randomly fancy a brew, to be first into the

---

* Also called the vomeronasal organ, it sits in the roof of the mouth and collects pheromones that inform us about each other. Humans don't have one, although you may have done at one time as a vestigial one appears in the foetus but doesn't develop. Just one more way we are superior to you.

kennels to clean them in the morning and still be mopping as the last handler put on their coat to go home.

They were privileged to run for all dogs and, because they were novices, were knocked down about ten times a day. The clever ones learned not to admit to bites after the first Dettol-ing. They walked whatever dogs happened to be in the kennels and of course we joined in the fun by dragging them about on the lead, getting into pretend fights with other dogs that they were expected to break up, and generally refusing to co-operate in any way by such means as mysteriously forgetting the meaning of words like 'Sit' when spoken by an S-S goon.

If they complained, they were out. One little, 'But...' or 'Not again?' and they were Gone Home.

It wasn't completely unfair. They knew the rules. Stick it out for two weeks and you were in. Get back up, laugh it off, dust yourself down, don't moan, don't complain, keep busy and work your socks off. They were there to be broken. They knew it and the handlers knew it. And they knew that they knew that they knew it and loved every minute.

It made our dog selection process look like a walk in the park. Someone frightens the living, err... daylights out of you and, provided that you don't actually, err... daylight yourself, you're in.

There were two other dogs in the kennels already pencilled in for my initial course, a laid-back black and tan with one floppy ear, called 'Arry (I don't know what his other ear was called*) and a manic grey feminist bitch called Ava, who was constantly trying to make up for her slight build with attitude. The remaining two, Donald and Dougie, had been bought in as pups and were coming with their handlers.

We were on the back-end course, starting in autumn and ending before the Christmas break. If all went well we'd be on the streets for

---

* Sorry, but it is a natural law that this response must be given or the fabric of the universe will tear asunder.

three of the busiest nights of the year: Black-eye Friday (when the boys from the building sites take their bonus cash and holiday belligerence straight to the pub at noon), Reverse-Santa (Christmas Eve burglaries - man comes into your house in the middle of the night and takes all your presents) and the traditional Boxing Day football match pitched battle.

But if all didn't go well, dog or handler would be ... Gone Home.

Day one of the thirteen week Initial arrived after I'd been incarcerated for three weeks. Already Don and Marie were dim in my memory. Not because I couldn't remember them, they were just dim and that's how I remembered them.

The usual hollering and clanking of slopping-out was interrupted by the opening of the office door into the compound; usually an auspicious herald as it was the portal to the Instructors' hallowed sanctum, our own Mount Olympus, where our fate was decided and Instructors entered our world to pass on the word.

On this particular occasion it disgorged three of the dodgiest looking human beings I had ever seen and two obvious old-hand dog handlers.

I recognised one of the newbies as a recent goon from an S-S course. A weasely streak of nearly seven feet tall, with hunched shoulders from permanently looking down, always hiding a cupped fag in his hand, sporting vivid acne and the sparsest of blonde moustaches dangling under a hooked nose. Jamesy smelled of ash, smoke, curry, dandruff, old socks and mints, and laughed like a braying donkey.

The second guy was eighteen inches shorter, ramrod straight to try to prove he actually was tall enough to be a policeman and hadn't lied about his height to get in. He was neat and tidy, with boots spit-and-polish shined, creases in all the right places (as opposed to Jamesy, who also had creases, but more randomly) and a shiny red face with clipped black moustache. It was said that in the dictionary under tho word 'dapper' was written, 'See Nuffer'.

Nuffer was so called because he had almost infinite patience with the drunks, wife beaters and other arschtücher, but just before he exploded into violence he would quietly say, 'That'll be e-nuff-er that from you now...' causing the aforesaid ne'er-do-well to believe that he was still being reasoned with when his face hit the wall and the cuffs bit into his wrists. He smelled of slightly too much after-shave, lots of soap, hair cream and deodorant.

The third newbie was young, a bit gawky with untamed hair and bushy sideburns. He self-consciously grinned a bit too much and wore fluorescent yellow socks in an attempt at flamboyance because he'd been told he needed to be a bit less reserved on his S-S course. Noddy smelled balanced. He smelled of promise.

The two old lags came as a double act: 'Round and Rounder'. You thought Mitch could lose a few pounds until you saw Mogsy, when you thought that you were seeing Mitch in a convex fairground mirror. Both were short on hair but big on confidence. They wore their blue woolly jumpers tight and with the snags and darned holes of a thousand barbed wire fences; creases were sown into pants to save effort.

Both smelled of dog-handler, that curious mixture of casual competence, leather, wet wool, moist wellies and exposure to the elements, added to which was the lingering odour of a diet too rich in fat, occasionally apparent even to humans. Their combined guffawing was usually at each other's expense.

'I've got an insect in me brew!'

'It'll be an earwig!'

''Ow d' you know?'

'I 'eard it shout 'ear-wi-g-o!' as it jumped in!'

Cue ten minutes of thigh slapping.

A word on the uniform, because after Health and Safety went bananas (always putting the skin in the bin to prevent slips-trips-and-falls, of course) they became festooned with more bits of kit than your average army and navy stores. Back then were the days of the stripped down version.

Handlers wore black serge police uniform issue pants and blue shirt with black clip-on tie, which was immediately discarded when away from a station. There were two official concessions to the unique nature of the dog-job. One was a fireman's navy woolly-pully instead of the jacket and the other was a pair of black wellies. Both of these were issued to all handlers.

In summer the jumper was discarded for shirt sleeves and in winter supplemented by whatever coat the handler cared to afford. The only one provided was the calf-length raincoat, which made running impossible and snagging their undercarriage on barbed wire fences almost inevitable, so they wore what they were most comfortable in. This made for a motley collection of anoraks, waxed jackets, ex-army camouflage smocks and cagoules.

Footwear had to be bought from the boot allowance, so most handlers had a pair they wore for best, but donned their issued wellies most of the time. A sure-fire way of identifying a handler on the beach was the bare patches on his calves where his wellies had rubbed the hairs off.

Official bits and bobs were added in season, like leather gloves or waterproof trousers, and unofficial ones when necessary, like the woolly hat or flat ratting-cap. All this was set off by a leather lead and stainless steel chain thrown over the right shoulder and clipped onto itself by the left hip in one easy motion.

For posh occasions where they went mob-handed, like football matches or seeing the pubs out, full police uniform had to be worn, but the rest of the time they looked like a gamekeeper that had fallen on hard times and had recently tuccled with a rough band of poachers.

They were still issued with a foot long bit of wood with a leather strap, which no handler carried but some occasionally threw for their dogs to fetch. On the other hand, most dog vans contained a three foot long pickaxe handle, which handlers claimed was for throwing for their dogs, but sported no teeth marks at all. Not canine ones anyway.

Handcuffs usually rusted in the bottom of the van drawer or foot-well. They were rarely needed by a handler holding a slavering beast in one hand and a pick-shaft in the other.

Thus attired and armed, without body-armour, extending batons, tasers, pepper-spray, rigid cuffs or any official training in prisoner-restraint and self-defence, they went to war.

As a 'back-end' course the weather was turning, so they were standing in front of my kennel in jumpers and serge trousers. They wore their shiny boots because wellies weren't allowed in the office and they'd not been through the drying room to change, coming straight out from the portal of the gods. As old hands, Mitch and Mogsy sported checked ratting caps and ruddier complexions than the other three, but they were all unmistakably dog handlers looking for dogs to complete their ensemble.

Mitch and Mogsy were out of the running because they'd already been teamed up with their pups, Donald and Dougie, but Ava, 'Arry and me had each been allocated one of Jamesy, Nuffer and Noddy. You might think it a bit of a lottery, but no, it was properly scientific. We were all personality matched through deep psychological profiling by the Instructors.

'If we put the two nutters and the two slackers together, that leaves Major with Noddy. D'you think he'll manage him?'

'Dunno. Guess we'll find out...If he hasn't eaten him by the end of the course it's a success – if he has, we can always get another handler. We're not wasting a good dog.'

And so it came to pass on that fateful morning that Noddy had the privilege to be allocated to me, Ava got Nuffer and 'Arry got Jamesy.

Now, some like to think of it as a marriage, but it isn't. It's more important than that. After all, if you get divorced you lose your home and your family, which in the circumstances is probably a blessing. But if you split with your dog, you'll be thrown off the dog section. From now until death-do-us-part we'd spend every day together.

First task was to take a walk to get to know them and we dutifully dragged them through the woods for a few minutes. Jamesy used it for a crafty fag-break and the others stood about whilst we dogs familiarised ourselves with each other. We all knew a bit about the others from our scent marks, but it's not as informative as a face to tail meeting. A bit like corresponding by email – you get the style and the general drift of the personality, but not the full flavour until you are up close and personal, nose to groin.

Donald and Dougie posed, puffed their chests out and stood on their toes, tails flagging slowly at three quarters mast. Ava stalked stiffly and curled her lip at over-familiarity. 'Arry relaxed and grinned, lifting his leg accommodatingly so anyone who wanted could get a better sniff. I adopted a 'take 'em or leave 'em' approach. I knew I could take 'em, so I left them alone.

Grooming is important, not just from a personal hygiene point of view, but as a way of bonding with your handler. Unfortunately, most pet owners think it consists of either packing you off to a parlour or dragging a comb down every bump on your spine. Police dog handlers are taught how to groom a dog properly and are expected to use that expertise every single day.

This was Noddy's first lesson with me and the whole class lined up along the grooming bench. Ten yards of solid plank set two feet off the ground; dogs standing front feet on the bench, back feet on the floor to stretch us out, handlers standing beside or astride us.

It starts with the whole-body massage incorporating the inspection. A vigorous rub with the fingertips that loosens dead hair and any dust caught in the coat, starting at the nose and ending at the tip of the tail, stopping off at every orifice and extremity to check for damage or ailment. Heaven. Transcendental bliss.

Dogs have been known to enter such a state of ecstasy towards the end that when their handler carelessly moves the leg that they were leaning against they actually fall over. But it has its practical uses too. Dogs kennelled after a hard night's tracking through undergrowth, or street-fighting amongst broken bottles, need to be checked for injuries. It's almost impossible in the pitch black, so daybreak is the first opportunity to check-up and patch-up.

Next comes the brushing, with a proper grooming brush, first against then with the nap of the hair, taking out all the detritus that collects in a decent double coat (soft fluffy under-hair with an overcoat of harsh guard-hairs). It invigorates the skin and sebaceous glands to maintain a healthy shine.

A handler is happy to look like a sack of spuds. It adds to their individuality and ethic that you can't stay smart and do the job properly. They like to look as though they've been dragged through a hedge backwards because if you're catching thieves you sometimes have to drag yourself through a hedge backwards.

But their dog must be immaculately presented. Smugness at their own scruffiness is in direct proportion to inordinate pride in their dogs' smartness.

Then the comb flattens out the stray hairs before the spit and final polish with damped-down palms along the length of the coat. All for free, every day. And who says there's no payment for a police dog?

All dogs groomed to perfection, we were introduced to the Skylark, a battered battle-bus that contained six dog cages and two rows of seats for the handlers. Fully marked up in police livery, it was an impressive sight rocking back and forth to the barking of six dogs outside the county's biggest football ground. A league two team, but nevertheless with their own brand of pond-life; single-celled self-replicating amoeba that lay in wait for unsuspecting opposition supporters. To be fair, as modern equal-opportunities hooligans they clashed with the suspecting ones as well, and with their own fans, and sometimes amongst themselves.

But all that was in the future. For now and every Monday to Friday the Skylark was the training bus - our transport and temporary day-kennel. It was here that Noddy made his first slip, in not getting me there quick enough. By the time we were standing at the back door, Ava, Dougie and Donald were in the bottom row of cages. Only Jamesy had lagged behind us, so me and 'Arry had the high jump.

I took the top-middle cage, because I'm a top-middle kind of dog, taking the vertical five foot leap like, although I hate to admit it, a cat.

'Arry on the other hand didn't have my natural agility and kind of chucked himself in the general direction of the cage on my left... and fell back on top of Jamesy so hard they both ended up in a heap on the floor.

It left 'Arry with a permanent reluctance to jump up, and there's no swapping cages after the course has started, so each time he had to get in Jamesy had to lift and manhandle eighty-odd pounds of floppy dog onto his shoulder to give him a bunk-up. Always good for starting the day with a chuckle.

The Skylark, Nuffer driving (ex-traffic, so a shoe-in for the role), Instructor in the front and the rest of us in the back - albeit humans in front of the bulkhead and us behind - took us the short trundle to the training fields. We were out for the day, so carried all we needed. Fresh water and bowls for us dogs, and sandwich packs for the handlers with flasks of hot water and the makings for the compulsory gallons of tea and coffee. The handlers had all their gear, wellies on their feet and lead slung over the shoulder, kongs, balls and tugs in their pockets, waterproofs, dumb-bell and tracking harness in their kit-bags.

But the tracking harness didn't stay packed for long, because our first lesson was tracking. Or, as Noddy was frequently heard to say, 'The most fun you can have with your clothes on!' (He didn't have much imagination for that sort of thing).

The tracking harness could probably have helped him in that regard. Made from finest quality saddle-leather it went over our heads and fastened around our lower chest, with a brass ring in the middle of our back as a fixing point for the tracking line, which was twenty to thirty feet of stout cord to which we tried to keep a handler attached.

As with most aspects of police dog work, tracking was fantastic on many levels. It is an absorbing and deliriously enjoyable activity for a well-bred dog, and a brilliant opportunity to have fun with your handler.

Totally immersed in following the scent, able to travel at twice the speed of humans and react three times as quickly, and held on twenty-odd feet of line that rips through the hands causing severe friction burns. And they can't tell us off because we're doing what they want! What's not to like?

Many's the dog that tracks to the sound of a zipping rope followed by the smell of burning flesh and muted curses, as once again the handler gets caught out. Gloves? No handler would track wearing gloves. Gloves are for wusses. Fetch the Dettol!

Of course there's a skill that they learn eventually, paying the line out and playing it back in as we twist and turn following the elusive scent of the quarry.

You'll never understand scent and what it means to dogs. Trying to explain scent to a visual creature like a human would be like trying to explain raspberry cheesecake ice-cream to someone whose taste buds could only experience cold porridge. You have an idea of the concept, but can't ever envisage the glorious depths and heights.

We started as generations of police dogs and handlers had done before us. Harnessed-up on a short line next to a pole stuck in the ground, handler tossing the ball to his Instructor who galloped off up the field in a straight line, waving the ball in the air to attract my attention, then he dropped it about a hundred yards away, before circling back to us marginally downwind of the leg he just laid.

I knew the ball was out there and roughly where it was, so I streaked off, line paying out behind me (slight smell of burning and a faint zipping sound). No need to track at all until I lost momentum, primarily caused by the dead-weight at the end of the line behind me, but when that first burst had gone, I'd lost the visual direction and used my nose. It was an easy track to follow, the combination of the rising crushed earth and grasses compressed by size eleven wellies melting into the human smell of the Instructor wearing them.

The wind was mostly on my back, with only occasional drifts off to one side or other, so as it blew the scent away from me I kept my nose to the ground, knowing that the ball would be in the centre, the strongest part of the thinning cloud that streamed away from me. Still running, but concentrating at the same time, then WALLOP the scent of the ball smacked me in the face as I shot over the top of it, twisting round and down to scoop it up.

This is my ball. Not just a ball. My ball. It is large and rubber. You would call it red, but it looks no different to the colour of grass to me. It has a hole through the middle and a short piece of old tracking line passes through it, knotted on one side and looped into a handle on the other. It looks like a medieval weapon (and is just as lethal if accidentally deployed at short range), can be chucked for fifty yards by a lanky handler, and gripped and tugged by a dog; it is almost indestructible and the Rolls Royce of police dog balls. And mine. The best reward I could have had for using my nose.

Even better than the hooting idiot behind me, whooping his delight and crawling towards me on his hands and knees in adoration. As he should. He couldn't have done that without me.

That was just the start of thirteen weeks of hectic activity, teaching them how to work with us. We began with the basics, tracking, searching for property, searching for people and the ever-present 'obedience'.

The obedience exercises would be considered brutal now, but were in line with contemporary dog training methods. 'Heel' predicted a short sharp snap of the lead and corresponding tightening of the chain around my neck. If you were bright you quickly learned to glue your right shoulder to his left leg, which alternatively made your handler gurgle with delight.

'Sit', 'down' and 'stand' were shoves you learned to avoid by assuming the positions and earning the chuckles instead. I can't say I ever enjoyed the obedience like today's kids do, with all their clickers and rewards, but it never bothered me much. I attempted to second-guess what Noddy wanted and tried to do it well because it made him happy.

Searching for people was more fun because I could use my nose again, but we didn't get the same rewards as they do nowadays. Now dogs get a ball for finding the person. Back then we got a clout around the nose to make us bark.

I couldn't believe it the first time we went to the disused warehouse. Mogsy ran off down the corridor of offices shouting my name and generally being as excitable as a porky poodle after a pampering.

Noddy held me back on the lead, although he encouraged me to pull forwards with, 'Where is he?! Where's he gone?!' as Mogsy disappeared around the corner, then loosed me with, 'Find him!'

47

I shot off, paws slipping on the tiled floor as I Scooby-Doo-ed after him. His scent hit me as I passed the door of the office he had chosen and I piled in to find him hunched in the corner. As I galloped at him he turned and smacked me across the nose with a riding crop. Talk about a short sharp shock! I went ballistic, baying at him in outrage, standing my ground but warily circling because of that concealed riding crop. Behind me Noddy was in the doorway, heaping me with praise of the, 'Good dog' type (I told you he lacked imagination), and he came forward to stand alongside me and pat my shoulder.

Emboldened by his support I bobbed forwards and bit Mogsy on the thigh. Not hard, but hard enough to let him know he couldn't whip me. I am not a horse.

He yelped as Noddy shouted, 'No!', but Mogsy said, 'It's fine. It's good to have a little fire. Don't want to discourage him from biting scroats.' After that I always barked as soon as I saw the hidden person move – and when warned like that, no one produced a whip again.

Everything got progressively harder. The tracks became longer and older, the person searches longer and more complicated. Property searching was still easy back then; no DNA to collect so we could just pick it up and bring it back, but the stuff we had to find got smaller and laid out for longer.

On week six we began biting. It started DTF with the padded sleeve my Instructor had produced in my first week of incarceration. I knew what that was for and put my heart and soul into grabbing and tugging it; digging in and pulling back as the Instructor gave ground and eventually let go. I trotted round with it in my mouth until Noddy tossed me my ball with a, 'Leave'.

Then it went up a level. The sleeve went onto the Instructor's arm and he stood in front of us, me on the lead. He held a stick in his left hand, about a yard long bamboo cane wrapped in water-pipe insulation. He crouched and leant forward into the stance of street-

48

fighters everywhere, face contorted into a grimace as he levelled his padded right arm in front of him, growled, 'Come on!' and waved the stick threateningly. I roared back and lunged, but was held by the lead, Noddy digging his foremost heel in with the effort.

The Instructor sneered into my face and my blood boiled with frustration at the unavenged insult. As I snarled and spat back he gave ground and as he turned to run Noddy let the lead go. My open jaws hit the sleeve and I clamped down harder than I'd ever done. My long, killing canine teeth were embedded in the hessian mesh, and I shook my head.

'Jesus bloody christ that's hard!' laughed the Instructor and I could feel him trying to wriggle his arm out of the inside of the sleeve, but I held him too firmly.

'I can't get it off. Leave him on for a few minutes and we'll get him to leave'.

I didn't know at the time but it was customary for the Instructor to slip his arm out of the sleeve to let the dog win it from him.

'Aren't you going to tickle him?' asked Noddy.

It was also customary for the Instructor to lightly roll the stick along the dog's head and flanks in the build-up to later hitting them.

'Not bloody likely. He's biting hard enough as it is without winding him up any more. We'd never get him off,' he said, grimacing with what I can only describe as a satisfactory amount of pain reflected in his eyes.

'He's coming down now, try him with the ball.'

The ball dropped past my head with Noddy's plea of, 'Leave!'

Get stuffed. I held on.

Seconds passed. The Instructor stood still. Noddy picked up the ball. My anger slowly subsided. The Instructor nodded. The ball dropped again but before Noddy spoke I darted my head sideways and grabbed it in my mouth. 'GOOD BOY!' they chorused. 'We'll take that down a bit next time...'

Instructors catch on quick.

And true to his word he didn't annoy me as much, stood further away, ran long before Noddy let me go and because I wasn't as infuriated I didn't bite him as hard. And I was prepared to let go for the ball first time, Noddy's, 'Leave' slightly more plaintive than before. Police Dog Instructor training is all a matter of balance. Let them know how to do it and they learn pretty quickly.

That week was all about the bite and the leave. They did bring the stick in and we were battered gently along our back and flanks, but as the stick was padded it all added to the fun.

All the dogs managed, none as well as me, but that's what you'd expect. Ava was sharp, 'Arry laid back, Donald and Dougie had done it before.

Then came control. Up to now all the revving-up excitable exercises had been done from the lead. We were wound up and let go.

On week seven I watched Mitch walk Donald out into the middle of the field, tell him to sit and, taking off the lead, throw it over his shoulder doubled over, but not fastened. The Instructor appeared wearing the sleeve and started to run. Donald stood up to go and Mitch bellowed, 'STAY!' Donald looked up at him, worried, and then Mitch yelled, 'Police-with-a-dog-stop!' and gave him the 'Hold 'im!'. Donald hesitated then shot off and took the Instructor as we all had before.

Dougie and Mogsy went through the same pantomime. Then Nuffer marched smartly onto the field, Ava prancing beside him, the tart. There was the same, 'Stay' as the lead came off and an odd half-sideways stance with the lead held over his shoulder by Nuffer.

'Police-with-a-dog-stop!', and Ava took off. In a blur the lead came down over Nuffer's shoulder and wacked her across the rump with a crack as Nuffer yelled, 'STAY!'

Ava curled to the floor in a heap and bared her teeth up at Nuffer as she rolled onto her back, half supplication, half threat.

The Instructor strolled back to his start point behind a scale jump. Nuffer gently patted his leg and encouraged Ava back to sit at his side. The Instructor ran again, 'Police-with-a-dog-stop', and this time Ava stayed put until Nuffer quietly let her go with, "Old 'im.' And she nailed the Instructor, but with less gusto than before.

In the van I bristled. My turn next. Noddy slipped the chain over my head as I dropped out of the top-middle cage and we walked to the position.

I heard Mogsy say to Mitch, 'Major'll kill him,' and Mitch reply, 'Watch.'

Then Noddy, for the first time in police dog handler training so far as I am aware, used his brain. He first took off my chain, slung the lead over his shoulder and fastened it there. Then he fastened a thick leather collar around my neck and threaded a short length of chord through the D-ring, holding it tightly in his left hand as I sat at his side.

The Instructor ran.

Noddy said, 'Police-with-a-dog-stop' and I went to stand up, except the chord-held collar stopped me and I sat again.

'Hold 'im,' whispered Noddy and I leapt forwards, the chord snaking through the D-ring as he released one end of it from his fist. I hit the Instructor and dragged him forwards, making him stagger to keep his feet. Noddy belted up behind me, grinning from ear to ear.

'I told you it would work,' he said with his best Cheshire Cat expression.

'Shut and get him off smart arse!' came the Instructor's, also grinned, response.

We'd just invented a kinder method of communicating with each other that they didn't actually want us to chase until we were invited to.

Police dogs of the future, you owe me.

We were on a bit of a cusp in police dog handler training about then. For years police dogs had been basically shoved and battered into the work, but the numpties were beginning to realise that we would perform better with an incentive to gain, rather than one to avoid.

It should have been simple really. Everyone works better for a reward rather than with the threat of a punishment hanging over you. In police dog handler training our reward was often just to be able to do what they wanted us to do anyway, like biting the Instructor. Waiting until they'd judged he'd had a fair start was the least we could do.

There were of course variations on the theme. Occasionally the Instructor would come at us waving the stick, or would stand his ground and fire a gun at us, but they always ended with the same bite.

They were still messing up our heads with what they called the Stand-Off though. Just as they'd taught us to bite and not back off, they wanted us to back off and not bite.

It started the same as a bite, same place, same, 'Sit-stay', same Instructor running off and same 'Hold 'im' command (we didn't have 'requests' in our day, we had commands – what do you think we were in, the Brownies?). But when we were about ten metres away the Instructor turned and faced us, hands folded across his nadgers as though for a football free kick. Except one held the whip. As I went in for the bite it lashed across my face and I remembered my first Person Search, and backed off, barking. The paroxysms of joy told me I'd made the right decision.

Ava wasn't so bright and spent a few minutes lunging in, biting, being stung by the whip, dropping off and lunging again, before she caught on. Stupidly brutal compared to how it is taught these days, but they didn't know any better – and we learned, although many dogs lost the edge from their bite because they were confused about when to stand-off and when not.

To be honest, it wasn't difficult to sus-out. Hands across the nadgers, stand out, anything else, bite.

And so it went for weeks, everything becoming more difficult. Tracks went from clean fields to romping across the countryside and through housing estates. Sometimes there was a runner and a bite at the end; sometimes we did night tracks in the dark. Searches expanded through woods, scrapyards and warehouses. Obedience was polished to perfection.

It was always hard but fun, and we had some laughs along the way. What is it they say? Find a job you love and you'll never work again? I never worked a day in my life.

On the Tuesday of week twelve Jamesy came back from his track with his nose spread over his face; blood everywhere. It wasn't unusual to pick up minor injuries, cuts from barbed wire or knocks from falling over, but this was a belter.

'Arry had tracked through a wood and up to the sheep-wire boundary fence. It was about four feet high and topped with a strand of barbed wire. Jamesy had laid his leg on top of the barbed strand to prevent 'Arry from catching himself on it and commanded 'Hup!' but 'Arry baulked. 'Hup!' but again 'Arry refused, although he see-sawed back and forth like he was trying to pluck up the effort.

The third time 'Arry refused, Jamesy, annoyed, said, 'Right 'Arry, get under then!' and bent down to lift the bottom of the fence to allow him to crawl through. Just as 'Arry leaped over.

The top of 'Arry's dome met the squishy part of Jamesy's beak, which exploded in blood and snot. The question of 'Arry's legitimate paternity was brought into spluttering doubt as Jamesy first picked himself up off the floor and then picked 'Arry up in his arms and threw him over the fence.

'Arry cleverly set off tracking again. They can't do anything to you when you're tracking because they don't want to put you off. Smart dog.

The last week was test-week. The Boss came and marked us

53

through our toughest exercises, clip-board in hand. He was a handler himself and as hard as they come, so he knew the intricacies of the job and how good we'd all need to be to master it out in the real world. And it was his dog section, so he didn't pass out sub-standard teams. Everyone upped their game when the Boss was on the field.

It was rare for a team to fail in the final week. The inadequate were weeded out long before and the handlers invited into 'the office'. It wasn't really an office, but a phrase used by Instructors that struck dread into handler's hearts. They could be all having a brew, us dogs lying quietly after an afternoon's biting or tracking, when an Instructor would beckon a handler by name with, 'Can you just step into my office...' as they walked away from the group for a quiet chat.

And that quiet chat could be anything from, 'How many times have I told you not to nag your dog when she's tracking? You're letting her down. Sort yourself out.' Right through to, 'That last half hour confirmed it. We've done everything we can and Pedro's never going to stop a runner for you. We'll start looking for another dog on Monday.' And by Monday Pedro would have gone home.

But we'd all come past that point and the Boss's scrutiny was mostly just to put the handlers under pressure, and officially record our competence.

So we all did the hour and a half old pattern track in a field with tiny articles in the grass and also the twenty-minute old track from an abandoned car in the housing estate, with a runner to stop at the end. We found and barked at two people in a warehouse, one out in the open and the other completely concealed so we were indicating on scent alone. We found four tiny articles in a twenty-five metre square, did heelwork off-lead in a line, send-away and redirect, sit-stand-down at fifty yards distance, the dumbbell retrieve, the hurdle, long and scale jumps, a straight chase, stand-off, stick, gun and an emergency stop.

And were we ever anything less than perfect? Too chuffing right we

54

were. The handlers were a bag of nerves: Nuffer kept putting his lead over the wrong shoulder; Mogsy had written L and R on Mitch's wellies in white paint – L on the right and R on the left of course – and Mitch had wiped boot polish round the inside rim of Mogsy's hat so he had a black ring round his bald pate when he took it off. Jamesy's voice was reduced to a squeak through tension.

There's an expression that, 'It goes down the lead', meaning that we dogs are effected by our handler's mood. I'm not sure that's how it works, but dogs are certainly sensitive to minute changes in their handlers. Ava accidentally swallowed a key, the second article on her pattern track, but Nuffer didn't realise and spent ages on his hands and knees looking for it in the grass. (When it came out three days later he washed it and presented it to the Boss, asking for his 10 extra marks for the track article. He didn't get them.)

Donald, who knew perfectly well how to send away and redirect, disappeared off to the right behind a low rise on the field and every time Mitch tried to direct him somewhere else he moved three or four steps left or right. Only his ears were showing above the mound, moving first to the left… then to the right… then to the left…

I bit on the stand-off. Don't know what came over me. Piled straight in. It just seemed like a good idea at the time. I saw the Instructor stop and turn and I just thought, '*Stuff it*' and took him off his feet. There was mayhem for a few minutes until the Boss said, 'I think we'll try that again shall we?' Second time was no bother. But I had to do another on Friday morning as well.

Meanwhile 'Arry plodded through everything, Jamesy's nose lighting up the winter gloom, until it came to the distance control (different positions on command at fifty yards) when he couldn't hear the squeaked '*down!*' or '*stand!*' and just sat there looking bemused. The Instructor saved him by advising Jamesy to use hand signals instead.

Friday (after my Boss-observed stand-off DTF) was cleaning day.

We were vacating our kennels and the Skylark for the foreseeable, and the handlers would leave them as they would like to find them; spotless. We waited in the holding kennels for the beginning of the next chapter, little suspecting what lay before us.

We'd learned the ropes and were going to work.

🐾🐾🐾🐾

I'd been home with Noddy for a few weekends towards the end of the course, so it came as no surprise when we were dropped off at his gaff on Friday afternoon.

Dog handlers lived in police accommodation with a kennel and run in the back garden, although the regulations had just allowed police to buy and live in their own property, so some were doing just that. They were still paid a pittance at that time and a police house was a considerable perk of the job, although they were increasingly becoming run down through lack of funds. It wasn't unusual to see peeling paint on the outside and draughts howling through the warped metal-framed windows, but our kennels were immaculate, and cosy.

We were on the edge of a not-too-bad council housing estate and Noddy could reasonably expect not to have his windows put in regularly or to find unpleasant stuff had been shoved through the letter box in the dead of night. The house was semi-detached to another handler's, so having a police dog in one of the two back gardens at most hours of the day and night also afforded protection from attacks by stealth from the rear.

We worked the northern force area in a team a four, covering the Town, several smaller towns and villages, and the surrounding countryside. The basic shifts meant that on any day one of us was on a day shift: 8-4 or 9-5pm, whilst another was on the back shift: 5-1 or 6-2am; one would be on Rest Day and another either be delegated to a special operation or training if it was early in the week, or an extra back shift at weekends. The shifts rolled so that we started after Rest Days on a 5-1am followed by the 9-5pm then another 5-1.

Between finishing the back shift and starting again at nine o'clock we took call, meaning that we could be re-called to duty for any jobs that arose. The handlers didn't mind because they were paid overtime, and we didn't mind because there were prisoners to be had. But it meant we could be working a full twenty-four hours before handing the area over to another dog.

We had three vans to share between us, but with one of them broken down, in for service or pranged at any one time there was little spare capacity, and handlers were forever picking one another up and getting a lift home.

That's how we started at five o'clock on the Monday before Christmas. Arthur picked us up from home, Noddy in the usual handler's half uniform – jumper and green anorak, but with a uniform jacket and cap chucked on the shelf behind the seats; wellies, one holding tracking harness and lead, the other stuffed with rolled-up waterproof leggings, stood in my cage just inside the back door.

Arthur was an old hand, a handler since the gods were in nappies so they said, and very well respected by all, not just for his capabilities as a handler, but also for knowing every dodge in the book. He was a real countryman who could shear a sheep, castrate a calf, purge a pig, chit a chicken and probably bodger a badger if the fancy took him. He knew when it was going to rain, and why, and where to find the best mushrooms, holly, mistletoe, pheasants and pie-shops, all of which he took advantage of when the time was right (mushrooms at daybreak for an autumn breakfast; holly and mistletoe to sell on to a market trader for cash at Christmas; pie-shops at four o'clock on a winter's morning, just as the first batch comes out of the oven and the baker has brewed-up; pheasants, when nobody is looking).

He was on first name terms with every farmer and magistrate for miles around and knew every footpath, lane, ginnel, alleyway and shortcut. Accordingly once he had sussed the direction in which he was tracking from a crime, he would often leapfrog the scroat and be waiting for him as he arrived home with the loot. He'd locked-up all the major thieves and, with fists like sledgehammers, knocked down all the major fighters. He had a slight smoker's cough and hard-men taking on all-comers in the street on a Saturday night would often hear, 'ah-herm' just before their lights went out.

His current dog, a shaggy yellow beast called Beddo, was just older than me, having graduated from that year's early course, and had a nice turn of sarcasm. He called me Marker – an insult that suggests I am so afraid that I have to go around marking every upright to boost my self-esteem. I called him Mark-seeker – a dog so worried that he constantly seeks out other dogs' marks to mark on top of them as the only way he can prove himself. We both quickly decided not to bother each other beyond a grumble whenever the other jumped into the van.

Arthur dropped us at the home of Big Ernie, the third of our four-handler team, where Noddy didn't knock but picked up the van keys from where they'd been left under the mat in the van cage.

Ernie was, even by dog handler standards, considered a bit odd. He was nearing retirement, but had lost his wife a few years ago. She hadn't died but one day, after twenty-three years of marriage, he'd come home from work to find she wasn't there. Bereft, he'd looked all over the house for her, but concluded he had lost her and consequently let himself go.

Now tattier than a Shih Tzu in an electric hail-storm, he had little time for shaving, bathing or other aspects of human personal hygiene. He spent most of his day-shifts on his allotment and most night shifts in the back rooms of various pubs. Again, even by dog handler standards, he drank a lot – sometimes when off duty too. He never turned up on training days, and on his days off he slept (still in his uniform), getting

58

up only to walk Gerald, his long-suffering partner.

Gerald was as laid-back as they come, eight years old and, through lack of grooming, as scruffy as Ernie. He spent his nights feasting on free pub crisps and his days snoozing on the allotment shed's veranda.

Like a grubby King Midas, Ernie's lack of hygiene extended to whatever he touched. Consequently when a handler picked up a van from Ernie it was a mess; full of damp cast hair (some of it dogs'), fish and chip wrappers, muck from the allotment and sometimes the odd spade or fork.

So it was that I was lying down outside the washing bay at the traffic unit watching Noddy clambering inside the van, battering away at encrusted muck with the hand-brush, when the call came through on the personal radio, 'Armed hostage incident at the Green Man – dog handler to the scene immediately.'

Dog vans had no blue lights; they'd only just been upgraded to a 'Police Stop' sign on the back door, as a nod in the direction of corporate policing.

There was a tug-of-purpose between those who saw dog handlers as sneaky takers of thieves, prowling around in a battered old van, and those who preferred to provide high visibility reassurance to an ever-nervous public. The sign on the back door was a compromise that could be illuminated or hidden by discreetly parking against a wall.

But it didn't help us through the Christmas rush-hour traffic. No, that was done by driving like a maniac, as we hurtled across town in a manner that was to become very familiar to me over my career. A manner that ramped-up the excitement because it meant that the game was afoot*, and the quarry to be hunted.

---

* (This is afoot-note) This is my second favourite Shakespeare quote after, 'Cry 'Havoc!' and let slip the dogs of war.' which always gives me a shiver and an urge to be slipped.

The Green Man was a sorry little pub tucked into a row of dilapidated shops and houses halfway up the main drag to the Shambles estate; the festering boil on the Town's backside.

Like many towns ours was laid out by people trying to get away from it. From the town centre there were major roads leading away in each direction, north, south, east and west. More minor escapes followed the river routes, where ancient peoples had come to conquer, realised there was nothing worth taking, and left again, leaving behind their less ambitious to breed with the locals and contribute to the scumming-over of the gene pool.

The Shambles was a result of the post-war council-housing boom of semi-detached homes fit for heroes, now a run down, boarded-up rat-run of homes fitted with zeros. Zero jobs, zero prospects, zero cash, zero morals.

You couldn't call them criminal gangs, because that would suppose some sort of organisational abilities, but it was populated by various hierarchies of illegal operatives. It's hard not to grow up a petty thief when shoplifted jars of coffee are hidden in your pram.

The way up was through drug dealing and the prime aspiration was to burgle a country house for the shotgun they could saw-off for a subsequent robbery.

TWOC-ing (Taking Without Owner's Consent – nicking cars and dumping them again) was the major hobby amongst pimply teens, who paid their younger siblings in drugs for syphoned petrol so they could while away the small hours taunting the police into a chase.

From there they graduated to borstal and eventually to grown-up prison, where they might meet their Dad, if they knew him. The ladies tended to specialise in benefit fraud supplemented by shoplifting and fencing the stolen gear. Being pregnant helped keep you out of prison, so large families were commonplace. Everyone knew each other and many were related. Yet others were rumoured to be the offspring of certain CID officers, all kinds of favours and information being negotiable currency. You could call it a sink-hole of rats, if you wanted to give rats a bad name.

The Green Man stood forlornly on the street that was trying to get in to the Shambles, usually fraternised by the sort that just want to drink, lots, and was now empty this early evening save for a lady doctor, two ambulance crew and a wild-eyed Fellsman holding them hostage at gunpoint.

The Fellsman lived somewhere out in the wild middle of nowhere and had been found wandering naked amongst his sheep. Whilst this wasn't a totally novel occurrence thereabouts, the absence of wellies had prompted his neighbours to call the doctor, who duly sectioned him, managed to persuade him to wrap himself in a coat, called the ambulance and was transporting him to hospital when he clearly fancied a pint.

Turning onto Shambleside Road he pulled a pistol from his coat and demanded they accompany him to the pub.

The half-dozen regulars enjoying mine host's hospitality turned to see a lady doctor and two ambulance men being propelled through the door. Unperturbed they turned back to their pints, only to be completely perturbed by the following nutcase, his coat and everything under it flapping wildly, waving a gun about.

Five bolted out the back door, the landlord ran upstairs to his flat and the sixth customer threw a chair at the Fellsman, who brushed it aside on his way to the bar. The local then calmly drained his pint and two others that had been left on the bar and walked past the Fellsman out of the front door, illustrating a degree of sang froid that only the truly slaughtered can achieve.

When we arrived in a side street a short distance away about five minutes later the road had been closed both above and below the pub by strategically placed Panda cars, blue lights whirring. The operation was in the third phase of the AFO*'s tactics of 'Identify, Locate and Contain'. The final tactical option, not yet reached in this case, was Blast The Living ~~Sh.~~ Daylights Out Of Them.

We bailed out of the van and Noddy donned his body armour, only recently issued to dog vans and kept in a bin-liner behind the seats to keep it clean. It didn't work. I relied on my natural agility to dodge any bullets that came my way. Like Superdog, only faster.

We took up a watching position across the road, just as the doctor and ambulance-men scuttled out of the door and away up the road to the waiting Panda.

When the Fellsman had decided to take a leak to clear his head and tottered off to the toilet, the hostages had taken the opportunity to scarper. Unfortunately they forgot to take the ambulance, which was still parked with the keys in outside the pub.

Now on his own in the bar, the Fellsman took to drinking steadily, helping himself from the pumps. The publican had phoned the nick from upstairs. He was only used to being threatened by fists, iron bars and pick shafts, and was seriously cheesed off at the loss of custom.

Time to crack out the crack troops. Within seconds the Firearms Inspector had picked out the place on his chest where his Queens Gallantry Medal would go and, pausing only to collect his well-drilled men and as many inter-continental ballistic missiles as he could carry, twirled his moustache and sped to the scene, bristling with weaponry.

Back at the nick, a high level discussion took place.

'Who can we blame if he gets away?'

'Better get more dog handlers.'

A short time after that, Arthur and Beddo joined me and Noddy in our side street, behind a parked van for cover but with a good view of the street and pub. Many other Plods had also turned up and were

---

* AFO – Authorised Firearms Officer – also known to dog handlers as the Technical Weapons And Tactics Squad

standing about ineffectually looking at the pub, waiting for the firearms team.

Noddy, noticing a discrepancy in Arthur's apparel, asked, 'Where's your bulletproof vest?' to which the reply was, 'Dunno.'

'You'll have to get one, it's regulations.'

'Whose is that...?' He said, pointing to one leaning against the Chief Superintendent's leg.

'The Chief Super's'.

'Well, he won't need it, I'll have that one.'

Ballistic armour has improved since then. Now it is sleek. Then it was of such bulk that had either of the handlers fallen over it would have taken two strong men to lift them again. Noddy's gangly legs gave him the appearance of a huge blue lollipop and Arthur looked like he should have been floating above a Michelin garage, although, had he done so, anti-aircraft batteries would have been within their rights to open fire.

Back in the firing line, the Superintendent, who had trained by watching every episode of Z Cars, was negotiating with the Fellsman by loud hailer from across the street. Standing not ten yards away, I distinctly heard him say,

'FRBK RPTRND PRQD DOKRNPZ PLK PUNDRKD', which I think means, 'The train now standing on platform three is the seven forty-five to Glasgow'.

There was no reply.

Upstairs, the landlord was providing a running commentary on the telephone to the nick...

'What's happening downstairs?'

'Nothing.'

'Can you hear anything?'

'No.'

'Has anything happened yet?'

'No.'

'What's happening now?'

'Nothing – wait...'

'What is it? WHAT IS IT??'

'Can I reverse the charges for this call?'

Meanwhile, the Firearms Inspector had arrived and was discussing his plan for gently encouraging the now rather pathetic figure to lay down his arms.

'A couple of stun grenades down the chimney and CS gas canisters through front and back windows should give us the cover to storm the door.'

The Chief Super had by now decided that enough was enough and, standing in the middle of the road with his hands in his pockets, asked the Firearms Inspector if something could be done.

The Firearms Inspector, attempting to see past the Chief Superintendent into the pub, climbed on top of a nearby van. Standing there, gun in one hand, binoculars in the other, and holding up a full-length protective ballistic shield with - well, I couldn't see quite what it was from where I was taking cover behind Noddy - he could tell straight away that he had no better view than he had before. He got down.

Under cover of the twelve pints of lager drunk by the Fellsman, a team sneaked forward and removed the keys from the ambulance. It was then that I first heard a piece of advice I was to hear frequently during my career...

'Will you shut that bloody dog up!'

Beddo, bored with the apparent inactivity, had playfully pinned two traffic officers and a portable generator against the wall. Teach them not to try to walk past on *his* pavement.

The Firearms Inspector decided to go for a look through the transom window above the pub door. After shuffling across the street carrying that full length ballistic shield in front of him in case of snipers,

64

he leant it against the door, pulled himself up by his fingertips, and peered over the top. There was another, solid, door inside. Unusual for a pub that.

Conscious that he had to negotiate the return journey safely to relay this vital information to his Entry Squad he picked up the shield again, executed a full 180° about-face, and shuffled back, the shield still protecting his front as he exposed his back to the pub door. Noddy and Arthur dissolved into fits of not very successfully stifled giggles. Beddo and I looked at each other in silent despair.

The Assistant Chief Constable arrived behind the van we were using as cover. Arthur, seasoned campaigner, suggested that it had been declared an Officers Mess, so we moved to a van we could call our own, nearer the pub.

'The only trouble with this van is that we might get caught in a crossfire,' he cheerfully observed, grinning and nodding in the direction of the fortuitously located next-door premises of the Funeral Director and Monumental Mason.

The Superintendent was now giving the departure times from Gatwick and the personal radio announced the arrival of the local TV crew. Instinctively everyone crouched lower, the Firearms Sergeant assumed a noble profile, and the Superintendent turned his best side to the camera - his back.

Another top-level conference decided that if immediate action was not taken, they would not make the nine o' clock news.

They would have to go in!

Cautiously, behind two full length angled shields this time, the Firearms Inspector, taking a Constable with him (teeth gritted as he imagined a commando knife clenched between them) in case he needed directions back, clattered across the road like two skeletons making love in a dustbin, to take a peep in the bar window. Looking up from his prone position plastered on the floor, our Fellsman (by now it

65

was impossible not to feel some proprietary affection for him) decided that the TARDIS observing him must be a dream and went back to his sozzled slumber.

Arthur and Noddy, nervous at being left on the same side of the road as the TV crew, crossed with us and hid behind the ambulance. Evidently they were quite prepared to be shot in the line of duty, but not by a television camera. Coincidentally this gave us the shortest direct line of sight should the Fellsman manage to lurch out of the door and make a stagger for it.

'Move in - move in', a whispered command and a dozen dark-clad beret-topped AFOs ran in a crouched position, guns outstretched, up the pavement past us. Beddo and I expressed our mild annoyance at being sneaked up on by a gang of what appeared to be scorched garden gnomes who had lost their fishing rods - all together now...

'WILL YOU SHUT THOSE BLOODY DOGS UP!'

The pub's outer door creaked open stealthily; the inner door flew off its hinges and hit the far wall. The noise may have woken the Fellsman from his twenty-seven pint coma, or it could have been the five burly Plods who landed on him a microsecond later and handcuffed several bits of him together.

The radio spoke, 'One man arrested, everything under control.'

Plods with guns emerged from behind walls, out of drains and under paving stones, bandoliers gleaming in the streetlight.

'I'll bring the van sir,' said the Shift Sergeant.

'Bring the van,' said the Assistant Chief Constable.

'Fetch the van,' said the Chief Superintendent.

'Get the van,' said the Superintendent.

'Time to go,' said Arthur.

The Fellsman, under the impression he was floating on a cloud, until his face hit the corrugated floor of the van, was escorted away from the scene to the sound of loud cheering from a group of about a

66

hundred concerned residents of the Shambles.

'Sink estate' probably isn't a fair description, unless the plug-hole was blocked with some particularly fetid gunk and the washing-up water hadn't been changed since... ever. Held back for their own safety by the outstretched arms of a rather crumpled looking Plod, this group, when allowed free access to the road again, were so anxious to assist that they all ran, screaming and howling towards us outside the pub. They'd seen riots on their (stolen) telly. They knew how the script went.

'Move them back,' said the Superintendent, 'Get them bloody dogs up here.' This is what Beddo and I had been waiting for! Free bites!

'Get them bladdy dogs away from those bladdy cameras,' roared the Chief Superintendent, contravening Noise Abatement laws.

'Time to go,' said Arthur. So we did.

The gun was found to be an unloaded plastic .177 air pistol that wouldn't have fooled a three year old, and when our Fellsman had sobered up he was charged with 'Keeping a doctor waiting for almost as long as doctors keep patients waiting,' and then bailed under the Mental Health Act to secure accommodation.

The Inter-Continental Ballistic Missiles went back in their box and the item made nine seconds at the end of the local news, the Firearms Inspector's profile looking every bit as noble as it did in real life.

And Arthur made two hours overtime for watching what could only be described as street theatre.

So it wasn't a waste of time and money at all.

Me and Noddy resumed our back-shift, him driving and me in the back, with the forgotten hand-brush and more hair than was hygienic for company.

The rest of the evening went off relatively quietly. We nosed around some burglaries in the Shambles. The more switched-on residents had realised that homes would be empty whilst the occupants were watching the Green Man panto so half a dozen break-ins had been reported afterwards, but there wasn't much for us.

They were all in off the street, down the side path and kick the door in, only portable stuff like radio-cassette players and video recorders taken. Not subtle, but effective. No property left behind for us to find, and tracks petered out quickly in the confusion of scents on the pavement. And *everybody* reported they'd had a video-recorder stolen, whether they'd had one or not. It wasn't for the insurance, because they didn't have any, but more a matter of pride that they didn't want you to think they couldn't afford a video recorder, even though you could see they had no carpets and were keeping warm by burning he floorboards lifted from the back bedroom.

Actually there was a theory that there was a video-recorder in the Shambles, but only one, it just moved from house to house regularly as it was stolen and sold on.

Noddy ate his bait* on the go, grabbing a sandwich and tea from his flask as we parked up in Station Square at pub kicking-out time.

The town centre at night revolved around the area in front of the railway station, where the main taxi rank performed the services of steadily removing the drunks to the outer estates and meanwhile concentrating them in one place for our entertainment.

Of course the Christmas party season was in full swing and the party-goers were generally in good cheer. Occasionally there'd be a punch-up in the taxi rank of the, 'Are you lookin' at my bird?' type. Given that the bird in question was probably in impossibly high heels and a micro-skirt, and at the time bending at the waist vomiting copiously into the adjacent flowerbed, hair held out of the trajectory if she was lucky enough to have a considerate mate, the only honest answer was, 'Yes.' However this would transform in the brain of the

---

*Bait, packed meal. Like many northern dialect words comes from Old Norse (*beite*: food). Hence bait-box and bait-time.

speaker into taxi rank parlance and come out as, 'Why would I want to do that? She's a reet minger!'♥

The questioner, not wanting to admit the, even temporary, truth of the statement would take exception and a swing or possibly a nut to the observer.

All this would happen before the Plod (one of several stationed close by to deal with just such incidents) had time to walk over, intoning, 'Van to Station Square please' into his radio. Both fighters would be lifted and dropped into the back of the van, which had been cruising with Driver and Sergeant waiting for such a call, where they could continue their discourse until arriving at the back door of the nick, prior to spending the obligatory night in the cells.

Noddy and I generally didn't bother getting involved in minor skirmishes, but watched from the van (we seemed to stay in the van more on nights when it was raining, but there again rain is known as the 'policeman's friend' because no one wants to hang around and fight when it's chucking it down).

On busier nights, like this one, we deployed out of the van and he stood in uniform and cap while I sat beside him, bristling with understated authority as we watched the ebb and flow of human detritus.

A small park area containing flowerbeds and some hefty mature sycamore trees ran alongside the taxi rank. In the trees several thousand starlings congregated at night, clustering together to chatter and gossip.

Not bright, your average starling. Their conversation revolves around, 'Found any nice worms lately?' and 'Did you see that wheelie I pulled as I came in to land?' But these ones were fun to play with.

We often stood across the square, watching the rank, and I'd wait

---

♥Reet Minger: unattractive lady, particularly to the sense of smell. Roughly 'a proper stinker', although I don't know how a puny-nosed human would know.

until plenty of birds were parked up, dozing in the branches, before belting out the loudest five seconds of staccato barking I could manage from a standing start.

A thousand starlings would simultaneously leap into the air, all screaming in fright, 'Shit!' and coincidentally performing the action at the same time – on the heads of the queueing rankers. Well, they say it's lucky…

Fun over, we went to bed.

🐾🐾🐾🐾

I heard the telephone in Noddy's room. Two rings and he was up and moving. I was waiting at the run gate as he hurtled out of the back door. He flipped the latch and we both leapt into the van.

Minutes later we were at the Farmers' Warehouse on the industrial estate. A huge open-plan building stacked with everything a farmer could possibly need, from wellies and clothes to wheelbarrows and horse tack, and it had been screwed twice in the last month.

The M.O. was the same again (*Modus Operandi* translates as Mode of Operation, or 'Ow It Were Done); they'd taken out two panes of glass from the louvre window above the door and climbed in. They'd previously got out by bursting the fire-door and legging it with a fairly random selection of goodies, but this time the fire-door was still firmly closed. They were still inside.

We knew they were inside because they'd set off a silent movement-sensor alarm that SOCO* had fitted and which alerted in the nick. There was already a Panda at the back and another at the front. It would have taken the Plods an age to search the whole place, so they'd called me out.

---

* Scenes Of Crime Officer – Plods with a permanent faint dusting of aluminium fingerprint powder - what they used to be until they had ideas above their station, copied the television, and became CSIs.

70

Noddy had knocked the lights off the van, cut the engine and drifted to a halt fifty yards down the road, and we walked up to the front door together. We didn't want them bolting out before we could get our teeth into them, but I was ready if they did. The key-holder had been called just after Noddy and he drove up to the door just as we arrived.

He opened up and I in took a nose-full of frightened scroat. The place reeked of two of them. Noddy slipped the chain from my neck and I sat at his side, quivering with excitement, as he bellowed,

'POLICE WITH A DOG! COME OUT OF THE BUILDING NOW OR I'LL PUT THE DOG IN!'

He paused as we listened for movement and shouted, 'LAST CHANCE, THE DOG'S COMING IN!' and looking down to me, 'Find 'im.'

We didn't really want them to come out because that would have ruined the game, but the police had this strange idea of justice. The shouted challenge was to show the key-holder we were being fair. He'd be our witness if there were any complaints that we hadn't given them a chance to give up later.

I already knew they weren't near the door – I'd have smelled them – so I shot off in search. The light switches were in the office on the other side of the building, so I was working by moonlight and scent. In the bottom corner, where the reek was strongest, were about a dozen circular racks of clothes, and right beside them I could see a man standing there, motionless.

My first collar.

I played it by the book and barked at one second intervals, the noise reverberating off the plate glass windows and bouncing round the building.

He didn't move a muscle, standing stock still as Noddy pounded up behind me with his torch illuminating... a headless figure!

It was a manikin... but the stench of scroat was so strong, how could I be wrong? The nose never lies!

Noddy looked at me in disgust as he envisaged his new-boy reputation being relayed down the nick. Our first prisoner a dummy. I could hear the japes from the Plods, 'Did he come quietly Noddy?' 'Who's the bigger dummy, you or your prisoner? Har har har.'

I stopped barking and, looking sheepish, radiated, *'Sorry – but the scroat-smell's so strong.'*

'Come out of there you pillock,' Noddy told me, his voice reflected his dismay, disappointment and embarrassment.

As I turned back towards the door, tail hanging low, a pleading voice came from the nearest clothes rack, 'Okay then mister but don't let the dog get me,' and a tiny urchin crept out from between the waxed cotton jackets.

Automatically I lunged forwards but Noddy's quiet, 'Leave 'im,' told me that this one was too small for sport – a tiddler we could only throw back – and I checked myself.

'Okay then, but only if you tell me where your mate is,' said Noddy.

'I'm here.'

The equally small voice came from the next roundel of jackets as a similar mini-scroat slinked out and stood in the classic you've-got-me pose of hands thrust into pockets and head bowed.

Now, Noddy hadn't known that there were two of them, but was using the assumption that they rarely burgle in ones and, as he'd got lucky, gave it another go.

'Right, how many more?'

'None, there's just me and Plug.'

'Are you sure? Because this dog's really pissed off now and he's going to rip apart anyone he finds after this.'

It was news to me, but what the heck, if it saves us some legwork...I gave the kid my meanest Elvis curled lip and Paddington hard stare. A tough look to pull off, I'm sure you'll agree.

72

'What about the other times? Was it just you two then as well?'

'Wot uver times? We ain't dun no uver times.'

Nice try Noddy, but even twelve-year-old scroats know better than to cough jobs you haven't proved yet. By now we'd walked the two kids back towards the Plod on the door, where Noddy handed them over.

'They're yours; we'll check out the rest of the place.'

We took up position in the doorway again and he bellowed,

'POLICE WITH A DOG. WE'VE GOT YOUR MATES. COME OUT NOW OR I'LL PUT THE DOG IN AGAIN.'

He looked at me. I looked back, narrowed my eyes and drilled, *'There are none,'* from my mind to his. He concentrated really hard, as though trying to understand the look on my face, then said, 'Find 'im.' Schwanzkopf.

Really people, when your dog is looking at you like that, he's trying to tell you something. Give us a break and make the effort back will you? Most of the time it isn't that important (quite often it's *Give Me That Biscuit*) but it would be nice if you met us halfway in this communication thing.

I wandered around the place to keep him happy, but I could smell there were no more. Noddy poked around behind me with his beam, looking inside the remaining racks of clothes, until he was happy there were no more of the Bash Street Kids stashed away and we left after resetting the alarm. The key-holder replaced the glass in the louvre and locked up behind us.

I didn't know if that was success or not. I'd made a bit of a schafskopf of myself by mouthing off too early, but on the other hand I'd made two (albeit pint-sized) burglars give themselves up. In one respect then it was a good job done – two nil to the good guys – but I'd let my biggest asset, my sense of smell, be beaten by my worst, my ability to make sense of stationary shapes. Arsch. I wouldn't let that happen again.

'Dog handler, are you still available?' The radio strapped to his chest gargled, making that scrustch noise all good cop-show radios make after each transmission.

'Just on our way back home...'

'Got another alarm. Council offices on Pratwell Square. Got a ten minute delay on it.'

'On our way, be there in five.'

Nowadays the bells sound as soon as the circuit breaks, but back then some insurance companies knew it was good to catch burglars inside premises and the alarm would trip at the central station whilst the bells remained silent to let us get there.

We were just around the corner, coasting to a stop again, when, 'Area two, front door's in.' The area Panda was there and confirming it wasn't a false alarm, maybe set off by the wind blowing through an insecure fourth-floor window or an over-ambitious stack of files dropping from a desk.

The Controller was an experienced Plod back at the nick. He knew the streets himself, having worked them for many years before specialising in the inside role. He sent a second Panda to the back street where she could see the fire exit door and monitor the end of the block, and a foot beat-bobby to the other end.

'Stay out – dog handler's on his way,' he told them.

He knew Panda drivers sometimes had a rush of blood to the head and dived inside, charging about like a headless chicken, hoping to come across a burglar on the job. He also knew that the chances of one finding such a scroat were minimal and that the scent of an over-anxious Panda Plod spread about inside did nothing to help me.

'At scene,' Noddy told them as we drove up to the front door, all need for subterfuge now gone. The door was indeed smashed in, which would in itself have set off the alarm, but was anyone inside, or had they legged it?

'POLICE WITH A DOG...' and off we went again. Burglars stink from the fear and adrenaline. I knew he was inside. But just one this time, and he was drunk. The building was massive and permeated by the scent of the paperwork that constituted the lifeblood of any council operation.

An old Georgian terrace had been knocked through to house the Town's council staff, and then the big rooms partitioned into smaller offices. It was a maze of open and closed door, after door, after door. One door would open into a cupboard stacked with files and the next into an office we'd just searched from the other side.

I tried to shorten it by scanning and walking out of rooms with no scroat scent in, and the ground floor went by quickly. But there were four different staircases and we had to be aware that he could double down on us when we moved up. The bells rang out when we were halfway along the first floor and accompanied us for the rest of the search, muffling any sounds that might have helped.

Methodically we moved from one end to another, then up a flight of stairs and back the other way, but by the time we'd reached the fourth floor even I wasn't sure we'd hit every room. Occasionally I'd catch the scent of the intruder, but the papery background scent was often too strong to track him and the combination of some doors being open and others closed made it swirl all over.

You don't know about scent, do you? You think it's a whiff of something, usually something strong, but it isn't like that for dogs (or, come to that, most other mammals except humans. Oh, and reptiles too. And fish. And insects. Everybody except you actually).

How can I put it? It's being able to see through walls, into the past and invisible emotions. As I scanned the planning department Chief Executive Officer's office I knew he kept chocolate digestives in the second drawer down of his desk, and that before they'd left for the evening he and his secretary had been very friendly on top of his desk.

Multiply those whiffs a hundred times and imagine each one to be a different coloured smoke, then stir them up into a multi-hued cloud moving in four dimensions. And through it runs the one disjointed thread I'm searching for, sometimes a wide ribbon, a tunnel leading me on, only to fade to gossamer, be blown sideways or upwards, or masked temporarily when a door opens and I'm hit by another kaleido-smoke.

I absolutely love it. But I wasn't loving this. It was too complicated and disjointed, with too many doors stopping and starting us. When we reached the lower level attic I wasn't really sure he was still in the building.

Because the houses in the original street were different heights, the attics of some of the houses were level with the top floor of others. This attic was used for storing files and papers tied up in pink ribbon, piled up in stacks three times as high as a dog. The entrance was a half-door in a wall and as soon as Noddy opened it I saw a figure, motionless in the dark, leaning against an upright roof support.

I wasn't going to be caught twice in a night barking at a dummy, so I trotted cautiously towards it. Then it moved. Or rather it legged it into the dark across the boarded floor between the stacks of files. I laughed inside and launched myself after him, nails scrabbling to get purchase, like a cartoon.

I heard Noddy behind me, 'Police-with-a-dog-stop! Hold 'im!' but I was already gone. I was rapidly gaining on the scroat when we cleared the last of the stacks of files and the boards underfoot ran out. I hurdled three joists, touching down on the ceiling plasterboard in between, hurled myself at his right arm, jaws poised to clamp down, and...

Nothing.

Nothing but a tearing and crashing sound behind and below me, followed by a dull thud.

I'd sailed over the scroat as he'd smashed through the plasterboard

76

and he was now lying on his back on the Chief Executive's desk. He was in more or less the same position the CEO's secretary had occupied some twelve hours earlier, but I doubt her leg was facing backwards, as his was.

Being considerably lighter than a human and spreading that weight over four points of contact has its advantages and, after peering through the hole at him, I trotted back through the attic and down to where Noddy was rather unnecessarily handcuffing our semi-conscious prisoner.

He turned out to be a drunken vagrant who had decided that the skip he usually dossed down in was a bit chilly and the council owed him a warmer spot. Kicking the door in was his first mistake. His second and third were in trying to hide from and then outrun me. His fourth and last was in thinking plasterboard could take his weight.

On the plus side for him the hospital bed where he was taken to mend his broken femur was nice and cosy.

As we left the building we passed the caretaker who had come to turn off the bells and secure the place. He was unmistakable in his caretaker's brown dust-coat. He smelled tired, but I guessed he'd been woken up the same as we had, and he was sweating slightly from the walk in to town, despite the cold.

'Got him, eh?' Caretaker asked Noddy.

'Yeah, a sorry state of a vagrant I'm afraid. Broke his leg when he went thought the attic floor.'

'Good. Serves the blighter right. Hope they throw the book at him.' Not a caring Caretaker then.

'They should lock up people like that and throw away the key. Thank you for catching him. If it wasn't for you officers of the law we wouldn't be safe in our beds'.

Noddy beamed slightly uncomfortably. It was nice to be thanked, but this grateful member of the public was going slightly over the top. He tried to be polite and changed the subject, 'Don't you feel the cold? Just the overall and no coat?'

'I'm on official council business. I have to dress appropriately otherwise standards would slip, and we can't have that, can we?'

'Err, no, I suppose we can't.' Noddy recognised the jobsworth mentality and sidled away towards the van, 'Well, we'll leave it with you then.' You can get stuck talking to jobsworths for longer than is good for your sanity.

'Phew, lucky escape there, mate. Who says, 'blighter' and 'officers of the law'?' Noddy asked as he drove off.

'No idea mate, he's probably got something to hide,' I sent back before I realised it was rhetorical exasperation rather than a question, and he wasn't listening.

We clocked off with Headquarters Control Room at five-thirty, Noddy stopping on the way home to let me clean out on a stretch of disused railway siding (Hey! It'd been a long night! I was bursting!), and were due back on at nine for the day shift. Little point in going to bed so I caught a nap in the van whilst he breakfasted.

At six o'clock he clocked back on. We could finish at two, and we'd have to take call until five when Arthur took over, but afternoons are quiet in response policing.

We responded to two different control rooms. Most work came on the radio around his neck from the local Town Control, who were also in touch with the Plods in the smaller towns and villages in the Northern Area we served, but we were a force-wide resource. The whole force, another three areas, was coordinated by the HQ Control Room and because dog handlers were so scarce, only four on duty in the force at any one time, we had to clock on and off with them on the radio in the van. If the effluent smacked the air conditioning we could end up anywhere in a county of over two and a half thousand square miles. What can I say? We were so good everybody wanted us.

Noddy went into the nick to check up on the night's crime from the rest of the Northern area, and sure enough people were waking up to find their houses had been screwed whilst they were fast asleep. Mornings were about picking up the pieces and maybe piecing some evidence together.

We rapidly formed a list of jobs to visit and Noddy prioritised them by which he thought might yield best results. First was a trip a couple of miles out into the country to a house burglary on the edge of a village. No sign of forced entry but a several grand's worth of jewellery and cash taken.

People lie. Dogs don't lie because we can smell when we are being lied to, so there's no point. When I say 'smell', it is partly olfactory, when the wrong emotion seeps through your sweat, but with attitude stitched in. The way you hold your body and tilt your head; the inflection in your speech, the truth in your eyes.

People often lie about what has been stolen from them. They lie that things they never owned are missing, because they can make a fraudulent insurance claim.

'Ooo officer I've been saving up for twenty years and they've taken me five thousand pound nest egg. Honest.'

They also lie that things they owned (but shouldn't have done) have not been stolen. That could include illegal items, such as recreational drugs or unlicensed firearms, or legitimate property they have come by illegally, for example by having stolen it from someone else.

I once found an antique silver salt-pot just over the back fence of a screwed house, clearly having been dropped by the burglar, and reeking of the householder. When we took it back the guy denied having ever seen it before, even though it stank of him. So Noddy took it back to the nick and guess what? It had been stolen from a big house job five years previously. The CID had a word with the guy.

Stupid thing was that if he'd just thanked us and accepted it back, we'd never have been suspicious about it. Arsch.

Cash, jewellery and silver are particularly easy to lie about, so when someone reports that's all that's been stolen, you take it with a pinch of salt, and when there's no sign of a forced entry, it sounds even dodgier.

We arrived shortly after the SOCO, who was still on duty, never having stopped from the night before. He'd be handing over to the day shift at eight, so this was his last call. SOCOs were a strange breed, not like the self-important CSIs you see on the telly (yes, of course I watch telly, what do you think I do when I'm lying in front of the fire?).

They were aging policemen of the been-there-seen-it-done-it variety. Inevitably world-weary, going through the motions of collecting evidence to put the bad guys away. In the days when DNA testing was a far-off dream their stock in trade was sellotape, dabbed on surfaces to pick up fibres and hairs, and smoothed over the aluminium powder that was carefully wafted over surfaces where fingerprints lingered, collecting the impressions left by sweaty hands. They would take plaster-casts of footprints and photograph other marks such as scratches at the point of entry.

That's what Jerry was doing when we walked round the back of the house into the garden, photographing the tiny bore-hole in the wooden window-frame that the scroat had made with an awl. The hole was so small that the householder hadn't seen it, but that's how the low-life had broken in. Bored the hole then pushed the awl through and flipped the window latch.

He'd searched the house, taken what he wanted, which was only stuff he could fit in his pockets, and let himself out of the back door.

'That's the third of these I've seen this week. It looks like he's back at it again.' Jerry punctuated his speech with despondent sighs.

'Bug'r,' replied Noddy, 'Busy time of year for doing any obs* though. Been in the garden?'

'I know better than to go tramping about the place. Point of entry's as far as I go, the rest's yours.'

'Cheers.' And then to me, as he looped the chain off my head and threw it across his shoulder to clip it into its parking place, 'Go and get busy.' That's handler-speak sending me for a wazz.

I know what you're thinking. Why the teufel would he tell me to have a slash in a garden that is effectively a crime-scene?

Because he's a dog handler.

Let me explain. There are *handlers* of dogs and people who go around with dogs – referred to by real dog *handlers* as 'dog-walkers' (who may also be employed as police dog handlers). *Handlers* of dogs are in tune with their dog. They know what their dog wants and their dog knows what they want. They use that cross-species knowledge to get the best out of their working relationship. Dog-walkers waste a great deal of time and effort trying to get the dog to do what they want, instead of using their heads to manipulate the circumstances to their best mutual advantage.

A police dog-*walker* (although they call themselves a *handler*) takes his dog into the garden and lets him off the lead with a 'search' or 'find' command. Now, what does every dog, police or otherwise, do when he's first let off the lead – especially in new territory? Correct. He cocks his leg on the first available vertical object and sprays to let the world know he was here. The dog-*walker* now has to give his dog a bollocking because he disobeyed a direct command and had a wazz instead. Then he has to ask his dog to search or find again, but now the dog's cheesed off and consequently not in the mood for working.

The dog *handler*, on the other hand, knows that his dog is going to

---

* Observations: staking out a likely place and waiting for scummy's next strike.

81

cock his leg at the first opportunity – it's canine nature – so gives his dog permission, then asks him to go to work. Having made his mark, the dog is happy and puts his mind to the job enthusiastically.

Any third party watching thinks the dog *walker* is a pimmel, which he is, and that the dog *handler* has such great control over his dog that he can ask him to empty his bladder before starting work.

So I did.

As I left my mark I also clocked the scent on the back garden fence where our current scroat had climbed in and out. You don't need to tell me about multi-tasking. I went over, gave a deep snort and followed the scent up the fence. Noddy checked the flower bed below and shouted over to Jerry, 'Footprint in the soil here.'

'Right –oh,' Jerry sighed, 'I'll cast it and add it to the collection.'

The wooden fence was five and a half feet so we could easily have scaled it, but there was a strand of barbed wire on posts over the other side to keep cattle from pushing on it, so we went round.

Barbed wire, the bane of a dog handler's crotch. Always too low for all but the shortest handler to duck under it, frequently too high to straddle. Noddy had acquired the knack by handler-lore osmosis; the art of observing and learning useful things that you just pick up without noticing it. If you'd asked him how he knew what the safest way over barbed wire was, he wouldn't be able to tell you – he just knew. It goes like this…

➢ If you are right handed support yourself on the nearest post with your right hand (left-handers mirror the whole process).

➢ stretch your left leg along the length of wire to your left, placing the instep of your boot on it, which weighs it down as far as it goes.

➢ your left leg is now resting lightly on the wire, your boot taking the weight.

➢ pat your left knee with your left hand and tell your dog, 'Hup!'

➢ he or she will leap lightly over your leg to the other side, without risking ripping his undercarriage or her nipples.

➢ flex your right knee and ankle, stand upright, straighten your right arm and then propel yourself over the fence, right leg skipping through the triangle formed by your right arm, left leg and the wire.

➢ land neatly on the other side on both feet.

Handlers become so practiced at this that they can do it on the run in a paused vaulting action. However, it can also go spectacularly wrong at almost every stage.

If it does, the least they can expect is ruined over-trousers. The worst, I'll leave to your imagination. But we avoided any risk that day by walking round, through the cul-de-sac and field gate, where I picked up the scent on the other side.

It had been a cool and damp night, and the day was barely warming up, so scenting conditions were favourable. He'd come and gone over the fence at about the same place, but there the track split.

He'd arrived along the fence and left straight out into the field. He was quicker when he left than when he arrived, his footsteps further apart and less hesitant, but not hugely so. Noddy clocked some marks in the mud, but they were less clear than the ones inside, and of less evidential value. After all, although they could place the pond-life in the field, it wasn't illegal to be in a field.

I checked and compared the scent on the two directions, then set off out into the field. Noddy could have stopped me and put my harness and line on (many handlers would) but he was content to let me pick my way over the track. We weren't in a hurry to catch the scroat – he was long gone – nor were we looking for discarded property – he'd sorted what he wanted when he was inside the house - but we were looking for clues as to the direction he'd gone home.

It was an old track, I reckon he'd been there about two and it was now approaching seven, but still workable in the plain grass field. There was plenty of light in the sky for me to work from, but Noddy would still be in the dark for another hour or so, until daybreak proper.

In no rush I picked my way across the first field to a gate into the second, heading cross-country towards the lights of the Town. After the third field we hit the railway line. It was a branch line, not electrified and with only a few trains each day. I stood at the fence, strings of horizontal plain wire topped with a strand of barbed at about four feet, and waited for Noddy.

'That's it kid, we ain't going on there,' he told me, as I heard the diesel engine leaving the village and boosting towards us with its carriages full of commuters. A few moments later we both stepped away from the line as it belched past, its stink wiping out any chance I had of following the scent in its wake.

We cast a hundred yards up and down our side of the line, then, checking carefully, crossed over and did the same on the other side, but no joy. Scroaty-boy had stayed on the railway, and if he'd stayed on for that long, he'd probably stayed on into the Town. We'd effectively lost him.

Anywhere you lose the scent of a track, like railway lines, main roads or big rivers, it is always worth checking both sides up and down in case they've done it to lose you and come back out again a few yards later, so I tend to do about a hundred yards on each side in both directions. If they've stayed on or in it for longer than that, it has become their preferred means of travel and they will only come off again when they need to change direction.

Noddy would log where we'd tracked on his dog report. He filed one for each job and a copy went to the detective in the case. He'd also call in to the collator's office and mention it to Harry, who collected information on his card index and inside his head. This scroat walked to his crimes and used the fields and railway lines, not roads. He worked alone, used an awl and took only what he could carry.

We went to a few other breaks as the day dawned into another damp and cold one. Nothing startling; a couple with nothing to show and one where I found some children's Christmas presents prematurely ripped open by some low-life who'd kicked open the back door and run off with them into the park behind. Once there, skulking in the bushes, he'd dumped them after finding he didn't really want a doll that wets itself, a toy harmonica and assorted clothes for a four year old girl. He took the little boy's bike though.

Merry Christmas.

🐾🐾🐾🐾

Wednesday was a back shift filled mostly with mopping up more Reverse-Santa breaks, and domestics.

Reverse-Santa jobs are always pathetic because not only do the parents lose the presents, they are left having to explain to the kids how come they had presents hidden in their house when they are supposed to be brought down the chimney on Christmas Eve by a jolly bearded fat man in a red suit.

There's rarely much to be had for me either – sometimes because they are straight out the front door and others because Dad's sold them to a bloke in a pub for beer-money and covered it by faking a break-in.

There is also an increase in domestics during the festive period. I hate domestics. Violence, screaming, yelling, drunken injured people sobbing. And I'm not allowed to bite any of them. I sit in the van, watching and hearing all hell break loose, and Noddy doesn't let me out to play. Not fair. We go for back-up in case we're needed. But I never am.

Occasionally the bloke is chucked in the back of the van and locked up for the night, but she always withdraws her complaint in the morning, turning up at the nick sporting her shiner and professing her undying love for him. If she's the problem and he's nursing a lump on

85

his head the shape of a frying pan, she'll be taken round to her mother's house to cool off for the rest of the night.

I have no idea why humans pair up like this. Dogs are far more sensible. I appreciate that you have an extended nurturing period during which you stay together to provide for your offspring, otherwise they wouldn't survive and mankind would die out, but what a weird genetic model to adopt. Ours is far superior (mind you, so is a cuckoo's).

We have a quick leg-over, often arranged for us by kindly people so we don't even have to do the whole chocolates and flowers courtship thing, and that's the dog's part finished. Even the bitch doesn't have a great deal to do; pops out the pups like peas from a pod and from then on, apart from a little light breast-feeding, she hands over care of the little blighters to people.

You lot gurgle and coo over them from the moment they are born, provide everything they need, and even find them homes where other people will pay to look after them for the rest of their lives. Now that's what I call a sensible way to spread your genes. And no domestics because the drunken swine's spent the week's housekeeping on beer or the filthy slut's not emptied the sink of dishes when he needs a slash in it.

Just after midnight we got a call to London Road. Every town has a London Road, even when it is in the far north. When the Town evolved it would have taken at least two weeks to travel to London either walking or on horseback, yet they called the road that pointed in that direction 'London' road. You have to admire their optimism that people wandering south were actually heading for London.

'Oh, yes, we're connected to the capital don't y'know?'

I wonder how they managed to overlook the fact that it passed through every other city, town and village on the way?

Anyway, London Road, being a major route out of town, is posh. Or at least posh enough to run past the scummier housing estates and eventually have fields behind it. And of course having fields behind means scroats only need to scale one wall, fence or hedge and they are in the back garden.

I know now that the tracks from breaks in houses like these follow a pattern. Out the back, over the garden fence into the fields and then towards the Town for a field or two until the open landscape is marred by the encroaching housing estate. Unless we are truly on their tail we manage a few streets before losing it in the maelstrom of scent. But this was my first one and I was still open to possibilities.

The householders had been out to a party and, when the taxi dropped them off, as they'd staggered in through the front door they heard the back door clash as the scroats left. Utter devastation met them, every drawer emptied out onto the floor, ornaments smashed and very large scheiße squatting steaming on the sofa. That last one's more usual than you think – scroats literally scheiße themselves through fear.

If we'd thought ahead to the possibility of DNA testing we'd have kept every one frozen in a bag, numbered and cross-referenced. We could now have a historical Scheiße-Squad DNA testing them and going round to the houses of middle-aged men, knocking on the door and lifting up the bag, saying:

'When you were seventeen you left this inside the scene of a burglary. With aromatic irony, you are now up this very creek without a paddle pal.'

The phrase, 'They've just run out the back, I heard the door clash as we came in!' is also very common, but at the same time mostly wrong. It's true that they heard the door, but not often true that it was the scroats leaving. You see, scroats don't go to the trouble of closing the door properly behind them when they leave, so when the front door opens it causes a draught through the house and the back door swings shut.

But this time they actually had just fled, and we were on to them. Noddy hammered the van to get there first and we bailed straight round the back. The exit point wasn't difficult to locate, they'd battered down the privet hedge as they'd crashed through it. We vaulted the gap with ease, me waiting for Noddy on the other side. It was bright moonlight, frosty, and the ground was like iron, with little grass cover in the worn-out field, but that didn't bother me. Their noxious stench hung in the air like a cloud of wasps at a picnic. Two of them. Noddy harnessed me up because he didn't want to lose me in the dark and I pulled hard towards Town.

I hadn't bothered to check the ground as the air scent was so heavy, and with little wind it was hanging obligingly for me, but after a hundred yards or so something seemed odd. They were moving too fast, even for hot-footing scroats. I should have been catching them, but I wasn't. The scent was, if anything, becoming slightly less concentrated and there was something else in it, something metallic, something oily. They were pulling away.

Noddy was jogging behind me, staggering occasionally, finding it difficult to keep his feet on the frozen field. I glanced down at the hoary grass and saw, instead of footmarks in the frost, tyre marks. They were on bikes.

I stopped, looked at the ground and up at Noddy.

'*They're on bikes.*' I thought hard at him, but nothing. I looked down and up at him again.

'What have you found?' he asked.

'*They. Are. On. Bikes.*' Concentrating really hard this time.

He flashed his torch at the ground.

'Bug'r. They're on bikes.'

He'd already told the Controller that we were headed for the

Riverbank estate and a Panda had been dispatched to park up and wait at the most obvious bolt-hole. Now he radioed in again because that widened the search. They could veer off into any part of the estate on bikes, and we didn't have enough Pandas to cover every rat-hole.

'Let us know when you can get us a definite direction.'

'Will do, we're heading for the play-park at the moment, but that's probably because it is the nearest ginnel. About half a mile away.'

We set off again at pace. Noddy dropped the line and ran alongside me, panting, 'Stay,' so he could catch up when I surged too far ahead. A hundred and fifty yards from the play-park we saw them break from the dark shadow of the hedges into the arc of the street lights.

'Play-park now, two on bikes, I'm a good hundred yards adrift.' Noddy gasped into his radio, gave up all pretence of tracking and we both ran.

I kept glancing back, '*Send me, send me, send me...*' I was drilling it into his brain, but he wasn't at home to Mr Telepathy. Yes, I could've gone by myself, but training is training and teamwork is teamwork. I won't pretend that I haven't made some decisions myself over the years, and maybe I should have gone this time, but I waited for the release command that didn't come.

The radio crackled loudly, 'Two just gone past me out of the play-park and cut through onto Garibaldi Road.' The Panda driver. They'd seen him skulking, shot out of the other side of the play-park and immediately through a pedestrian alleyway into the next street. And now they knew we were coming. Useless arsch.

Like many parts of the police family, they've been invented and reinvented in various guises over the years, but the value of Plods with local knowledge just can't be underestimated. At the time they were called Resident Beat Officers, or RBOs, and were allocated a part of the Town to call their own. They walked or cycled their beat and the better ones knew all their residents by name and sight. Hamish was one of the better ones.

He'd been hitching a lift home with the Panda and when the break was called he knew where to head. On a hunch he'd positioned the Panda at the obvious spot and headed off into the estate on foot.

We both heard the clatter as two bikes hit the road, the sound carrying clearly in the cold night air. Noddy didn't notice but just before the racket I also heard the hollow 'whump' that Hamish's helmet made as it bounced off the head of the leading scroat, chucked unerringly by the RBO from where he stood, just back into the hedge at the end of the ginnel onto Garibaldi Road.

The force of the blow knocked the scroat sideways off his bike, and his brother ploughed into the wreckage from behind. Hamish stepped out and grabbed Colin Doyle by the scruff,

'You're in serious trouble now Colin, riding a bike with no lights? They'll throw the book at you.' Paul, his brother, scrambled to his feet, disentangling himself from handlebars and spokes, and automatically started to run.

'Paul, seriously, don't waste your energy. If you run now, I'll go knock your Mum out of bed and tell her. Maybe do a full house search.'

Colin and Paul were eighteen and twenty years old, but still scared to death of their Mum. You could look at it as them being respectful, or you could look at it as because their Mum would have them battered by one or several of their uncles for first getting caught and second giving the police an excuse to visit her house.

Big Claire Doyle was a shoplifter, fence and firmly embedded as the matriarch of the whole Doyle clan, which comprised of her numerous brothers and their offspring. Many of them were also called Doyle, and there were also sub-clans related by parentage but not necessarily legitimate marriage. It was said that when a girl partnered up with a Doyle she became family, and family shared. It was a lucky (or deluded) Doyle that knew exactly which Doyle was their father.

90

Doyles regularly swapped identities and it was difficult for the system to keep track. They were a Traffic Plod's nightmare – trying to match the Doyle with the details on the registration, insurance and driving licence. But Hamish knew each one by sight. He was sometimes picked up and driven across the county to identify which Doyle had been pulled over by Traffic.

Fraudulent Doyles' heads would drop when they saw Hamish alight from another traffic car. Sometimes, if they were just lying out of habit, the mere threat of sending for Hamish could make them come clean.

Paul decided he'd better wait with Hamish and Colin for the van, and so we found them a few moments later, Hamish smoking a micro-thin roll-your-own.

'Ah, hiya Noddy. Tracked all the way?'

I sniffed at the two dejected scroats, their pockets bulging with jewellery and silver.

'Aye, Hamish. I'll do you a statement.'

I'd followed a trail of scent from the scene of the crime to the feet (well, wheels) of Colin and Paul, and they were in recent possession of the property stolen from the house. Result.

But no bite again.

The night played out with a couple of alarms from smashed shop windows - drunks kicking plate glass windows in for entertainment was a frequent problem. Of course it set the alarm off and we'd have to search the premises to make sure no one had entered, but I knew they'd never set foot inside because there was no scent. Quite often Noddy would know too, from my lackadaisical approach, but it still had to be done.

Un-blooded, we went to bed.

Thursday morning was still bright and crisp, frost slowly thawing. We went to another Walking Man break that backed onto a school field, tracked across the field and out of the gate. When frozen grass melts it releases trapped scent, so it was easy enough to follow in the field. I knew it was the Walking Man from the scent, and the MO was the same as usual. I lost him in the melee of the traffic as he crossed the road in front of the school six hours earlier; his scent wiped out on the opposite footpath.

From there we were asked to go to a corner shop that had no alarm, but had been visited during the night. Somebody had been hungry on the way home and kicked a glass door panel in, then crawled through to take boxes of Mars bars. They were probably too drunk to notice that they'd cut themselves, but the blood spots remained visible on the pavement even eight hours later.

I'd never been trained to follow blood spots but, hey, I'm a dog; blood's one of my favourite things. Noddy could see the spots at first, but he harnessed me and let me follow the trail to get my nose in. Occasionally I'd pick up a whiff of the scroat that went with the blood, but mostly I was a blood-hound. There were places where we lost visual because it had been walked over and scuffed away, but the scent remained enough.

The route was short but complicated. He'd walked through the estate, using all the cuts to make his most direct way home. We picked up four Mars bar wrappers on the way and when I took Noddy into a front garden (tastefully decorated with rusty tin bath and a broken bike-frame) we could both see the blood on the front door knob.

It's true what they say about zero tolerance. If this scroat had been jumped on for dropping litter and the council had made him keep his front garden tidy maybe he wouldn't have thought it was alright to midnight snack on somebody else's choccies.

The CID had been taking a statement from the shop-owner, so they arrived just as Noddy's hammering brought a dishevelled scroat peering round the door, heavily blood-stained tea-towel wrapped

92

around his hand.

Ever eloquent in the face of adversity, he opened with, 'Wot?'

'Police. Can we come in and have a word?' said the younger detective of the two.

'Wot fo'? Ain't dun nowt.' (Translation for southerners: 'For what purpose? I have done nothing.')

'I suspect that the gash on your hand was caused during the course of a burglary during which a quantity of sweets were stolen. I'd like to ask you some questions.'

The young detective was a classic of his era: shiny suit, big knot in his tie, coiffured mullet and luxuriant Zapata 'tash. The older one too had a 'tash, but clipped more in a military style; military haircut too, and a cheap suit. Out of the corner of his mouth he said, 'Leave it with us Noddy' and as the midnight snacker watched us turn to go, his own front door smacked him down the middle of his forehead, propelled by Zapata 'Tash's shove.

As he staggered backwards the two followed him through the now open door, and as it swung closed behind them I heard Military say,

'Right, show us the Mars bars and let's have a proper cough or I'll lock you up for the job, your missus for handling and have the kids taken into care.'

Black Eye Friday was the last Friday before Christmas, when the building site foremen paid the week's wages, and often a Christmas bonus, at lunchtime. Traditionally they went straight to the pub with pockets bulging for a 'quick half' on their way home. 'Half' would turn into 'many', and insults and fisticuffs would inevitably follow in another fine Christmas tradition.

The Town always put on extra staff in preparation and Noddy and me were to do a twelve hour shift, 4pm to 4am. This was the day before and Noddy had to go to a briefing to prepare for the upcoming mayhem. I don't know why he needed a special briefing; how difficult can it be to tell him to get me out of the van and let me bite them? He'd parked up in the station yard and I could hear the Inspector call the briefing room to order.

The Task Force were there in their usual gang. Another invention/reinvention of the same idea with different names, sometimes the Tactical Support Group, sometimes the Special Patrol Group, occasionally Operational Support; there has always been a place in the police for a gang of highly motivated thugs with special skills, chief amongst which was cruising round in a van until called for, then beating the living scheiße out of whoever they were pointed at.

Sorry, what I meant was 'a highly motivated group of men and women who can be deployed as a team at short notice to cover tactical emergencies and respond quickly to emerging disorder.' I always liked them.

'Now this year we are having a change of tactics,' started the Inspector, 'The powers have decided that Black Eye Friday is a pejorative term that is self-fulfilling. If we look for black eyes, we will find them.'

A whisper went round the room in several voices,

'What's 'pejorative?''

'Means it's got holes in it, like a colander.'

'No, that's 'perforated', you tosser.'

'You'll be perforated if you call me a tosser again.'

'It means contemptuous, much like you two.'

'My Granddad was an Old Contemptible.'

'Was he in the war?'

'No, that's what my Grandma called him – she couldn't stand him.'

'I can see you're a chip off the old block.'

'I'll chip a lump off your block in a minute.'

'So' said the Inspector in a much louder voice, to get their attention,

94

'To lighten the mood and expectation, we're now calling it 'Festive Friday'.'

'Not so bleedin' festive when a bloody scaffolder's coming at you with a table leg in the snug of the Golden Lion...' The Task Force Sergeant was a big man, with a whisper that boomed around the room.

'Look', said the Inspector with a sigh, 'I don't make this bollocks up, I just pass it on from the rarefied heights where it masquerades as making a decision. So this year's plan is for you to be nice to the brickies, scaffolders, plasterers, joiners, decorators, hod-carriers and all the other tradespeople that are belting the living daylights out of each other. They will of course become bosom buddies the moment you arrive, bury their differences and direct an allied attack on you, so the best of luck with that.'

There was a group guffaw from the Task Force and a sigh of relief from the RBOs who were present and had the misfortune to have one of the builders' pubs on their patch. It would be business as usual. None of the RBOs were afraid to go into a Black Eye Friday pub-ruck, but it's nice to know the cavalry are coming to back you up.

The Inspector started allocating Plods to beats when the Controller stuck his head around the door.

'Armed robbery at the Shambles Post Office. Two men, medium height and build, one jeans and black bomber jacket, the other jeans and dark blue anorak, both in ballies*. Threatened staff with a sawn-off and left with one mailbag. On foot, towards Talavera Road. No vehicle seen. I've sent the area Panda but she's not there yet.'

'Keep the scene clear, I'll try for a track,' Noddy shouted over his shoulder down the corridor as he led the scrum of Plods cramming through the doorway heading for the back yard.

In TV shows the Plods to rush to major crimes, whereas in real life

---

* Balaclava – the favourite disguise of the scroat, which had not yet been supplanted by distinctly posher ski mask.

they plot up away from the scene to watch for anything that might be slightly out of the ordinary; a car with anyone matching the description, or one carrying a male driver and two male passengers. There wasn't a lot to go on – the descriptions were rubbish – so our job was to try to get a direction of travel for the toxic waste.

If we could follow them on foot we might find someone who saw them getting in a car round the corner, and then we'd have a colour for the car, which is at least a start. But tracking at 11am in a busy estate is tough. How would I know which of the many tracks leaving the post office were the toxics? We were in luck. The Panda-Plod had established that they had run across the road from the Post Office and then cut down a ginnel – a footpath between two corner houses. And even better for us, she'd made sure nobody else walked that way after she arrived. Sometimes they aren't as stupid as they look.

We harnessed up and I cast around, quickly picking up the two freshest scents there in the ginnel. They were unmistakably scroats, hardly unusual in the Shambles, but additionally tinged with adrenaline. It was a well-used thoroughfare so there were many other human scents there too, but I stayed with the adrenaline as the main feature to distinguish these from the rest. Noddy wasn't convinced, and held me taught on the line, making me keep my nose to the floor, but I was happy I was right and pulled hard into the harness to tell him.

The day had remained cold with still air, but the hedges acted as a funnel and the air scent had blown up and through, with little collecting on the sides, forcing me to check footprint to footprint.

We were now fifteen minutes behind them and moving at a slow walking pace as I checked and rechecked the ground. I kept losing one scroat, then regaining it, then losing the other as we passed out of the ginnel onto the open footpath on Talavera Road. I was trying to keep both scents in my head and filter them out of all the others, so I could tell if they split up. Halfway down they turned left along another ginnel and came out on Salamanca Street, another fifty yards then right through another ginnel, still both together, but walking now.

They could be a mile of twists and turns ahead of us, so we had no chance of catching them, but they still hadn't got into a car. Walking suggested the first phase of the getaway was over. They'd probably taken the ballies off, or rolled them up onto their heads (nobody would have looked twice at two blokes wearing woolly hats on such a cold day) but they hadn't chucked them or I'd have found them.

Noddy was keeping Control updated with our progress as I tracked out of that ginnel onto the footpath in the cul-de-sac end of Corunna Road when the scent went haywire. I didn't lose it, but it went from next to nothing to being everywhere. There were puddles of it. I checked and found it carried straight on again, slightly fresher, then after another ten yards it disappeared at the edge of the curb. They'd got into a car.

I stopped, looked at Noddy and thought, *'Car'.*

He'd obviously been expecting it, looked back at me, 'Sure?'

'Yep, car.'

He shouted it in on his radio and Stevie the RBO popped up as Noddy was unharnessing me; he'd been shadowing our progress on parallel roads through the estate.

Noddy and Stevie started discussing scroats' names and where they lived, trying to fit the pieces together: descriptions, knowledge of the estate, direction of travel, access to sawn-off, and so on.

I wandered back to the scent puddles I'd found at the end of the ginnel and found there was a side track up a garden path. I thought the scent puddles had been left by them waiting for the car to pick them up, hanging about on the corner, but no. They'd come down the ginnel, turned into the first house at the end of the culdy, (culdy-sack, French meaning 'bottom of a sack'; very apt for this estate, which was in many ways scraping the bottom of a sack) then come back out and got into a car. The puddles were caused by them walking back and forth as they

97

went into and came out of the garden.

I nosed the gate open and tracked up to the door. The double track went inside and came out.

'What you got mate?' from Noddy.

Stevie said, 'It's empty. Has been for more than a month. D'you think Major wants inside?'

Amazing. It must be like having second sight. There I was, scratching at the door with my paw and pushing at it with my shoulder, whining, and he's able to interpret that as 'Major wants inside'. Genius.

I couldn't have been more explicit if I'd etched 'We need to look in here,' into the peeling paintwork.

Noddy followed me up the path and when he put his shoulder to the door, the yale latch popped and it swung open.

Stevie again, 'Hang on. They've got a sawn-off. If they're still in here we'd better wait for the TF.' Task Force were also AFOs and in view of the nature of the crime had been issued with firearms.

'I'm pretty sure they'll have gone. We tracked to the kerb. Tell you what, call TF and I'll put Major in. It'll only take a minute to search.'

Great. I knew they weren't inside, but Noddy couldn't have been a hundred percent. So did he bravely venture in? No, he did not. He sent Major in to risk his life. And what thanks do I get? A gallantry medal? A pension? No, a pat on the back - maybe.

Noddy slipped a chain over my head and excitedly whispered into my ear, 'Police with a dog, come out or I'll put the dog in!' over and over and... I couldn't help myself. I can't now. I never could. It just winds me up into a frenzy every time. Just the possibility of the chance of a find. I feel almost dirty for the way he can manipulate me, push my buttons, twist my tail, but I still loved the feeling. The rush! The buzz! And when he slipped the chain off again I shot into the house like a steroidal whippet.

Downstairs, no scent past the hallway. The rooms were empty of furniture, but more importantly, empty of scent. The toxics hadn't set foot in the living room. I passed Noddy crouched to one side of the doorway and took the stairs five at a time. Upstairs was curious. There was scent there, but only in the back bedroom and the landing. They'd been in the back bedroom, but there was a lot of scent hanging on the landing. Their scent and other stuff. Dust. Paper? Mailbag. There was mailbag scent. Noddy could see me on the landing as I followed the drifting scent with my nose... upwards.

Two TF arrived in a squeal of tyres and with guns drawn as they jumped out of the car, having watched too many episodes of The Sweeney. Regan and Carter had a lot to answer for.

Did you know that the best position for you to hold a handgun is pointing forwards, about chest height, with both hands loosely stretched out in front of you? Police officers have to be trained out of holding it vertically, pointing it at the sky, right next to their face. This is because they, like everyone else, have been brought up watching TV cops holding it like that. TV cops hold it like that not because it is the most efficient way to hold a gun, but because it is the best way to get the hero's head and the gun in close-up camera-shot at once. It makes more dramatic TV. But because life imitating art will increase your chances of being dead, real police are trained out of it. Mostly.

'Give us a sec, Major's onto something. Let him work it out.'

Noddy held them back in the doorway as I slowly pirouetted onto my back legs, following the scent up the bannister to... the loft hatch. I dropped back onto all fours and stared at Noddy.

'Loft,' I telepathed.

'Shit.' He said quietly. 'They've been in the loft. Or maybe one's still in the loft. We tracked to the kerb about ten yards down the culdy, so I'm pretty sure they were in a car, but Major says 'loft'. I can't be sure they both got in the car.'

'Shit.' Both TF and Stevie in unison.

'No, you ärsche,' I thought at all of them, 'There's some _thing_ in the loft, not some _one!_' But they let me down again. No contact.

'We've got an entry kit in the car...' That's TF for you, prepared for anything, except listening to dogs.

Minutes later the two TF were stood one on the landing each side of a folding A-frame ladder. One smacked the loft hatch with a door-buster, a one-person held battering ram. Stevie threw two lit torches through the opening and the second TF yelled, 'Armed Police!' pointing his pistol (correctly), directly at the hole.

The loft hatch cover clattered to one side and the torches lit up the roof-space. One landed in the loft, shining into the gloom, and the other fell back down the hole onto the TF door-buster's head, making a dull clunk and tipping him back off the ladder.

The torch, eighteen inches of aluminium with extra batteries for high power, hit the wooden floor and bounced on its end down the stairs, one step at a time. In the film version, it will switch to slow motion, but even in real time it slo-o-o-o-o-owly boinked end over end on each hollow wooden step.

We all turned to watch it in disbelief. Boink, boink, boink... Fourteen times, like a depressed slinky, into the hallway. On each boink, it got funnier and funnier. By the time it finished Noddy was bent double and Stevie could hardly say, 'oops, sorry' for laughing. We had announced in no uncertain terms to anyone in the loft that we were coming to get them and we meant business but, however much we tried, we couldn't really take ourselves seriously.

The TF stepped slightly unsteadily back onto the ladder, smoothing down his hair and his dignity. Of course, from there they could only see immediately around the hole. Someone was going to have to stick his head into the loft. That would be a really good time for a cornered scroat to blow it off with a sawn-off shotgun.

'Can you lift Major in?' asked the TF with a lump on his head.

Oh, not so brave now eh? It's always, 'Call the TF, we are the heroes, go anywhere, do anything, all singing, all dancing...', but who do you call when you want someone to stick their head into the loft?

I didn't care. I could smell there was no one up there.

I jumped into Noddy's arms – a trick we'd perfected in our spare time and handy for occasions just such as this – and he boosted me into the loft from the ladder, a TF standing each side, armed and pointing. Now I *was* worried. I was far more likely to be shot accidentally by the TF than by a non-existent scroat.

Quickly moving out of the way of the open hatch I clocked a pile of gear. Two jackets, a full mailbag, two ballies and a sawn-off shotgun. They'd changed coats, stashed the gear and the gun and took off in the car. I brought one of the ballies to the hatch and let them see me.

'No-goddy 'ere', I thought at them, my thinking voice strangely affected by holding a bally in my mouth.

'They've left some gear, but looks like they've gone,' said my genius handler, 'Major'd have told us if they were still there.'

Noddy came up the ladder and shouted down to the TF to bring some evidence-bags. I hung around in the background whilst they passed the jackets, ballies, mailbag and sawn-off, suitably bagged, back down the hatch and into their car.

At that point I realised I'd have to come down from the loft. I hadn't really thought of it until then but it was an eight foot drop, straight down.

People are fine, they can sit on the edge and lower themselves halfway, or use the ladder. I couldn't do either. Dogs only have one way of dropping, and it's head first. I wasn't dropping eight foot onto the landing. I'd end up like the torch, in the hallway having hit every stair on the way down.

Noddy started down the ladder, 'Come on son, I'll catch you.'

'Nope', glaring at him and standing my ground.

He climbed back up the ladder and took hold of my neck with both hands. As he pulled, the ladder wobbled under him and I pulled backwards out of his grip.

'Blood-i-ell.' He sounded annoyed, then climbed back into the loft, unclipped his lead from his shoulder and dropped the chain over my head. The other end of lead dropped out of the hatch.

'I'm going to stop him backing away, can one of you pull the lead and catch him as he falls?'

Stevie replied, 'Errr, is that safe?'

'Course it is, just don't drop him.' Stevie climbed the ladder until his head just poked through the hole and as Noddy pushed from behind my head tipped towards the hatch, bringing my nose within inches of Stevie's cheek.

'Come on Major son,' he said as he pulled gently on the lead.

I growled, starting low in my hoden, and reached a snarling crescendo, lips curled and ears flat back, my spittle spattering his face.

'Errr, Noddy, how about if I push and you pull?' Stevie said ever so quietly.

'What? Oh, okay, you come up and I'll come down.' Noddy walked me away from the hatch whilst Stevie came up and round behind me, then started down the ladder himself. Time slowed as things happened in very quick succession.

Stevie stepped towards my backside with his hands outstretched like a wicket keeper shooing chickens; I turned around and lunged at him, roaring my defiance at being pushed through a hole; Noddy took hold of my lead near to my throat and took one step down the ladder.

The consequences were that I was off balance when Noddy pulled on the lead, which made it lighter than he thought, so he toppled off the ladder and landed on all fours at the bottom. His full weight coming off the ladder dragged me through the hatch upside down and heading for a heavy fall onto my back. Until, being the supreme athlete I am, I turned lithely in mid-air and skipped lightly off his back onto the floor.

Well, I thought it was lightly; Noddy didn't agree and lay there groaning. I licked his face in conciliation.

'Stop playing with your bloody dog Noddy, we've got to get out of here and get an alarm in.'

Sympathy was a skill the TF didn't train in.

We had a quick look round and searched the route back to the Post Office, finding nothing, as SOCO placed a silent alarm on the loft hatch. When anyone opened the hatch, we'd be the first to know.

I sat in the van for the rest of the shift as Noddy wrote up his statement and helped prepare the response plan for the alarm. We definitely wanted to be involved and I was hoping they wouldn't come back tonight, when we were off duty and Smiddy & Slade were on.

Smiddy was the remaining member of our four-handler team working the Town, with his partner Slade. He was the joker in the pack, always smiling. His quick wit and repartee was a big hit with the ladies, and his van was often to be found parked in secluded places and rocking, but not to the sound of barking. He was known as the Potter's Dog; all ribs and libido.

Slade was not named, as everyone thought, in honour of the '70s Brummie glam-rock group, but after the old English word for an open space in a woodland or valley; a peaceful secluded glade; a place for quiet contemplation. It couldn't have been less apt. Slade, how can I put this... Slade was an out and out dog of war. I mean, I've never been slow to take the opportunity for a bite, but Slade was in a league of his own. He was the section's Gurkha's Kukri; once out of the van he had to be blooded and he didn't get back in without biting somebody. He wasn't big, but he was fast, ginger and he only had one mood. Bad. He didn't bother us other dogs, in fact he was happy to work alongside us so long as we didn't get in his way of biting people.

Tracking and searching didn't mean a thing to him. He would do

103

either, but took no pleasure in them other than as a means to bite some people at the end of it. I often thought he saw Smiddy in the same way, simply as a facilitator that allowed him to pursue his favourite pastime. He didn't bother with searching for property at all.

When Smiddy rocked up in his van at a job, all the Plods quickly found a reason to be somewhere else, or jumped back into their Panda cars before Slade got out. Most of Smiddy's conversations at jobs took place through half an inch of wound-down window. It just goes to show how good he really was with the ladies. Imagine how successful he'd have been with a fully open window.

Finishing at 4 o'clock, we were handing the van over to them for the back shift, but as they lived next door it wasn't too onerous. Another shift in with only a low-life chocolate-thief to show for it.

Still, I was hoping for big things out of Festive Friday.

🐾🐾🐾🐾

The day dawned bright and cold again and, after our morning walk round the field behind the estate, I spent it lounging about. On the walk we practised a desultory bit of distance control and a spot of heelwork, which we did most mornings just to keep us from getting rusty, and Noddy groomed me as he did religiously every morning. I wasn't losing much hair at that time of year and my guard hairs were plumped by a thick undercoat that kept me warm whatever the weather. I often slept out in below-freezing temperatures in those days. When you're young, you don't feel the cold as much.

After scrubbing out my kennel and run Noddy left me to my thoughts until he walked next door and picked the van keys up from Smiddy, who was just finishing. Smiddy had done a four-to-midnight and then an eight-to-four, so was up to date and able to brief Noddy. I charged out of the kennel run and leapt into the back of the van, and when he'd climbed into the front Noddy told me the news.

104

'Could be a good night mate. The alarm's still in the Corunna Road loft and they haven't been back, and the Town's bouncing already.'

It was Black Eye Friday (stuff 'Festive Friday') and made all the more so by the fact it was the 24th. Christmas was tomorrow and work had finished at lunchtime when the pay packets were handed out, with bonuses.

We were always supposed to go to the nick so Noddy could check the messages and keep up-to-date with crime trends, but we'd had the benefit of Smiddy's quick turn-around and when we were halfway there we were diverted to the Catholic Club, where George Brian Hanrahan Rafferty had ripped his shirt off and was taking on all-comers.

In an obvious case of narrative causality 'GBH'* Rafferty had grown into his name and become that worst of pub bores, the drunken fighter.

Six foot tall, with the barrel chest of the layabout labourer (always gave his occupation as 'labourer', but hadn't worked since leaving school at fourteen), at the age of sixty his major weakness was his double-barrelled belly. GBH was living on past dreams. In his youth he had been a bare-knuckle fighter, brawling in arranged bouts in the back yards of pubs for a few quid, regularly mashing the faces of his opponents and having his own face pulped in return, so he could spend his winnings at the bar.

These days, his major talent was being able to stand relatively upright whilst younger men hit him, and when he ran out of dosh he would challenge the whole bar by roaring and ripping off his shirt.

Usually this would result in people buying him a drink to shut him up, but this being Black Eye Friday a young plasterer had taken up the challenge for sport and then an old friend of GBH's stepped in to stop him, then a mate of the plasterer's had waded in and pretty soon everyone was hitting someone in defence of someone else, except the

---

*'Grievous Bodily Harm' – Section 18 of the 1861 Offences Against the Person Act - and defined succinctly as 'really serious bodily harm'.

ones whose wives were there, who were trying to prevent them taking the opportunity to settle scores by lamping 'that slag' with a bottle in revenge for some bygone imagined insult.

The Catholic Club was in the town centre and had an extended license for the afternoon Christmas Party in the function room upstairs. Noddy abandoned the van in the street outside and ran in to find out the current state of play. He knew (and I was hoping) that to take a police dog into a confined space would cause mayhem.

In a very tight space everyone would get bitten: police, innocent bystanders (obviously there's no such thing – anyone innocent should have left before we got there) and guilty scroats alike. If it was over he wouldn't need me and if it wasn't it would only take a moment for him to come back for me and release havoc (my unofficial middle name).

Noddy had heard of GBH – everybody had, he was a legend – but not met him. I found out later that when he'd run up the narrow staircase he'd come face to face with the aged pugilist staggering out onto the landing, blood streaming from a burst nose.

Noddy had placed a hand on the barrel chest and said, 'Whoa, big fella, are you alright?' to which GBH bloodily spluttered, 'D' youse kna' who I yam?' and Noddy came back with, 'Why? Have you forgotten?' prompting GBH to swing a haymaker at his head.

All police officers have quick-comeback replies to the stupid things that are said to them and are constantly looking for opportunities to use them. Other replies to 'Do you know who I am?' include, 'No, but we could look for a label inside your jacket,' and 'No, do you?' or even, 'If you hum a few bars I'm sure I'll be able to pick it up and join in.'

Noddy leaned back out of the way of the telegraphed fist and the momentum of missing his target toppled GBH forwards. There were no witnesses, so it was the word of a fine upstanding police officer against that of a drunken and somewhat embarrassed former bare-knuckle champion who alleged that Noddy booted him up the backside, making him bounce head over heels down the stairs, crash through the door and come to rest sprawled on his backside in the street.

Noddy followed him down, rolled him over and handcuffed him behind his back, leaving him stranded like a beached whale, rocking on his belly and groaning.

Muttering quietly, 'I don't give a shit who you are mate, you're nicked,' Noddy went back up to check on the function room.

The rumble, through the lack of its main character and the presence of two Town-centre Beat Plods, was fading into people wandering towards the door, standing toppled chairs upright and mumbling that it was nothing to do with them.

When they made their way into the street and saw GBH trussed and waiting like a bale of rubbish on the kerbside for the section van to collect him, their sullen belligerence turned to hoots of laughter. This made GBH very angry indeed and he swore loudly at them whilst thrashing his legs trying to get enough purchase to right himself, only succeeding in propelling himself in a circle, his slow pivoting depilating his belly.

Eventually, to loud cheers from the encircling crowd, the Section Sergeant turned up with his Van Driver and, taking an arm and leg each they lifted GBH, trussed like an overstuffed Christmas turkey, into his luxury transport to the custody suite, adding another chapter to the fall of a legend.

Noddy booked GBH in as a common law breach of the peace because it involved the least paperwork and, leaving the van at the nick, we deployed on foot in the town centre, Noddy in full uniform and flat cap.

Some forces insisted on dog handlers wearing helmets but ours sensibly considered that it was difficult enough holding a lunging dog in one hand and a struggling scroat in the other without having to balance a coal-scuttle on their head at the same time, so flat cap, peak slashed like a guardsman* it was.

I've loved foot patrol in the Town over the years. So many opportunities for bites. Obviously night-time is best, when the drunks come out to play, but Black Eye Friday is like an extreme Saturday night, in the afternoon.

The shoppers had gone, weary-footed and weighed down with the responsibility of having bought the wrong gift, and most of the stores had closed at 4pm to let their staff away early for Christmas. If you haven't bought your presents by 4pm on Christmas Eve, somebody's going to be thrilled in the morning to open a brown paper bag containing a fan belt and a bottle of screen-wipe.

Those that were left thronging the streets were revellers; revellers revelling in the knowledge that work was done for at least the next three days, the eight pints they had already consumed, the anticipation of the next eight pints and the certainty that although they would be in deep, deep, trouble when they finally flopped up at home, that wouldn't be for another several hours yet.

The men, youths, some no more than boys, were mostly in gangs of mates, staggering, slurring and whey-hey-ing at passing ladies; alcohol conferring in them the vastly mistaken impression of their own desirability to the opposite sex.

Neither sex seemed mindful of the cold, tee-shirts for the blokes, and mini-skirts for the fairer cellulite-dimpled sex.

Women, some mistakenly thinking of themselves as 'girls' also roamed as packs, tottering on heels, or carrying them slung on one finger, so convinced of their attractiveness they'd given up acting demurely (if they ever had).

There's a theory of evolution that suggests that animals handicap themselves in order to demonstrate that their genetic fitness, thus

----

* Ask your grandad sonny.

securing the finest or most mates. Hence the peacock's feathers are impressively beautiful and also prove that even whilst waving half a palm tree from his bum he can avoid predators and pull the birds. And whilst a stag that can roar the loudest proclaims his superior size, he also debilitates himself over the course of the rutting season so much that the lack of food and the parasite burden can kill him if he isn't in the best of condition when he starts.

There's a thought that inebriation serves the same purpose for humans; that your ability to cope with being sloshed, wasted or otherwise smashed shows off your superior constitution. If you can pull when you're paralytic, your genes must be winners.

There is a slightly undermining counter-theory, which is that if you are pie-eyed you are likely to be in the company of other like people and everyone looks better when the beer-goggles are on. The counter-counter-theory is that if a man can still perform when nissed as a pewt, he truly is a man, my son.

Like a vast slow-motion Benny Hill-esque tableau, pubs would disgorge one group to lurch purposefully to the next venue, which would in turn tumble out another mini-gang. Occasionally two clutches would bump into each other on their rambles, either two female, two male or one of each, and someone would make a remark or look at someone else the wrong way, or remember how she had bullied her at school.

Fights split the sexes*; men's head's butt, fists fly and boots thud home; women's handbags flail wildly, nails gouge and hair is scragged, but always to the refrain of wild shrieking from on-looking women and shouted encouragement from men.

''E's not werf it Barry!'

'Go on Bazza son, smack 'im one!'

---

* This distinction is not apparent in any other species (except insects but the things they do to each other are just plain weird).

Life imitating soap-opera imitating life.

Our brief was plain: Break them up, but don't lock them up unless you really have to. No Custody Sergeant wants their cells full on Christmas morning.

Time and again we ambled towards just such an affray, to make sure they had enough time to realise we were coming and leg it. I'd bark my deepest magisterial warning as we approached and each time they'd split and run, or at least sway to their feet and teeter on their way, clutching hands to their wounds or half carry-dragging inert mates.

Noddy did his best to hold me back (probably), but I managed to stretch out and nip a few of the slower ones. More of a love-bite than a proper mouthful, and another proof of the genetic fitness theory of inebriation. And anyway, we didn't want to incur the wrath of the Custody Sergeant by taking bleeding prisoners in.

Carousers more reluctant to shift, or those too far gone to get out of the way, were shoved back by Noddy's friendly hand in their chest or on a shoulder with, 'Get yourself away home – you don't want your bum bitten for Christmas!'

In between we stood prominently on street corners to watch over as many pubs as we could, barking our loud proclamation to the merrily sloshed world that we were there to keep order, with a bit of calculated lunging at anyone foolish enough to approach too closely.

'Foolish enough to approach?' I hear you ask. Yes, I know, there's a big ugly policeman holding a slavering baying hound and you'd think people would avoid them, wouldn't you? But no. We seem to be a magnet for every dipstick with an unrequited death-wish.

Up they come with hand outstretched, 'Can ah give 'im a pat, pal?' Now you have to bear in mind that I am lunging and snarling at the end of my very shortened lead, but still managing to reach up to face height. Do they really think I would like to be patted? Is this how they think dogs act when they want to be patted?

Actually, no dogs ever want to be patted. It is patronising and not at all sensuous, but mostly it is extremely impolite to be that familiar with someone you've only just met.

Noddy's replies vary depending upon the occasion. Because it was Christmas he was tending towards something non-inflammatory such as, 'Thanks for the offer mate, but he's not in a very good mood,' whilst turning sideways on, body-blocking me so that I couldn't get at them and fending them off with his free right hand.

The more offensive peacocks and stags come up to us to impress their mates (or themselves) with variations on a theme.

'Ah cud kill yon dog y'kna'. 's easy. Just pull 'is front legs apart an' it busts t' heart.'

Yeah, right. What do you think my jaws would be doing to your face whilst you're trying to get hold of my legs?

Noddy replies resignedly with, 'Yes, thank you, now go home before you get locked up', followed by a rather less friendly guiding hand.

Except this one didn't. Having been shoved away from me once, he came back in an arc and settled on one hip in front of me; clearly drunk, but not incapable. Early twenties, with the tan of an outdoor worker and broad, with big farmer's hands; old waxed cotton jacket and jeans, with the aroma of cows. He was carrying a hot pizza in a box. Double pepperoni if my nose served me right, which it always did.

'Ah cud tak' 'im.'

'Enough now mate, get away home with you before your pizza gets cold,' said Noddy, still trying to be friendly.

Let me have him, please?' I drilled into Noddy's head.

Nothing.

'Ah wanna gan doon yonder,' said the nuisance, indicating down the street, right over my head.

'That's fine, off you go.'

111

'But yer in me way. Shift yer dog.' We weren't in his way; there was plenty of room to walk round us. He was becoming an annoyance now and, with a small crowd stopping to watch, we weren't going to move for him.

'Go round. Now.'

''sa free country an' Ah wanna gan yon way. Yers can't stop me.'

He walked straight at me, confident that Noddy wouldn't let me bite him and that he would make us move.

Noddy let his left hand, which firmly grasped my lead, slip forward six inches in a short underhand jab, and my momentum drove me into his midriff. I closed my jaws on jacket and flesh, and he went backwards to the ground with me on top of him.

I shook my head rapidly from side to side in a rat-kill and ripped the front from his jacket before letting go for another bite, but Noddy hauled me off. The smell and taste of blood flooded my veins with the anger of long dead dire-wolves, making me want to throw back my head and howl my wrath, but I stayed professional and stood squarely over him, daring him to move.

'Why did you walk into my dog?' said Noddy, loud enough for the crowd to hear and alter their perception of what had just taken place, and thus the reality of it. The dog hadn't gone forwards, the idiot had walked straight into it. Served him right.

'Ah didn't think 'e'd bite mi.'

'Schafskopf.'

'But you walked straight into him.'

'Yea, sorry.'

Two Task Force who'd been watching from a little way off had called the Van and it arrived from just around the corner before he'd got to his feet, which he was in no rush to do, with me standing bristling for another shot in front of him. A square torn from the front of his coat hung limply from its hem and blood was starting to seep through his

112

fingers from where my four canine teeth and twelve incisors had gouged their path across his belly.

He could take me, eh? Another moron disabused about the speed and power contained in such a handsome package. Anesthetised by the alcohol, he wouldn't feel the full effect of the pain for some time. But he would eventually.

As they shoved him in the back of the van he shouted, 'Hey, what about my pizza?' and the box was frisbee-ed in after him.

At the nick the Custody Sergeant would understand; anyone properly bitten was always locked up, and this arsch had been asking for it, even on Christmas Eve. We stayed out rather than take a valuable resource off the streets to book in a prisoner, and pizza-man was dropped into a holding cell to wait until it quietened down.

Unfortunately the holding cell he was dropped into was also a temporary home to three scaffolders who'd been brought in for busting up the Golden Lion and, moreover, refusing to pay for the damage.

They hadn't had their tea and when he refused to share with them he took a good-hiding for his bad manners and they dined on thirds of pizza.

Then the alarm went off at Corunna Road.

No time to pick up the van, we hopped in a passing Panda, Noddy in the front and me on the back seat, alternately licking the driver's left ear and growling in his right. Always time for some fun, even on the most serious job.

The Controller was sending each resource to their appointed place: a Panda to each corner of the block, covering the rat-runs but staying well back, with no blue lights; armed TF in a plain car to the front, but blocking the culdy end until everyone else was in place before walking up to the door; Section Sergeant and Driver in the van to back them up when they needed prisoner transport.

We covered the rear, in through the back garden of a house on the parallel street and across the wasteland that passed as a children's playground, despite the exuberant little scamps having burnt out the roundabout and ripped the chains off the swings.

The Panda driver paused briefly to drop us off, pleased to be rid of me as we bailed out, running as we hit the ground. There was an eerie silence on the estate, like the world knew something was happening and was holding its breath to see how it would turn out.

Our panting breath and pounding feet sounded loud as we turned in the front path, down the side and into the back garden, the bright streetlight at the front dwindling into dim twilight behind the houses.

We could that see the back of the Corunna Road house was in darkness. The alarm sounded only in our control room, like the first one I'd ever attended in the Farmers Warehouse. It had been placed on the attic by our SOCO, so we knew the scroats had come back for the postbag. SOCO had also placed a dummy postbag there to delay them, but by now they'd have rumbled that they were rumbled, or more likely, be standing there scratching their heads.

'Front covered.'

TF were in place, and one after the other four Pandas shouted in that they too were in position. We were still running. Noddy had a torch in one hand, but hadn't used it; he'd slung his lead over his shoulder as he ran and I was bounding freely alongside him after his whispered, 'Heel,' through clenched teeth.

The back fence into the wasteland was broken and battered down in several places – Noddy had checked out the route as we'd left after the robbery – and we barged our way over it as we heard, 'Armed police, stand still!' called out by TF around the front and repeated immediately by his mate.

I crossed the playground in five bounds to arrive at the mesh fence separating us from the back garden of Corunna Road, Noddy only a second behind, just as a fleeing scroat hit the other side of it at full pelt.

Noddy smiled and said very quietly, inches from the scroat's squashed face, 'Police with a dog, stop. Stop or I'll send the dog,' and grinned hugely as I rumbled a deep throaty growl.

The radio crackled, 'We've got two out the front, but one's gone out the back window.'

Noddy replied, 'If you pop round the back, I've got him at the fence,' and then to the scroat, who was looking round wildly for avenues of escape, 'Go ahead, run - make his day,' nodding down at me (I told you, a quip for every occasion). I pulled my nastiest snarl and as his eyes dropped down he gulped and stayed rooted to the spot.

Noddy was of course bluffing. We could see there were no nearby holes in the mesh fence and I couldn't jump it from a standing start. If the scum had run for it the best we could have done was for Noddy to pick me up and throw me over – and it was six feet high. Naturally I can scale six feet, but not vault it; I'm a dog, not a grasshopper; I need a run up. By the time we'd done that this wiry scroat, built like a racing-rat, could have been another garden away. But bluffing often works when you're dealing with the hard of thinking.

He was already wetting himself when he hit the fence, and we were the cow-pat that topped off his midden. He'd lost the ability to rationalise (not that he'd had much to start with) and stood with a terrified expression, tears welling in his eyes as he realised the most fun he would have in the next five years would be slopping out.

The TF seemed to take an age and Noddy didn't dare move for fear of breaking the spell of weakness we'd cast over the scroat, but eventually they'd cuffed, searched and stashed the two that had burst out of the front door, and came around the side into the back garden.

They yell a lot, the armed police, and so it was now. They worked as a team, one covering the other and ordering the scroat to the floor before cuffing him behind, searching him, then dragging him to his feet

115

and off to the waiting Panda. Each scroat went into a separate vehicle to the nick; they'd be kept apart to prevent them getting their heads together to invent some story about being in the loft to catch wild pigeons for Christmas dinner, or that they were practising coming down chimneys to surprise their children.

As soon as the TF had the scroat we scaled the fence, Noddy boosting me from behind and clambering over after me, then we went round the front to search the house. Much like before it stank of scroat and fear, but again only in the stairs, back room and landing. The place was empty and although we hung around whilst TF went up the ladder, we knew we had them all.

We finished off with a quick but thorough search around the garden, not surprisingly finding nothing; they'd come to collect, not to bring stuff with them, and their car was parked by the gate.

Already the rest of the TF were simultaneously kicking in doors where our three robbers were known to reside, and CID were visiting the scroats in their cells for a pre-interview chat. The final wheels were in motion to wrap up the job that wouldn't have started if it hadn't been for my track. I love it when a job comes together.

The rest of the night was an anti-climax; the kind of night I would come to know well; one of traipsing round late break-ins with nothing to show for them, interspersed with shouts for assistance at pub-brawls or domestics that we would rush to, only for them to be under control when we got there. Noddy booked pizza-man in, wrote out a statement and left him to be charged in the morning.

It was our first Christmas on the section so we naturally picked up any jobs on Christmas day, but there weren't any. The Town was dead. All shops and workplaces closed, no one on the streets. The population all either wrapped up in festive family bliss, wrapped up in their hangover, or tho especially painful double-jeopardy of both

There was a skeleton staff presence, an Inspector, Sergeant, five Pandas and a Van Driver, but they were all drinking tea in the nick, waiting for calls that never came. We dropped in for a biscuit mid-morning after Noddy had clocked on by radio and we'd had a leisurely wander round the field behind home. Sometimes you take your pleasures from the simple things, and I've never tired of collecting information on our regular walks; just sniffing around and waiting for something to turn up.

We left the nick before the Chief Super turned up to prove that life was just as tough for him as it was for the poor Plods that had to turn in on Christmas Day, which it wasn't because he just showed face then naffed off again to his turkey and pud.

That was the only bit of the whole festive tosh I enjoyed, the delicious bits of turkey chucked on top of my tea after we'd knocked off for the day.

Christmas. I just don't get what you lot see in it. Big celebration because some beardy-guy was born in a stable and promised to save mankind. I think you should ask for your money back, because he hasn't done a great job of it up to now.

In fact, I'm doing a better job than he is, steering mankind onto the road of righteous behaviour, and I was born in an under-stairs cupboard! Instead of turning the other cheek maybe he'd have been better off biting some people too.

But Boxing Day, that's what I call a celebration.

🐾 🐾 🐾 🐾

Real Boxing Day was a Sunday, which Noddy had been given as a day off to make up for working Christmas Day, so like most days off I lazed around and waited. If I'd been in a western I'd have taken my gun apart, oiled it and put it back together again fifty times, or idly thrown a knife into the stump of a fencepost. But I am a dog, so I lay down and

117

watched the back door for the movement that didn't come until Monday.

We're good at watching and waiting.

It was a ten o'clock briefing for Smiddy and Noddy, with Arthur and Big Ernie coming on at noon. We also had dogs and handlers joining us from around the county in a proper show of force for the Boxing Day Match.

I heard one of you once said, 'Some people think football is a matter of life and death. I assure you, it's much more serious than that,'* and that is how the local yobbos felt about the pre and post-match feuds with their rivals.

I can't use the word 'supporters' because they weren't. They were scum who used football matches as an excuse to show off their low self-esteem by casually slashing like-minded scum with a Stanley knife, and it was our job to stop them; or at least stop them ambushing and damaging the real supporters.

Playing with them was great fun every other Saturday or so in the winter, but Boxing Day was always well attended and this one was more so because it was a local derby. It was even more well attended because people who had thought the extra-long Christmas break a good idea were now bored out of their tiny brains and were looking for any kind of entertainment.

The day was bright and crisp with the winter sun slashing just over the roof-top horizon, never shifting the frost from the north facing pavements and gardens all day.

We cruised round in the van for the first couple of hours, with the pubs steadily filling up from opening time at 11am. Despite the freezing cold, yobbos would congregate on the pavements outside, consuming their courage as they watched for opposition supporters.

---

* Bill Shankly, a Scotsman who played for Carlisle Utd and Preston North End, quoted during his managerial career with Liverpool, where some people thought he was a god. He wasn't, he was held in much higher esteem than that.

We would park up and keep an eye on the groups that contained some of the more well-known and occasionally move them back inside. Much as I hate to bring felines into it, it was a game of cat and mouse as we hunted them and waited for them to make any kind of move.

At noon we left the van outside the railway station and foot-patrolled the patch we had been delegated. The main road past the football ground also connected the motorway to the railway station, so most supporters would use it from one end or the other.

Handlers were given stretches of it to walk, whilst others patrolled the main car park and around the ground. We'd drawn the end nearest the railway station, but we'd missed the first running battle when thirty yobs had arranged a rumble with a similar number of visitors down a back-street off the town centre.

By the time we'd heard of it and made our way there, they'd already legged it. Task Force, our own roving hooligans, had been first on the scene and had bust a couple of heads locking up two minor scum.

Now, I don't want to give the impression that this was some sort of organised gang, because they were about as organised as a bunch of feral cats – sly, devious and whilst they would play along with each other when it suited them (mostly to do with safety in numbers), they would equally drop each other in the brown and sticky if it was necessary. However, to give them their due they seemed to have been born with a collective low cunning that allowed them to turn up en-masse at a fight before it knew it was happening, and fade away again just before we arrived, often leaving bleeding people in their wake.

They never operated in groups of less than four or five and always endeavoured to outnumber their opponents before making a move. They would split up and scout for victims, selected for their size, flamboyance, gobbiness or some other quality that made them a target, then the glaring would start.

'Glaring' is a collective noun for a group of tomcats, and particularly apt as when the yobs assembled, but before they attacked, they would eyeball their victims from across the street as they pretended they were walking to the match.

We were also subjected to the glaring as an insult about which they knew we could do nothing; even a tomcat can look at a king. Mind you, an insult is only insulting if you allow yourself to be insulted by it, and Handlers laughed it off in the knowledge that when they finally did catch them doing something illegal they would be more than glared at.

I treated all football hooligans alike, whether they were home-yobs or visitors. So far as I was concerned they were all scum that deserved to be bitten if I could get at them, and I spent my time roaring and lunging at anyone stupid enough to come anywhere close. Noddy held me on a very short lead wrapped around his left hand.

We passed the first hour on foot rushing from one just-finished battle to the next, never catching a sniff of real trouble, but watching a lot of glaring.

The Firm, as they dramatically called themselves, consisted of half a dozen or so seniors. They were the ones who had been around for a while and organised the rumbles with other teams' like-minded scum.

They were followed by a fluctuating number of minor minions, many still at school, who hero-worshipped them. They would in turn become elevated to the more serious ranks as they proved themselves in what they believed to be combat, but was more just kicking people and running away. The arsch-dribbelt at the top would eventually grow out of it, either by getting married and settling down or doing time when they were caught once too often, thus ensuring room for the next generation.

They all had the same smart-casual clothes and stout shoes. Docs or leather brogues were fine, but no trainers; not so much a footwear fashion statement as a weapon. They didn't wear the team's colours as they didn't want to be identified, but a scarf could be secreted in the pocket to be brandished at the enemy at the right time.

There were two trains to be met at the station, the first at one o'clock, and about fifty away supporters were gently pushed together to form the flock we would escort the mile to the ground.

The difficulty with this bunch was that they were early for the three o'clock kick-off and wanted to go for a pint. We knew if they did they would immediately become targets for our abschaum, to be picked off for a kicking, so our main job was to keep them together and moving towards the ground.

There was a happy holiday atmosphere amongst them as we herded them onto one pavement along the shop fronts. Smiddy & Slade were at the front, with Nuffer & Ava and Jamesy & 'Arry down the road-side, and me bringing up the rear with Noddy.

We were all supplemented by one group of Task Force and a sprinkling of RBOs for their local knowledge of the abschaum. The Task Force battle-bus took the lead, driving down the road to push oncoming cars out of our way.

Although we were mostly pretty new to it, it wasn't a hard concept. The fans would try to peel out of the column towards a pub and we would persuade them it was a good idea to remain within it for their own safety. The RBOs did it by cajoling and joking with them and I did it by lunging and trying to grab them if they dawdled or turned around.

The supporters were singing their chants and all the dogs were barking and straining into their chains. Slade became so frenzied at not being able to turn around to confront the noise behind him that he bit Smiddy's leg in frustration. After a short bout of under-his-breath-swearing Smiddy changed places with Jamesy so Slade could lunge at supporters alongside him instead.

Across the road members of the Firm occasionally appeared, to be approached by RBOs dropping out of the column for a chat, to let them know we knew they were there. About halfway to the ground around a dozen Firm appeared behind us, walking quickly and whistling the Laurel and Hardy theme* in loud but tuneless unison. The tune was used as an insult towards the police in general and was usually, as in this case, accompanied by an exaggerated plodding walk, hands clasped behind the back.

Noddy bided his time to allow them to tire, but when they came too close turned and grabbed the closest by the throat. He was about nineteen years old and had the appearance of a weasel that had been dressed by throwing it through Top Shop.

Whilst he had a chat with the yobbo Noddy held me at arm's length and I directed my snarl at the rest of the bodensatz, who were trying to give the appearance of gathering round us threateningly, but managed to do so whilst staying far enough away from my teeth to remain safe. They were about as threatening as a Chinese Crested Powder Puff.

Finishing his chat Noddy thrust the weasel across the road and I herded the rest of them along with him. Noddy must have thought weasely had an infectious disease, because I heard him finish with '... cough and if you get in the way again, being nicked will be the least of your worries.'

A cheer went up from the away support, who had turned to watch in amusement, as two RBOs peeled out of the line and, crossing the road, walked alongside the Firm explaining that the dog handler was a nasty man with a brute of a dog and that they should never make him cross because of the terrible things he does, agreeing that he shouldn't hurt poor little football fans' feelings in front of their friends.

The Firm glared at us from across the road. We'd made enemies, but they were never going to be our friends and, if not first blood to us, then a solid broadside had been fired across their bows. They knew

---

* Dance of the Cuckoos - adopted by Laurel and Hardy to musically reflect Oliver Hardy's pomposity and Stan Laurel's ineptitude.

who we were and we were taking no lip from the likes of them. Round one to us. At the next street corner they split up and melted away like pond-scum in the sunshine.

The rest of the walk to the ground was uneventful and we handed over to Gerald and Beddo, who had been patrolling there from the start, while we hitched a lift back to the railway station in the TF bus. The other three escort dogs walked back up to their respective patches, but we'd been away for a while and the town was bouncing.

Most of the half-drunk supporters were still in a holiday frame of mind, but with that many morons kocking about they were only an insult's throw away from kicking off. As we jumped out in the main square we saw two Firm hanging about the station entrance, but they quickly sidled off when they clocked us.

We took up a position on the traffic island in the middle of the square, with a good view of the station front and down each road radiating away. It was a good vantage point and a highly visible warning to yobbos. I added my highly audible warning at frequent intervals, roaring my challenge at anyone staggering or chanting, which was almost everyone.

The pubs were emptying fast onto the streets. Punters knew they would need to leave the town shortly after two to walk down and queue to get through the turnstiles before kick-off at three. Perfect timing for the two o'clock train, with over two-hundred hammered away supporters pouring onto the platform and eager to be on their way.

They'd been drinking solidly since boarding. Not in the nice Mediterranean habit of sipping a glass of wine to pass the time on the journey, but in a northern European type feast where ale was quaffed in order to get as smashed as possible before venturing out into the freezing cold to clash in glorious battle with similarly inclined nut-jobs. Think of Viking hordes dressed in jeans, t-shirts and puffa-jackets, with bobble-hats for helmets.

Six dogs and handlers met them at the station entrance and held them there.

Mitch & Donald and Mogsy & Dougie had joined us, having been the last pair touring in their van, and together we formed a semi-circle facing the fans. The problem this time wasn't that the supporters wanted to slip off to the pub. It was that they wanted to charge headlong to the ground. If we let them go they'd end up straggled out and we'd have no chance of protecting them. They had to be kept together.

I felt glaring and looked over my shoulder to see the weasel and half a dozen younger Firm loitering at the far side of the square. I sensed movement to my front and as I turned back a troll-like man with a nice line in neck-tattoos and an ugly scowl strode out of the crowd jabbing his finger towards Noddy's face. I lunged and missed the finger by a breath as Noddy dragged me back. The man's scowl grew uglier, but he turned two shades whiter and stepped back.

The mood of this column was distinctly different. No more banter with the RBOs, just spittle-mouthed vitriolic chanting about who's going to get their 'kin'ed kicked in. All six dogs escorted them and we were barely enough. When a group of the scum broke out and crossed the road in a lightning attack on three home yobbos who'd been stupid enough to return a chant, all hell broke loose.

Task Force were rolling in the middle of the road with prisoners they'd grabbed and 'Arry got his first bite on the thigh of an away yob. It was a fair bite on the coward who had run across in front of him, smacked an opponent twice in back of the head and was running back to the safety of the crowd when Jamesy tried to grab him. He missed, but 'Arry lunged and bit hard. It was a good bite, a full mouth of thigh, and that was the problem. If his mouth hadn't been so wide he could have held the bite, but it was and he couldn't sustain it. When he let go the unge rinfor half fall baok into the melee and was shielded by his

124

mates pushing him to the back. He wasn't worth pursuing.

Slade was going mental. His eyes had glazed and he was frothing at the mouth as he lunged and bit. Smiddy was using him as a clearing machine, fanning him around. Anyone in front of him was bitten and released before they knew it. Bang, and on to the next one.

Donald and Dougie held the front of the column and Ava and I faced them down the length of it to stop everyone joining in. Ava was red-eyed and snarling. Noddy had me on a long-lead in the middle of the road and I was working as much of the column as I could, back and forth, letting no one step out of line.

Four prisoners were bundled into the back of the van that had arrived, siren screaming, and left just as quickly. Order restored, Mitch stepped Donald aside and let Mogsy & Dougie lead them on again.

Bringing up the rear was the easy job as they were moving anyway, and it gave us the advantage of being able to see right down the length of the column. The deafening noise made communication impossible as the chants echoed in the confined spaces of the three-storey Georgian terraced streets.

Occasionally Noddy would hear snippets on his radio about the Firm picking off stragglers in the side streets, but there was no way we could leave this rabble. Every time we reached a side street some pond-life would try to break away, even though we had Panda drivers leap-frogging to block them off, and as back-marker we had to quickly round them up again. Gives you a whole new respect for sheepdogs.

Three-quarters of the way there the front tried to push past Dougie. At first Mogsy just quickened his pace, but when they did the same Mitch clocked what was happening and, waving to Jamesy, led him at a run to make a stand. Dougie, Donald and 'Arry lunged and barked them to a halt again. Meanwhile as the rest of the column caught up it became a target for the yobs on the other side of the road, whose number swelled rapidly from the side streets as we neared the ground.

125

Slade, Ava and I worked back and forth between the two factions, first pushing one pavement horde back, then the opposing one. We were all mentally in a bad place. We saw everyone as a target and anyone could be bitten. All the handlers were pushing people out of our way, including the uniforms.

At the ground the plan was to direct the column down one side and around to the away supporters entrance gates, but we lost it. The road was blocked by stationary cars and both pavements by home supporters. We had lost our leading TF bus, stuck in traffic at the last junction, and we had nowhere to lead them. Sensing our hesitation the column spread all at once and as they filtered away we could no longer keep distinct boundaries between home and away fans.

All the dogs were on their back legs by now, necks pulled high and tight by handlers to prevent us biting randomly. Of course there were genuine innocent supporters there, they were in the majority, but we no longer cared. I'd been taunted and sneered at, goaded and mocked; I'd been threatened by schweine who refused to come close enough for me to bite. My red mist had descended.

It was then that we spied the rocking shoulders of the weasel and four Firm wearing no colours on the far pavement, a sure sign that boots were making an imprint on the body on the deck, and repeatedly yelling 'Move!' at the top of his voice Noddy shoved our way through the throng.

As we skirted a slowly moving car the Firm squirmed away and the Chief Superintendent, who had also seen the fight and was heading in the same direction, stepped in front of us.

So I bit him.

On the buttock.

Obviously I didn't mean to bite a Chief Superintendent. I didn't know who he was from behind. We'd never been introduced, And when people are jammed together like that it's very difficult to tell them apart.

I knew we were going to a fight and so I bit what was in front of me. Clearly I was a bit hasty, but there again, he shouldn't have got in the way. Anyway, what was he doing there, leading from the front? He should have been in an office somewhere, not trying to do my job (at which I was considerably better than him anyhow).

It was over in a flash, and it was only a nip, but it left him with a beautiful tooth imprint that could be clearly seen on his left bum-cheek, through the flap of trousers that I had ripped away. And his hat had flown off from the accompanying whiplash of his head. Ripples of empty space cleared around us, propelled by the force of embarrassment.

He was embarrassed because he'd been bitten by one of his own police dogs. I was embarrassed because I'd bitten one of our own bosses. Noddy was embarrassed because he'd let me. A nearby TF carrier that had arrived just in time to witness the unfortunate incident was rocking to the sound of unrestrained laughter.

'Right!' said the Chief Super, as he bent to retrieve his cap and felt a gust of fresh air where there shouldn't have been one, 'Clear the bladdy street! And I'll see you two in the half-time briefing!'

He pushed his way through the fans to a passing Panda, where he opened the passenger door and, gingerly lowering himself in, barked, 'Bladdy Infirmary!'

Clearing the street wasn't an option, it would clear itself, but I'm sure it did him good to give an order before he left. Noddy sheepishly dragged me around into the car park. The fans were rapidly clicking through the turnstiles as three o'clock fast approached, and other than keeping an eye on the outside of the ground it would go quiet for us for the next ninety minutes or so.

After all the fans were inside the handlers had a brew whilst we dogs gratefully drank from the offered water-bowl, then caught our breath in the back of the Skylark, parked there especially for the purpose.

The half-time briefing was given to respond to developing events and provide feedback for the earlier ones, and boy were we going to get some feedback.

The Chief Super was a disciplinarian, famed for his lack of tolerance of anything sloppy, and penchant for hauling Plods over the coals for any kind of real or imagined laxity. Noddy had already been delegated to attend on behalf of the dog section as we were foot-patrolling the side of the ground outside the main stand, under which the briefing took place.

I wasn't frightened of any human, and I'd already decided that the Chief Super could go stuff himself. Only an idiot walks in front of me when the red mist is upon me, so he only had himself to blame. But I knew Noddy was bothered, not so much by my indiscretion, but in readiness for the savaging he was heading for.

When the half-time whistle sounded I walked smartly to his heel into the briefing room, like gladiators to the fray. We, who are about to see the chords bulging in the neck, the blue vein throbbing in the temple and the spittle in the corners of the mouth of the Chief Superintendent, salute you.

The rest of the group commanders, Sergeants and Inspectors, were already in, standing in front of the Chief Inspector, who was holding court.

We already knew most of what he had to say: that the away supporters would be held back in the ground at the end of the game whilst the home scum were pushed away as fast possible; then we would escort the away lot past the coach park where some would board, and the rest would be walked back to the railway station.

The only bit we hadn't expected was that the dog handlers were now on standby for an anticipated pitch invasion at the final whistle.

The TF Inspector admitted we a lost the away column in front of the ground, blaming the traffic jam caused by the traffic warden on point at the car park entrance, who blamed the club stewards for not parking the cars fast enough inside the ground. But apart from one, (ahem) minor incident, we'd got away with it.

The Chief Super stepped from behind the Chief Inspector, resplendent in new trousers, and started by blasting the Town Inspector for his Panda drivers for not moving fast enough when cutting off the side streets for the escort.

'I want them there before the bladdy scum, not bladdy afterwards! And that applies to the bladdy rest of you as well, bladdy get stuck in as soon as you see them massing. Bladdy shift them! Keep them bladdy moving! And you,' his finger accusingly singling out Noddy at the back of the room, 'Bladdy well done for getting bladdy stuck in, but next time bladdy shove me out of the way of that bladdy dog! My arse is not here for your target practice!'

Noddy grinned and snapped to attention, lead held looped in his right hand,* 'Sir! Yes-sir!' and the Chief Super grinned back. He saw the bite as a mark of his own desire to get stuck in, and knew that he would go down in football match policing legend as the Boss who was so much in the thick of it that he was bitten by a police dog. It was a badge of honour that showed the old man could still mix it with the best.

They'd be talking about him in the Chief Officer's briefing at HQ in the morning. Of course, from a Chief Super's rarefied viewpoint, the only thing worse than being talked about in the Chief Officers' briefing at HQ was not being talked about in the Chief Officers' briefing at HQ.

The Chief Inspector took over again, 'Everybody know what they're doing?' and when the room collectively gave the police affirmation to a senior officer of, 'Sr!' 'Then get out and get on with it.'

We were first out of the door, Noddy still sheepishly grinning ear to

---

* Dog handlers don't salute because they hold our lead in their right hand. Instead they come to attention, or at least as close to it as they can.

ear. We wasted no time in getting back to the rest of the handlers to relate our brush with the Almighty, and to place them on alert for the prospect of a pitch invasion.

And sure enough the intelligence was right. The RBO spotters inside had clocked a large Firm contingent behind the goal in the home paddock, which was unusual in itself. Often the abschaum wouldn't go inside the ground, but hover around outside, busying themselves with throwing bricks at the away buses, or lying in wait for the late to arrive and early to leave. That's why we patrolled outside; but today they were conspicuous by their absence.

The final whistle blew and they came over the barriers from both ends, meeting in the middle of the pitch with fists and boots flying.

I know what we should have done. We should have closed the gates, told everyone else they could stay in and charged a small fee to watch the contest, awarding a cash prize for the last man standing in the middle of the pitch. But the police are big on restoring order, so we went in instead.

Stewards and pitch-perimeter Plods were trying to pick off individuals by grabbing them, but what were they supposed to do once they caught one? There were another ten running amok for every one grabbed. Arresting each one individually wasn't an option.

As soon as we'd been given the order all the dogs lined up at the gate, led by Arthur & Beddo. On Big Ernie's command we marched into the ground in single file down the terrace to the pitch perimeter, along to the halfway line and with a smart right turn spread out across the middle of the pitch. The scum parted before us and when we halted the line Big Ernie bellowed, 'Outwards turn!' and every other dog and handler turned right or left and marched five paces forwards, where we stopped, four dogs facing each way, about fifteen yards apart. A file of hastily-assembled TF similarly marched down the halfway line between the two lines of dogs and likewise turned outwards. They were there to

130

pick up the pieces.

Arthur and Big Ernie nodded at each other and both yelled, 'Clear the pitch. Forwards march!' and both lines of handlers stepped out into dog-bite heaven.

Dogs see faster than humans anyway* but my world went into slow motion as the battle rage came upon me. We were second in our line, commanding a strip of pitch from the centre spot, where Mitch & Donald were on our right, to two-thirds of the way to the touchline, where Arthur & Beddo were on our left. Ava was at the far end of our line and 'Arry, Dougie, Gerald and Slade worked in the opposite direction.

All the dogs were on extended leads, arcing in front of the handlers, so with only the minimum of lateral movement we covered the whole pitch. We were barking, snarling and lunging, straining on our leads. We all still wore chains in those days, but the handlers had clipped them back on themselves so we couldn't choke out.

The scum ran, and where they could, they tripped opponents into our path. We could have bitten them all, but the handlers' orders were to walk slowly and keep the line, to allow them to escape. The bosses wanted the scroats off the pitch, not carnage.

A home scroat thought he'd spotted a gap in our line and tried to dart between me and Donald to get back to his own end. I was moving forward towards three Firm who, knowing the game, were deliberately walking slowly just out of my reach. The runner was level with me when I saw him out of the corner of my eye and raced low towards him. Coming up onto his forearm, I sank my canines in and pulled hard back and down. He went face-down in the mud and my blood-lust went up.

In another world I heard Noddy yell, 'Leave' but it was too far away

---

* Our flicker-fusion rate, the rate that eyes take each picture to send to the brain, is considerably faster than it is in humans – we see more frames per second than you. The world is slower and so we react quicker than you.

and I shook the arm manically back and forth, feeling the muscle rip in my teeth as the pond-life screamed.

'Major, leave 'im!'

Desperation seeped into Noddy's voice, and the training kicked in. I dropped the soggy arm and turned to my front again.

The battle wasn't over.

TF picked up the sobbing scroat and passed him down the line whilst two of the three Firm who'd been dawdling in front of me legged it. The other maintained his disdainful meander, just out of range, looking back at us with a smirk.

Noddy looked at me, smiled and took two quick paces.

''old 'im.'

I launched myself at the clown's insolent back and hit him mid-spine, knocking him flat. As he rolled over to get up I placed both front feet on his chest and snarled, spitting flecks of foam into his face.

The line had halted and all eyes were on us.

'Not so clever now sonny,' Noddy smiled at the prone scroat.

'Y'... y'... y'... c'..c..an't do that...' it whined.

'Really?' said Noddy, 'You must have tripped in your rush to vacate the pitch. Here, let me help you,' and taking my chain to pull me off him, he took the scroat's collar in his other hand and swung him back towards the waiting TF.

Spectators still in the grandstand, watching the best entertainment they had ever seen on this pitch, spontaneously burst into applause.

The line moved forwards again, but this time no one dawdled in front of any of us, the remaining toe-rags quickly diving over the nearest hoarding to safety.

Pitch cleared, we stood guard on the perimeter as the ground emptied, fans piling onto buses and being herded into a column ready to head for the railway station.

I smelt him first, his unique papery signature-scent rolling down from the terrace off to my left. I looked up and honed in on him, taking the scent first in my right then left nostrils as I pinned down his location. Medium height, medium weight, trimmed light-brown hair topped with a bobble-hat, camouflage jacket, jeans, t-shirt. And size seven Adidas trainers. Walking Man was watching us from the crowd. Too far away to make out his features visually, but the scent gave him away.

I stared at him, '*I know who you are and I'm coming to get you,*' and saw him flinch as the intensity of my thoughts hit him. Ever felt a cold shiver that you didn't expect? 'Someone walking over your grave'? It's a bolt of raw emotion you've picked up from someone. In his case, me.

I pulled towards him growling but was jerked back, 'Heel!'

'*Noddy! It's the Walking Man! He's there. We can get him!*' I implored and pulled again.

'Heel, man!' Noddy was annoyed because he thought I was randomly picking on football scroats. Great useless lumpen dolt.

And as the stadium emptied I watched Walking Man walk away.

The genuine home fans and the ones who had brought their children for a Christmas treat headed home or back to the car park to join the queue to get out. The Firm, and other random dolts who'd been caught up in the collective battle-fever, melted away to regroup and plan ambushes.

Once we were sure they were on their way we headed for our allotted tasks: Arthur & Beddo and Big Ernie & Gerald doubled-up mobile to be directed to any trouble-spots; Mitch & Donald and Mogsy & Dougie headed off up-town on foot to so they were ahead of the column, and the rest of us were to escort it back to the railway station – Noddy and me at the front, Nuffer & Ava, Jamesy & 'Arry on the flank with Smiddy & Slade bringing up the rear.

As we took up position at the column's head the huge double gates across the back of the stand penned them in, although the wide open space of the training pitch offered them room to move sideways and not be crushed from the back. And it was across the training pitch that the mob decided to make a break for it. Fed up with being held back for what must have seemed like ages whilst we had cleared the pitch, about a hundred scarpered towards the other side, where a public footpath cut through between two houses out onto the main road.

The TF Inspector wasn't having it.

'We'll hold these. Dog handler, head those morons off and herd them back here!'

Noddy and I dutifully legged it up the back street towards the ginnel where the errant crowd would bottleneck trying to get out onto the road, and not surprisingly we missed the first dozen because of the head start they'd had on us. Of course I'd have beaten them on my own, but when you're dragging a human after you, it does tend to slow you down.

Noddy put on a burst as we neared the cut and saw we were losing some, so we were going at quite a lick when we reached them.

In fact so quick was Noddy moving that he lost purchase with his boots on the frozen puddle that hadn't seen the sunshine all day.

I stopped, attention focussed on the rabble pouring down the path between the houses, as Noddy slid past me, on his back, almost to attention, before hitting the garden fence with a loud crump. His cap followed, slowly rolling on its rim, wobbling past us like the wonky wheel from a clown's car, eventually teetering round and round before toppling to a halt upside down.

I could tell he wasn't injured by the speed at which he leapt to his feet. But I could also tell his pride was a bit dented when I saw he had his baton drawn. It was just a bit of wood and about as much use as a mouse in a dog-fight, but it added emphasis.

His anorak was rumpled up from the slide, he had icy mud all down his back, and he was so red in the face I thought he might actually

134

steam.

He dropped into a fighting crouch, brandishing his baton in one hand my lead in the other, and spat 'Right!' at the smirking and now slightly bewildered crowd, 'Who's first?'

There were no takers. The ones who had been about to push past him, and the ones who were about to point and fall about laughing, all thought better of it and started to melt away backwards whence they came, muttering words like 'looney' and 'head-case', whilst keeping one eye on him.

If Noddy had looked foolish when he ice-dived, he'd moved up to ridiculous and was now bordering on embarrassed nut-job. It is a special kind of embarrassment where you know you did something that made you look stupid, and you tried to cover it up by doing something even more stupid, and now everyone (including you) knows it would have been better if you'd stopped at the first stupid, but it's too late because now people are pitying you and wondering how you're going to salvage at least some self-respect.

It could have gone two ways. He could have charged the crowd and laid about them for being witnesses to his stupidity, but thankfully he chose the second.

'Right then. Fair enough,' he said.

He smoothed down his hair, straightened his coat, flicked at the mud caking his trousers (surreptitiously slipping the baton away again), bent down and, slipping the chain from my neck, said, 'Fetch.'

I knew exactly what was required here.

I shot out, flipped the cap up by the headband with one paw, neatly caught the rim in my front teeth, and flew back to execute a perfect sit in front of him, cap presented peak first.

The crowd went wild, clapping, cheering and laughing. Face saved, Noddy donned his cap and on the slightest nod of his head I shot round his legs to a perfect heel-sit, head presented up to take the chain dropped over it, and we marched the remains of the errant fans back down the footpath to join their fellows at the gates.

The escort back to the railway station was raucous. The two-all draw was enough to keep the away lot in high spirits and they chanted all the way. We led them and kept the pace up, and would occasionally see Firm waiting ahead of us, in shop doorways or down side alleys. They mostly melted away but occasionally Noddy asked Mitch & Donald or Mogsy & Dougie to make sure they left.

About three-quarters of the way back we passed a narrow dark alley. I smelled scum and pulled Noddy towards it, but he heaved me back with, 'Leave it, there's nothing there.' Nose trumps eyes though, and when the column was halfway past the entrance a dozen Firm mushroomed out like a bacterial infection and hit them with boots and fists.

We were stuck at the front and had to hold our position, but Nuffer & Ava and Jamesy & 'Arry punched their way through from the road side, the less culpable fans making way for them and the slower or more stupid ones being bitten out of the way. Then the front of the column tuned and pushed back towards the melee in the middle, filling the road around the fight. We had nothing left to hold back, so we too turned and joined the push.

It was like swimming though a sea of idiots, Noddy yelling 'Move!' at the top of his voice and shoving shoulders aside. I was on my back legs roaring and lunging, sometimes grabbing clothing and dragging its wearer behind us.

Naturally the Firm had left when we got there, but Nuffer & Ava and Jamesy & 'Arry had their backs to the alley, surrounded by scum shouting and gesticulating angrily, wanting to give chase.

Smiddy & Slade had pushed their way through from the back and the four of us formed a line, a teeth-wall, and held it fast, lunging at anyone foolish enough to come within range. As we held the scum

136

back, Mitch & Donald and Mogsy & Dougie took up position at the front and back respectively and Arthur & Beddo and Big Ernie & Gerald abandoned their van and shoved from the far side. Slowly the massed crowd was shaped into a column again.

Many scroats were able to proudly compare their fresh scars on the way home later that evening.

The Firm were hanging round the railway station, but didn't break cover as we ushered the column through the entrance and parked it on the platform. Arthur & Beddo and Big Ernie & Gerald guarded the portal to prevent locals getting in and visitors getting out. They could handle it from here.

We picked up our van and headed home; another satisfying day at the office. As we left I spotted a Firm lifting his t-shirt to show a TF the teeth-marks on his back, but the shrift he got was very short.

They both knew that anyone bitten today had deserved it.

Everyone bladdy did.

🐾🐾🐾🐾🐾

At 2am we were taking the air on an industrial estate on the edge of town before finishing for the night, in that quiet time between Christmas and New Year when boredom awakens a scroat's urge to burgle.

The back shift had been quiet, with the only activity a flurry of domestics after the pubs emptied. We were almost back to the van, Noddy huddled into his coat against the biting wind that was blowing the sleet in, when the alarm went off at Boodles Jewellers in the middle of town. I heard the alarm bells even though they were the best part of two miles away* and quickened my pace towards the van.

Noddy called me back, 'Hoi, what's the rush?' and I drilled back at

---

* Yes, hearing is something else that we do better than you. Higher and lower pitches, distant, weaker volumes and direction location – all better than you.

him, *'Town centre alarm,'* staring hard to help the telepathy, but luckily his radio told him as well and we both ran and jumped in the van.

In those days there were often delays on the bells ringing outside the premises, while the alarm company contacted the local police to try to catch the burglars bang to rights inside, but this one rang out as soon as the window went in, smashed by a block of paving.

The two dregs who had heaved it quickly scooped the contents of the window display into a rucksack before roaring off on a Kawasaki 1100 motorcycle that, when the number was checked, was found to have been stolen earlier that day in Newcastle.

In the silence of the night even Noddy heard the bike heading our way in the distance. As we reached the main road to the east the bike sped across in front of us, two-up doing over seventy, and we gave chase as they turned away from the streetlights and wound the bike through the back-roads and villages.

Noddy's local knowledge compensated for their speed advantage and although we couldn't catch them we stayed in touch, throwing the old van around corners sideways. I too was flung around sideways in the back, but I didn't mind; I knew we needed to get close and then I'd be in with a chance of a chase and a bite.

Noddy was chanting, 'Police with a dog. Stop! Stop or I'll send the dog!' and the words worked their magic on my brain, adrenaline wiring me for pursuit.

The scroats realised their mistake; they weren't losing us through the villages, so when they hit the main road again they stayed on it in a straight blast for freedom. Much more comfortable for me, but the old van began to groan under the strain.

The increase in speed on the open road was both their advantage and downfall because, although we'd dropped half a mile behind them, they lost control of the bike on the sleet-drenched road, left the carriageway and ploughed sideways across the wide verge, before

138

colliding with the 'Welcome to Northumberland' road sign.

Noddy was still flogging the van for all it was worth when we saw the bike's headlight describe a beautiful arc in the air in the far distance before disappearing.

Arriving moments later we expected to find body parts, but the schlacke were gone. The bag which had been crammed with jewellery had burst on impact and scattered gems, rings, necklaces and bracelets over fifty yards of overgrown grass verge. The bike was a mess of mangled metal, reeking of hot petrol, wrapped around one leg of the sign that was now groggily pointing towards the ground.

Bikers these days ride in a protective cocoon of full-face helmets, padded Kevlar jackets and trousers, and boots and gloves that wouldn't look out of place on an astronaut. Do you know what hospital consultants call them?

'Donors'.

Not, 'People whose lives can be saved after they have been in an accident', but accidents that are a potential source of organ harvesting waiting to happen.

These two Geordies had no helmets and no biker gear (keep up, of course they were Geordies: bike stolen from Newcastle, heading back east, don't know the local back roads). Wearing t-shirts, jeans and trainers, with puffa jackets the only nod to the almost freezing temperatures, they had not only survived a ninety mile an hour crash, but had got up and had it away on their toes before twenty seconds had elapsed.

I was screaming in the back of the van whilst Noddy scanned his torch around for bodies, but saw none. I shouldered the door aside as he let me out and, still wired, rushed back and forth excitedly looking for the bite, before I could settle down to using my nose.

I picked up the tracks away from the bike. They were confusing because the vermin had come off the bike in different places over the fifty yard slide, the passenger almost immediately and the rider later, but both had tumbled forwards with the momentum.

Imagine trying to work that out as a scent trail. You visual creatures have no idea what it is to have this puzzle of the past laid out before you. You just see what is there. We smell what *was* there, but sometimes not exactly when*. Working it out occasionally takes some time.

Sticking together like scum does, they'd gone straight over the fence into a field of sheep. The sheep had scattered as they'd run through them, but then converged back on the fence again to see what the commotion was. Not that they'd understand it.

Stupid creatures sheep, ever both curious and scared; deciding it might be dangerous and running away, before wanting to see what it is, and coming back for a look if it doesn't chase them. And they stink. Not just of sheep, musky wet lanolin and herbivore faeces, but of humans, sheep-dip and drench, a strong disinfectant odour.

Noddy harnessed me up but annoyingly the tracks had been trampled all over several times and the thin winter grass churned to mud. I struggled to pick them out.

I'll try to translate it into visual for you. Imagine a white sheet of paper and draw a red pencil line across it. Look at the paper – it's easy to see the line right? That's what a fresh track across grass is like. Now draw two red pencil lines wiggling across another piece of paper and wash the whole sheet in a rainbow so some blotches of it reflect colour and some don't. Scribble all over that with different coloured pencils and take a potato-print dabbed in black ink and repeatedly stamp it down randomly. How well can you see the lines now? Whilst they're still

---

* Albert Einstein is credited with consolidating the idea that space-time is a single interwoven continuum, in his special theory of relativity, but dogs have always worked in space-time. The greatest brains in human physics are still trying to catch up with what we already know and use.

140

there, they're not as apparent as they were. Tough to follow eh?

Okay, now see that as varying intensities of coloured smoke drifting in a three-dimensional box measuring a hundred yards on each side. Then add breezes blowing at differing intensities from different directions and at different levels. That was my sheep-field track.

I stared at the sheep, '*Which way did they go?*' I asked, but all I got back was rank fear. You might see your own dog staring at other animals for a brief moment, before moving on. We're communicating with them and reading their thoughts back. Sadly they are mostly too stupid to have anything interesting to say. Still, it was worth a go. I was young and optimistic. I was later to find out that the only use sheep could be was in observing the direction of their running and panicked bleating, when it could help pinpoint fleeing scroats who had spooked them in the distance.

Even though the sheep ran away (again), I made slow progress and the dross were making ground on us. I was relieved to be at the next wall, over which were looking... a herd of bullocks. Bullocks: living warm wet leather, wetter scheiße, methane and part-fermented grass, tinged with the arrogance of a herd mentality.

Cattle can be not just a nuisance, like sheep, but positively dangerous. If they take a dislike to you they'll gang up and try to trample you. Obviously they don't have the speed and agility of a superbly fit German Shepherd Dog, and if our handler lets us off the lead we can avoid them, but we can't work at the same time.

We jumped the dry-stone wall together and ran at the beasts, Noddy waving his lead around his head so it thwacked a few of them on the rump as they stampeded away across the field. Slightly ironic given that the lead used to be one of them.

Then I started the slow business of picking out the scents across the muddied grass again. The bullocks came back and followed at a less than discreet distance, snorting and pawing their displeasure at the second pair of intruders in their field, but without the bottle to follow through with a proper charge.

Concentrating on scent is hard when there's a herd of bullocks on your tail, and I had to turn and lunge at the leaders when they got too bold, but I picked my way to the next wall, and onto the road into the village.

Lost scroats generally head towards lights, and it had been a fair bet they'd hit the road in the village. We could have gone straight there, but how stupid would that have looked if they'd been sitting behind the first fence? And we'd had no back-up to send there to head them off.

Neither did we have a radio signal, here in the valley bottom. Once on the road the track petered out to nothing; too cold, too hard on the tarmac and now too old. We were twenty minutes behind and we'd lost them. A scarpering scroat can cover two miles in twenty minutes, even over rough ground.

Exasperated, Noddy decided we had to go back to the van, which was far enough up the hill to have signal, so we could radio in with an update to stop them worrying about us.

We spent the next hour of the early morning searching the village gardens and back lanes, but with no joy. I couldn't tell if they'd gone to ground or kept moving, I couldn't get a whiff of them.

The lack of radio signal in the village was a problem. Normally we would keep searching until daylight brought people moving about. Two non-local youths would arouse suspicion and some police activity in the area would alert people to report sightings of them.

But to receive or transmit we had to trek upwards. We could either search in the valley bottom, where the Geordies had last been, or we could sit at the top of the hill and hope they would be reported.

Figuring they were laying low not too far away and wouldn't break cover until after first light, to try to lose themselves amongst the populace going about their legitimate business, we waited the night out

142

by returning to the crash site to pick up what jewellery we could. Most of it wasn't too difficult, and we collected quite a lot, but my heart wasn't really into searching for property. I wanted the scum that got away.

A double-crewed Traffic Car turned up eventually and had the bike collected on a low-loader, but there was no point in them hanging round, so they waltzed off in their warm cocoon to their next brew-spot.

I've never been able to work that out: on nights Pandas went single-crewed to brawls and domestics, where most murders occur, but Traffic, reporting little old ladies for not wearing seat-belts, were double-crewed. Of course these days none of them go out alone, except dog handlers, and only then because we are there to look after them.

The valley was the route to the next town where there was a modicum of civilisation. There was only one road across the surrounding hills. Called the Military Road it was built by the English to move troops and supplies when fighting Bonnie Prince Charlie's Jacobites in the 1740s. It paralleled the older Roman road so they'd nicked the original stone from Hadrian's Wall to build it. And by all the ancient gods, it was bleak.

You could stand on the road looking north and with no imagination at all conjure images of hordes of woad-tattooed ginger savages brandishing spears and claymores, emboldened by the local firewater, screaming unintelligible insults through the driving sleet.

Much like Glasgow holiday week at Blackpool.*

The chances were that when the scroats did move they would stay towards the valley.

When daylight groped its weary eyes open Noddy decided our best bet was to search the village and valley farms and occasionally drive up the hill to clock in for any information on the radio.

The first hour was quiet, and brought us nothing in the way of

---

* I am an equal opportunities insulter. I can't abide most people and I despair of other animals that aren't police dogs, and most of them are arsch-fällt.

143

Geordie scum, but we'd been joined by Big Ernie & Gerald and Jamesy & 'Arry, who should have been on a training day at HQ but had been redirected to our job to help.

The three vans were travelling up the far side of the valley to split the remaining farms between us, passing an old rotting fingerpost with the local names etched indistinctly onto the pointers, when HQ sent a message blind over the van radio. We were leading and consequently picked up more of it than the others due to our extra elevation, '...suspicious males at Greensyke Lonnin...' and then it died again.

Noddy had no idea where Greensyke Lonnin was but, thinking quickly, slammed the brakes on. Big Ernie pulled up behind and Jamesy behind him. Noddy ran to Ernie's window, wound down in anticipation of the conversation.

'Greensyke Lonnin! What did that last signpost say?' hoping Ernie had spied and deciphered it.

'Never spoke to me,' came Ernie's deadpan reply.

Noddy looked at the impassive face and fell to his knees, shaking uncontrollably with laughter. Jamesy climbed out of his van and rushed towards him, 'Never spoke to me,' giggled Noddy, climbing to his feet and leaning on the van for support.

'What did that last signpost say? Never spoke to me.'

I think he may have been delirious from the cold and lack of sleep.

It was a little while until Noddy and Jamesy composed themselves and were able to drive up to the top of the hill to ask for radio directions to Greensyke Lonnin.

When they parked in a rough layby where a side lane dropped away from the Military Road, looking down over the village from the other side this time, they saw two figures near the valley bottom, trudging with their heads bowed, heading east across empty fields, towards the dim lights of the next town.

Ernie elected to drive down to head them off should they make for

144

the road. Jamesy bailed out of his van with 'Arry and set off straight across the fields towards them, and Noddy drove us halfway in between, where we too abandoned the van and gave chase on foot.

We started a good three hundred yards behind them, and although we wanted the two figures to be our Geordies, Noddy wasn't sure enough to send me. They just could conceivably have been ramblers out for a morning constitutional. The road had turned a corner and Ernie was driving parallel to us another couple of hundred yards downhill. Jamesy & 'Arry were angling towards the pair from above at a fast stumble over the boggy moorland.

They turned round and looked at us... and didn't run, just turned away and continued trudging towards the distant town. Hmm, could be ramblers. We were doing Noddy's fast walk-jog. He thought it was a quick way to travel without arousing suspicion by running.

He was of course completely wrong, because he looked like an ape that had heard about running and had dropped out of the trees to try, but couldn't quite get the hang of it. Jog, jog, jog, long-step, long-step, hurried-step, hurried-step, long-step, jog, jog - about as natural looking as a St Bernard in a bikini.

Anybody seeing him heading towards them would think that not only were they being pursued, but by a person who was at least partially disabled and possibly deranged.

As we gained upon them Noddy had to make a decision. There were two of them. If he hailed them and they took to their heels, he had to be sure I could take one down. Not a problem even at two hundred yards. But he also had to judge if the other could be taken by either 'Arry or Gerald, or by me again after dropping the first.

We were about seventy yards away when he shouted, not a proper challenge, but, 'Excuse me, Police, can I have a word?' and then under his breath to me, 'Police with a dog, stop. Stop or I'll send the dog...' and repeated it as they turned to look at us.

Two young males, one walking wrongly; not obviously limping, but not straight, like he was trying to hide it. Same description: jeans, trainers and dark puffa jackets.

'*Run, chickens, run,*' my telepathy kicked in and yelled at them, but they stood and looked as we rapidly closed the gap between us, Noddy now properly jogging, thank goodness.

'*Run, run, run! Please, run!*'

'Morning guys, out early?' Noddy left the question hanging.

'Aye, just on us ways home, been to clear us heads like, after last neet,' the non-lame one volunteered.

The lame one looked grey, his eyes glazed.

Jamesy arrived with 'Arry. I could tell by 'Arry's bounce that Jamesy had been chanting the mantra as well; 'Arry was wired and ready to go. I guess I looked the same to him, bristling for the challenge.

We'd stood slightly off the two suspects, giving us room to manoeuvre should they make any kind of move, either towards or away from us, and lining up an individual each. I knew I was taking Non-lame and 'Arry knew he was taking Lame if they ran.

But Lame was running nowhere with his ankle sticking out at that angle. I'm no expert in human anatomy, but I'm pretty sure feet should point forwards, not sideways. Broken ankle. Common injury from coming off a motorcycle, especially if you're only wearing trainers.

'Where's home then?' Noddy was still keeping it light.

'Doon there,' Non-lame offered.

'Where exactly, what street?' Noddy was playing with them now. He'd already given Ernie the thumbs-up behind his back.

'Not sure what you call it, it's his girlfriend's place we're staying at, but I can find it.' Good attempt by Non-lame.

'What's the town called?' Game, set and match to Noddy.

As Non-lame looked across at Lame, rapidly trying to weigh up their chances of either legging it or kicking the scheiße out of us, Lame came awake and stretched his hand out towards my head.

'Nice dog, ish he friendly?' he slurred slightly in his pain.

Noddy smiled as Lame's hand reached towards me and my world slowed down in anticipation.

'Try to touch him and he'll rip your bollocks off,' Jamesy warned, and as Lame recoiled I belatedly made my lunge, snapping only air as Noddy held my short lead tight.

Laughing, Noddy said, 'Come on guys, back to the road, there's a nice detective wants a word with you about a motorbike and a jeweller's window.'

Their shoulders slumped even more as they turned, then Lame dropped his piece de résistance, 'I can't walk, me ankle's broke.'

'Really,' said Jamesy, 'How did that happen?'

'Errr, I slipped?'

'Yes, I know, off the back of a motorbike.'

'But I really can't walk,' Lame wailed now.

'A minute ago you were not only walking, you were thinking of running,' said Noddy this time, 'Now get your bloody arse back to that road before I kick it all the way for you.'

And in a true espirit de corps Non-lame supported Lame, arms entwined over shoulders, back to the roadside, to where a plain car was waiting. Driven by a young detective with a coiffured mullet, big-knotted tie and luxurious Zapata moustache, his older military-looking partner in the passenger seat, they'd taken a hunch that not only would the Geordies break cover in daylight, but that we'd scoop them up as well.

'Cheers lads,' said Military, as our new-found friends ducked into the back of the car, 'We'll take them for a little drive before we head back to the nick. I'm sure they'll be wanting to tell us all about themselves by then.'

As they drove off, Noddy looked at Jamesy and Gerald, 'That's me off then. I'll drop the jewellery I've got, scribble a short statement and then off to bed.'

We'd been on the back-shift, so should have done the quick-change onto days today. It was nearly ten now, and by the time Noddy had finished the paperwork it would be twelve. He'd take a couple of hours time-off and we'd be done until back-shift tomorrow. New Years Eve.

'I could have a look round the site for any more gear, that's as good as a training day,' said Jamesy. ''Arry was always a good property-searcher, so it was right up his street.

'Well done boys,' said Ernie, 'No point in going through to HQ now. I'll find some day-jobs to do.'

Of course he would.

On his allotment.

🐾🐾🐾🐾

New Year's Eve has never really been a police dog occasion. Blokes tend to be joyously drunk and happily shake the hands of policemen and women they would normally not cross the street to spit on if they were on fire. The Plods make sure they are wearing their gloves.

Women seem to think it acceptable to kiss policemen as a display of their bonhomie and some policemen become adept at the air-kiss so as not to offend. Others embrace the whole situation and lead their slobbering new-found friend down a ginnel for three minutes of fun and weeks of antibiotics.

Blokes on the other hand rarely had the bottle to attempt to kiss policewomen, and those that did were usually dissuaded by a well-placed knee to the groin.

I have always seen my primary job as defending Noddy from all-comers and did not allow anyone to come close, with a friendly bark-lunge-snap warning, for which Noddy was grateful

'Oh, he's a right grump isn't he? Sorry...' he would tell people whilst fending them off with his upraised right palm, after he'd given me the secret signal for, 'Kill, maim, disfigure.'

We had a couple of rehearsed signals for me to go into defensive action. The general one when in a sitting position was the back-heel nudge - a tiny touch of my rump with the heel of his right foot. The scroat in front of us never saw it, and it propelled me in the right direction.

The other rehearsed covert signal was the use of the word, 'Inspector'. Sometimes bosses liked to walk the streets to keep up their cred with the troops. Often they didn't like to be alone in case something happened and they had to deal with it. It's one thing to be seen to be mucking in, but actually mucking in had to be avoided at all costs. Consequently they would tag themselves onto a Plod who was walking a beat and walk with them to the next Plod, safe in the knowledge that if anything happened in front of them they wouldn't have to sully their notebook. There are notable legendary exceptions to this general rule, who become legendary because they are notable exceptions.

Noddy's favourite perch when on foot patrol was on the traffic island smack bang in the middle of the square and sometimes bosses would want to linger there with him, seeking his protection until the next Plod came by. But Noddy didn't always appreciate their company and so we had the signal.

If it was a boss Noddy liked he would greet him with, 'Evening Sir...' On the other hand we had the fall-back of 'Evening Inspector...' at which I would launch at them baying and snarling as arranged. The rank above was Chief Inspector and if we were graced by the presence of a Superintendent he could start with, 'Evening Sir, seen the Inspector lately?'

Naturally all were followed by an apologetic, 'Sorry boss, he's wrong side out tonight...' and the boss would rapidly leave.

We'd been in the square for half an hour and I'd seen off several ladies of negotiable affection and one Inspector when the call came, much to my relief. There's nothing quite so boring as having to bark and lunge when you know there's no chance of a bite from it.

The north was experiencing a cold-snap and at eleven o'clock it was already dropping past minus four. Dogs don't really bother with quantifying temperature; what matters is how we feel, and standing about makes you feel cold. We dogs operate at higher temperatures than you to start with. A dog my size is most comfortable at a body temperature of 38-39°C and the general rule is that smaller dogs are hotter and bigger dogs cooler, but humans are colder still at about 37°.

We don't sweat, except through our pads, which is why you see our damp paw-prints on the kitchen tiles on a hot day, but the few sweat-glands there are more about scent-release than cooling.

Overheating is controlled by panting, highly efficient on its own, but more so when you consider that we have a special heat exchange mechanism between veins and arteries that prevents our brains overheating even when our body temperature rises, such as when we exercise. Add in to that a comparatively bigger spleen than yours, which allows us to release and pump more blood-cells when we heat up, spreading the load and cooling the whole body, and the insulating properties of hair that can be puffed up or laid flat, and we yet again beat a naked ape hands down*.

Keeping warm is easier too. We fluff up our double coat to trap an insulating layer of warm air, harsh guard hairs overlaying soft downy undercoat, and we can curl up into a ball, keeping surface area to a minimum by tucking our legs in and covering our more vulnerable faces with our tails. Of course not all dogs have the same hair and I'm only

---

* Editor's note. not the best expression to use Major – shot yourself in the foot there…

talking about the best quality German Shepherds, like me.

Tonight was one to keep warm, a thought uppermost in our minds as Noddy drove us to our job.

Albert was a war veteran. In 1943 as a young man he was one of three thousand 77 Brigade Chindits who walked into Burma at the behest of Major-General Orde Wingate, to demolish the railway supplying the occupying Japanese army.

A slight but fit man when he went in, he'd walked a thousand miles there and back, carrying a sixty-five pound pack on his back. They'd reached the limits of air support and frequently missed the drops from the single squadron of six RAF planes supplying them, so like many others he'd suffered from the effects of malnutrition.

Drinkable water was scarce, in temperatures of 43°. A third of the force didn't make it back, and a third of the two-thirds who did were never fit for combat again.

They'd sabotaged the railway in over seventy places, but the efficient Japanese repaired it, it is said, within a week, and with good reconnaissance and patrols that far outnumbered them, the Chindits were boxed in.

Wingate had given orders that the wounded and others who couldn't keep up must be left behind, so Albert kept up. When he was stricken with dysentery he marched naked from the waist down through the rivers and swamps, cutting paths through the jungle with his machete.

After fighting his way back to India through the Japanese army, he and his colleagues were described as 'splendid examples of courage and hardihood', but the war was over by the time he recovered.

Like many others Albert didn't talk about his bravery, but went back to work rebuilding his country. He retrained as a fitter, repairing the production machines in the local biscuit factory, met his lovely wife and had two lovely children. But as he grew older, watching them grow up, he never lost his love of walking.

He walked every opportunity he could: up fells on his days off, in Scotland on holidays, and later, when his body started to fail him, in the parks around his home, leaning on a stick.

It is not surprising then, when his dementia became so bad he needed constant care and his family reluctantly found him the best care-home the equity in his house could afford, he occasionally went walking.

Tonight he'd walked out of the front door of the home shortly after eight o'clock. The door should have been locked, but the New Year's Eve skeleton staff were rushed off their feet.

Someone remembered seeing him after tea, dressed in pyjamas and dressing gown, readying himself, they thought, for bed. But no, Albert had donned his slippers and set off to walk back to India.

He felt slightly ashamed that he had been captured, but knew that if he could get a head start he could evade the Japanese patrols. After all, he'd done it before. He wasn't quite sure which way India was, but if he could just keep walking…

'He can't have got far, he's left his stick,' the care home manager, a rotund woman with too much make-up and a harassed smell, told Noddy. 'Nobody noticed him missing until we did the last round. We've been so busy y'see'.

The local Plod was there too, 'We've searched the home and grounds. He hasn't been seen since about eight-thirty and it seems from the clothes left in his room he's in dressing gown, jim-jams and slippers.'

The Plod had done his homework. He knew that most missing people turn up very close to home, if not inside it, so he'd done the preliminary search himself before calling us.

I stared at the manager, 'Do the maths lady. He's been gone nearly *three hours. Travelling at one mile per hour he could be anywhere in a radius of three miles. At two mph, a radius of six miles. That's a circle twelve miles across. He can't have got far? Schaf-gehirn.'*

I must have got some of the meaning through, because she looked at me then quickly away, embarrassed.

Noddy took over, 'Get as many patrols on the roads as you can, but stay out of the fields. We'll take care of them. Three hours is a very cold track, and it's freezing on top of it. We'll be lucky to get a start, but we'll try in the grounds.'

Sometimes it's the things you don't say that resonate the loudest. Nobody said, 'Don't fancy his chances out in this cold.'

They didn't have to.

Albert had ducked out of the front door and gone left, closing it quietly behind him so as not to alert the guards. He kept to the building line out of the floodlights then headed across the lawn, climbing the five-bar gate into the field beyond. Freedom! He hadn't felt this good in years.

To get home to India from Burma he had to travel west and the cloudless night helped him as he kept the North Star on his right. He had to stay off main roads in case of Jap patrols, but that was okay, he was in open pastureland with the cover of hedges. That would change when he was away from the village and into the jungle though.

The Burmese villagers were usually friendly and sympathetic, but he couldn't risk bringing the wrath of the Nips down on them by asking for their help. No, concealment was his key. He stealthily pushed his way through the next hedge, the thorns snatching at his clothes.

I couldn't pick Albert up in the grounds, but did get the turbulence left when he'd gone over the gate. He'd left more scent hanging there because it was his first exertion and he'd wrapped himself over the bars as he'd climbed it, dropping full length on the other side, releasing crushed scent from the frozen grass.

153

I nodded at Noddy, '*This way*,' and jumped the gate. He couldn't help but get my meaning and followed.

The night was bright so Noddy wasn't using a torch, which was a help because I didn't have to keep adjusting my night vision. We see better at night than you do (we are in every sense a superior being) but it mucks it up having to switch back and forth. I believe you have a similar effect, just not as good.

I lost the track as soon as we were into the field again, so followed the hedge looking for his way out. There was nothing on the air, so he was long gone and we were clutching at straws.

The little wind that there was drifted in different directions depending upon the terrain, but further down the hedge I picked up the strong incongruous scent and ran the fifty yards. When Noddy caught me up he shone his mini-torch into the hedge where I was pointing.

'Bug'r,' under his breath, when he saw the ripped dressing gown snagged on the barbed wire strand, 'How the hell did he get through there?'

As he pulled the dressing gown free and hung it on a branch I sent back, '*Don't look at me, I can't see a way through!*'

He must have got some of it, because he pulled his coat tightly around him and backed into the hedge, flattening the branches. When he leaned sideways and laid his leg over the barbed wire strand a hole opened up big enough for an agile dog to jump through. I hopped over and landed lightly on the other side, as Noddy fell backwards, ripping his pants-leg and landing heavily on his shoulders. I know you shouldn't laugh, but…

The Japs were still patrolling the main thoroughfares and so far Albert hadn't needed to cross one, but that was about to change. He'd already turned north to keep to the hedge-line, so needed a left to get back woot again. That meant crossing the road.

154

When he came to a gate it was slightly open, so he pushed his way through and immediate ducked down as the lights of a patrol came around the corner. He rolled into a ball in the hedge-bottom as they drove past, turning his head so they couldn't see the white of his face, and waited until they were out of sight around the corner before stooping low across the road.

As soon as he set off he lost his footing on the slippery banking, but staggered to his feet in a headlong fall and toppled into the gateway on the other side. He lay stunned for a moment until, seeing more lights coming, feverishly threw himself into a roll over the gate. Landing like a sack of spuds, he lay winded, gasping for breath, but safe. They hadn't stopped or opened fire.

Noddy scanned the field, but I'd already decided to check out the gate onto the road diagonally opposite. Albert's dressing gown had an interesting scent. There was fear, but also determination and courage. I could smell this guy was on a mission.

Sure enough, he'd crossed the road. I smelled him in the gateway, exerting himself, terrified and yet brave far beyond the need to be when crossing a road.

His slippers were on either side of the next gate, starting to freeze to the iced grass, a useful confirmation for Noddy that we were literally on the right track, but there was no sign of Albert himself.

Albert picked himself up and thought, 'Idiot'. He couldn't stay by the road. He'd seen the Japs spraying roadsides with machine-gun fire from moving vehicles. He had to keep moving. West. To India. But he was too exposed. He needed to find some cover.

Fifty yards to the west he saw the jungle looming. Ideal. Tall trees with undergrowth that would hide him. But first he would have to cross the river. He heard it rushing over the stones before he saw it and reflected that in better times it would be a pleasant spot for a picnic.

155

Funny, the things that come into your head when you're under pressure, he thought to himself as he took off his trousers and rolled them into a tube. No need to get them wet, he slung them over his shoulder and walked across the stones into the icy water.

Although it was flowing fast the river was shallow here and even in the middle it only came up to his thighs. He stumbled a couple of times and went down on one knee in the shallows on the far side, but being barefoot helped him keep his footing. He was soon across and striding towards the jungle, but getting tired now. Very tired. He would have a nap for five minutes once he could hide, he thought, as he climbed over the iron fence.

'He's heading west, terrified and determined.' I drilled at Noddy once he'd shoved the gate open, and he looked up at the sky and back towards the low security twilight home for the intermittently bemused. Even he could see we'd made a straight-ish line. Albert had kinked to hit the gate, but the general direction was consistent.

'Oh, no,' he groaned, 'C'mon, let's look at the river.' The river cut across the field, north to south. In a straight line from the gate, heading west, was a cattle-ford, where the bank sloped down gently into the water and back out the other side. The water was too deep for Noddy's wellies to get him across dry-footed.

We stood and for a moment contemplated Albert's fate if he'd gone in, and then...

'Across!' I beamed at Noddy. *'Across, across, across!'* and I danced up and down the bank to write the message hard in the frost.

'Oh, no,' he groaned again, 'Go on then.'

I ran into the water and it quickly took me off my feet, but I struck out hard for the far bank and soon felt the stones under me again. I briefly shook myself, my guard hairs having saved me from being soaked to the skin.

I picked up the bundled pyjama trousers I'd scented from the opposite bank and turned to face Noddy.

'*Rook at dese*' I stared at him past my mouthful.

'Down, stay!' he grinned and started running back to the gate... and didn't stop as he vaulted over, up the road, over the bridge and back into the field on my side of the river. I stood and waited for him. I understood why he wanted me to lie down – so I didn't wander away from the place I'd found the pants - but it was minus six and I was still dripping icy water. I reasoned that I was the better judge and he could get stuffed.

The jungle was thick and Albert was struggling to make any headway; he wished he'd brought his machete. Would have been useful if he came across any Japs as well. But for now, he needed to rest. He'd just sit down here for five minutes then he'd be fit to go again.

The leaves were crunchy but surprisingly comfortable as he sat down, snuggled in and almost immediately drifted off, still dodging, running and fighting a long-ago war, in a fenced copse on a freezing night in rural England, soaked and naked from the waist down, with his cotton M&S PJ jacket hanging from his bony shoulders the only thing between him and hypothermia.

I couldn't pick him up on the far side of the river. I reckoned from the PJ pants that we'd made up time on him, but his track was freezing as soon as it was laid. The field had been grazed bare, so there was little grass-crushing and the soil underneath was hard as iron.

'The copse is the next thing to the west,' said Noddy, 'We've nothing to lose, let's give it a look.' So we jogged over.

The copse was not an uncommon feature in the local fields. There were about a dozen mature trees, oaks, sycamores and elms, corralled by an iron fence, a relic of the grand estate it was once part of. The undergrowth was a barbed tangle of brambles, blackthorn, gorse and bracken, with the odd crab-apple and dog-rose here and there. They were a haven for wildlife, rabbits, mice, shrews, pheasants, grouse and songbirds, but impenetrable to anything bigger than a cat.

The life-smell was weak, but unmistakably human, and it hung on the broken foliage, trapped by the tree canopy. Albert had certainly been here, but had he gone through and left? I nosed the air to left and right, but the scent was equally weak to both sides.

Noddy shone his torch, illuminating the spiky morass in front of us, but not penetrating more than a few feet. Broken branches and trailing bramble runners showed where Albert had entered, but they'd sprung back into a spiky barrier again. If he'd gone straight through we'd waste valuable time struggling after him, but if he was still in there…

'Go round,' Noddy indicated to the right.

We needed to see if we could pick up an exit as easily as we'd picked up the entrance from the field side. I loped off until BANG, on the opposite side Albert's scent hit me like a brick in the nose.

I stood up on the fence, then tried to push myself through between the bars, but my muscular shoulders wouldn't fit. I was whining with frustration and about to leap over when Noddy arrived, jogging behind me. I didn't need advanced telepathy, this time he knew we'd found him by my excitement.

'Stay!' He said. Jumping over the fence into the dark thorny vegetation was a risky business and Noddy didn't want me to impale myself. Then he saw the pale figure slumped against a tree, just feet away, and not moving.

'Judas H. Priest! Albert!'

Still no movement as Noddy flicked on his beam and vaulted the fence, crashing through the bushes into the tiny clearing at the bole of the tree.

Albert jolted from… he wasn't quite sure where he was from   but he saw the searchlight bearing down upon him and the man dressed in black behind it. The Japs had found him, but he wasn't going down without a fight.

As the figure bent over him he scooped up a handful of earth and flung it towards the Jap's face then, using all the strength he could muster, whipped his fore-head forward, catching the Nip a hefty crack below the right eye.

As the Nip soldier fell back, bellowing his war-cry, *'Kin-ell!'* Albert was up and scampering back into the jungle.

Plunging through the brush his jacket was grabbed from behind and he was dragged to the floor on his back. Rolling over, his fists bunching to meet his assailant, he came eye to eye with... a dog.

I watched Noddy bend over Albert's prostrate form. I couldn't see him breathing and the scent of his life-force was weak. He looked like a ghost and must have been almost dead. Then the wizened stick-man exploded into life, throwing dirt into Noddy's eyes and following up with a classic Glasgow Kiss.

Noddy staggered backwards, clawing at the leaf-litter stinging his eyes, as I hopped over the railing. Albert was quickly away into the bushes, but I was quicker. Four legs good.

In two bounds I had him by his PJ tail and tugged backwards to drop him onto his back. As he rolled over, his fear smelling more like heroism now, I lay down in a play-bow, nose to nose with him and licked his face in the friendliest gesture I had.

'Albert, we're on your side. We've come to rescue you.'

All the ancient cultures know that humans can commune with animals when they are in an altered state of consciousness. Some starve or endure extreme pain to enter that state. Albert had done it inadvertently by nearly freezing to death.

In that moment he and I connected at the most basic emotional level. All he had to do was translate my concern into a practicality he could make sense of.

'Bloody Nora, it's a dog. The Nips don't have dogs. You must be Yanks!'

'Shucks, that's right limey, we Yanks have come to save your sorry ass.' I quickly got into character.

Albert collapsed into the mulch and started to weep. Not from pain or cold, but from relief.

'Are you alright mate?' Noddy also had tears streaming from his gunged-up eyes and was still rubbing at them with his fists.

I looked hard at him. Soaked, frozen, worn out, half-naked, having failed to evade capture then been plucked from the jaws of death *was Albert alright?*

I know his eyes were full of scheiße, but was his brain too?

'Got any K-rations Joe?* Better than that bloody compo any day,' croaked Albert. Noddy realised Albert was talking of soldiers' food and tuned in with me.

'Sorry bud, no rations for now, but we're taking you back to base. We're going home.'

Noddy dressed Albert in his jim-jam trousers and wrapped his own coat around him. We'd left the slippers, but Albert was too weak to walk anyway, and as Noddy picked him up he fell unconscious in his arms.

On the way Noddy called in and arranged for an ambulance to meet us at the now-increased-security home for the partially befuddled.

We looked a sight as we made our way back along the road, on the coldest of nights Noddy doing his great-ape jog-trot in wellies and with no coat, his breath steaming around him with the effort of carrying a limp bedraggled Albert wrapped in a jacket three sizes too big for him. I trotted alongside pretending I didn't know them.

---

* Joe = GI Joe = every American soldier.

160

We dropped Albert at the maximum security retirement home for the unbelievably heroic just as the ambulance turned up. They wrapped him in tin-foil and took him away, alive, but only just. For the second time he'd beaten the Japs and made it home, only to be hospitalised.

So, having escaped the slobbering masses and associated cold-sores at midnight, which had passed as we either: (a) took back the pathetic self-destructive old fool, or (b) had the honour of escorting home one of the bravest men we ever had the pleasure to encounter, we went to bed, Noddy still blinking the grit out of his eyes and gently dabbing the egg-sized lump on his cheek.

But as it turned out that wasn't the coldest of nights.

As we were to find out, the next one was.

We turned out for our day-shift at nine to a list of breaks on the outskirts of town. Three had the unmistakable M.O. of the Walking Man – a tiny hole drilled in the window-frame and only cash and jewellery gone. It made sense. He knew we'd be busy on New Year's Eve and had taken advantage. He'd probably done another couple that the occupiers hadn't yet noticed too.

As usual, there was little for us. The tracks were still frozen where they existed, but most were straight out of the back gardens into the field at the back (there was always a field, or a school field or a railway line at the back) and from there to the road. I got a strong whiff of him around the windows where he'd climbed in, but couldn't follow him amongst the traffic on the road. With no property to discard, there was nothing for us to find.

We had a look at a couple more jobs on the housing estates, poor-on-poor break-ins where the neighbours preyed on each other. I found a faux-leather handbag from one dumped in bushes beside the playground out the back, which Noddy handed in to SOCO for supergluing*.

Quite often scroats didn't take gloves when burgling, but so they didn't leave their prints all over the job they took their socks off and placed them over their hands. When they left they put their socks back on their feet. Obviously they didn't like to go far carrying jewellery boxes and handbags, as that would be a bit of a give-away as well - nasty little scroats don't usually carry handbags. Another ruse was to stuff as much gear as they could, like jewellery boxes or even the contents of whole drawers, into pillowcases, and sort it out as soon as they thought they were clear, discarding the less-valuable and later fencing the better bling. They'd take their socks back off their hands to sort through the loot, so when we found the chucked gear it was very likely to have fingerprints on it.

Many an Officer-in-the-Case has been pleased to be given a scroat's name with the positive identification of a fingerprint found by Scenes of Crime, on discarded property found by a police dog and identified by the householder as being taken in the break. Teamwork; I love it when a plan comes together.

That took us until mid-day, when the steward of the golf club opened up and found the place trashed. The back window had been smashed and the fire-door opened. The cigarette store was bust open and the contents all gone. The spirits had likewise been spirited away. The bandits (slots, fruit-machines), those beguiling flashing temptations that are no more than tax on the triumph of human hope over experience, had been broken open and the cash taken.

The only blessing was that the steward always banked the bar

---

* It's called Cyanoacrylate Fuming and seems to have been discovered in Tokyo in the late 70s. A superglue solution is warmed in a cabinet into which the evidence is placed. As the fingerprint warms the water in it evaporates and is replaced by the glue. The print can then be dusted or photographed.

takings on his way home.

Ten sofa cushions had been unzipped of their covers, which were used to carry everything away. There had either been ten of them, or two scum had made five trips.

'Ah', I hear you thinking, 'They probably had a car,' and that's what Noddy thought as we drove up into the fells, because this wasn't the local Town golf club, it was the Moor golf club.

The highest in England, the Moor golf club is perched on the Pennines at fifteen hundred feet above sea level. We were traipsing up there for nothing; you can't screw a golf club in the middle of nowhere for that much stuff without a car. But in this job you always expect the unexpected.

Noddy parked the van out the front. There were no golfers as the course was closed by the foot of snow that had laid there for the past month. The club house had been used for parties over Christmas and New Year's Eve, but golf itself was off for the foreseeable future.

We went inside together. Noddy gratefully accepted a cup of tea with the local Plod and tossed me a bag of beef crisps donated by the Steward. I popped the bag with a paw and scoffed all except the last one, which I pushed towards Noddy. It's only fair to share. Make sure you leave the last portion of whatever you're eating for your dog. They might not do the same for you, but to be honest would you actually be grateful for the end bit of a bone or a rawhide chew a dog's been gnawing on? I thought not.

'I'll stick with the tea thanks,' Noddy wasn't hungry then.

I polished the crisp off, licked the bag, then licked the carpet clean of crumbs. Interesting flavour, golf club carpet. Salt and leathery, with a strong tang of umami and spilt gin.

The points of entry and exit were round the back and we could see two distinct types of footprints that had come and gone many times in the flattened snow. Both sets had the distinctive tread-pattern of

163

wellies. Best bet was a trail through the snow leading up to the main road where the car had been parked.

'Have you followed these?' Noddy asked the Plod.

'Not my job Nod, I don't want a rollocking from a dog handler for messing up the track,' he smiled back.

'Or to go too far from the warm,' Noddy smiled back. It might be bread and butter stuff for us, but with the scroats and the gear long gone, we were looking at stale bread spread very thinly with margarine.

We followed the footprints in the snow. The party had finished at one o'clock and the steward locked up by half-past two. By my reckoning they were gone by eight or ten hours and although I was scenting a hint of difference in where the track was and wasn't, it was more obvious to see than to smell.

The trail led away from the back of the clubhouse to a drystone wall from which the snow had been dislodged. On the other side were indentations in the snow where the cushion-covers full of booze and fags had been dropped.

The minor road was higher to our right and led about a mile back into the little town. In the other direction it led to the back of beyond. There was nowhere for a scroat to live for miles until you reached places to which the Geordies had given affectionate names to make them seem more welcoming. Names like Barney, Bish and Darlo.

Already the local Plods had contacted their more eastern colleagues on the assumption we were dealing with travelling Geordie scum who'd nipped over the tops and back again.

But the trail went left, dropping towards the valley bottom. There was a road a couple of miles away across the steep valley, but that was a bit of a trek, five times carrying sacks of bottles and fags, and they'd have to cross the South Tyne river each time. In the moonlight, at ten degrees below freezing.

The river there wasn't very wide, but it was fast and boulder-strewn,

164

with deep pools. One slip and they'd be icicles.

We followed the footprints embedded in the foot-deep snow downhill to the left, away from the road and towards the South Tyne. The day was overcast and the light was seeping away, taking what little warmth there was left with it. The snowy landscape took on the ghostly role of illumination as we crossed the next two fields.

The pattern was the same, snow-cleared drystone walls with the impressions of the cushion-covers on the other side; the same two sets of wellie-prints pointing in both directions; both of which were the wrong direction to make any sense.

In the third field we hit footprint chaos. At right angles to our two-scroat double trail was a twenty-yard wide super-trail of countless footprints. Many were fresher than our two, but some older too. The vast majority were walking-boot tread. It was like a herd of people had migrated along the side of the valley to and from the little town, but we were still a mile from habitation. Dozens if not hundreds of people had walked in both directions.

Then it dawned. We'd come across the Pennine Way; two-hundred and sixty-eight miles of walking trail along the backbone of England, from Derbyshire to Scotland.

People are stupid. You invent brilliant modes of transport from cars and buses to trains and aeroplanes so you can get to wherever you want to be, and what do you do for fun? Walk. Not just walk, but find the most remote places to do it.

I know you think dogs like to 'go for a walk' and some dumb pooches get all excited when you say the words and pick up their leads, but honestly, we don't. No dog walks for pleasure. Walking is incidental to what we do when we are out.

It's a bit like saying 'we're going for a breathe'. Breathing isn't the point of the exercise, it's just something we do when were are performing the preferred activity – which changes.

Don't get me wrong, we like to go out. In fact pet dogs' lives are so boring I don't know how they stand it. I'd have been mental if I was a pet. Same-old same-old every day. Dull, dreary mind-numbing tedium.

No wonder they go silly at the words, 'Would Tiddles like to go walkies?' It's the highlight of their day.

But 'walking'? No. Sniffing, checking out the local pee-mail; who's been past and left a mark; what's happening to who; who's happening to what? All the gossip in handy scent and pheromone packages.

And that's just the start. Imagine how exciting it is to chase a squirrel or a rabbit, or to follow the scent left by a passing cat, or start a rumble with a poodle, especially if your only other excitement in life is to bark at the postman, who never comes in anyway?

That's why we love 'walks'. Not for the walking but for the incidental excitement that comes with them.

But with humans it's all, 'Oh Jacinta, let's go to the Lake District for a walk. We can walk up a mountain and back down again. How exciting!'

Exciting? Have you never chased a squirrel?

Noddy and I looked at the path but neither of us could make out our scroats' marks amongst the multitude. We checked the other side of the pathway. Nothing. We checked fifty yards each way on both sides of the pathway. Nothing. Our scroats had stayed on the path, brilliantly camouflaging their tracks.

At least that ruled out crossing the freezing river below us. But it was a mile into town. Had they walked a mile each way five times? That was three hours walking! Plus the time inside the clubhouse filling the cushion-covers and smashing up the bandits.

Okay, think. They hadn't gone to the road to a car. There was no scroat habitation close enough to walk to with all the gear. They hadn't had enough time to walk to the town and back again five times. They'd stayed on the path for at least fifty yards one way or the other.

They'd stashed the gear somewhere.

A stash made most sense. Take as much gear as possible a short distance away, hide it and come back the next night. But they must have known, dim though most scroats are, that we would follow the footprints in the snow. That accounted for them hitting the path.

It wasn't a coincidence, it was a plan. If they knew about the path and they'd walked there, they were locals. Which meant they'd walked from the town.

Noddy and I looked at each other and I knew that he knew what I knew.

'C'mon.'

We both said it at the same time and set off to find the stashed booze and fags… in opposite directions. Noddy turned towards the town and I turned towards the bleak wilderness.

'Seriously Major, c'mon,' he said again, walking off, 'we've got a stash to find and the light's almost gone.'

I stood my ground and, concentrating as hard as I could, I sent him, *It was a plan. They knew we'd be here. They knew we'd follow them to the town because there's nothing the other way. It's a huge amount of booze and fags. They've either got to go off the path to hide it, in which case we'll see their footprints, or hide it next to the path, in which case we'll find it easily. Except if we aren't looking in the right place. So they must have gone the other way.*

'Major, I dunno what you're doing, but let's go.' Humans. The lights are on, but there's really no one at home is there? I set off up the path towards the bleakness, leaving Noddy to either catch up or go his own way.

'Hey! Okay… I get it, we're going this way then.'

After two hundred yards the path dropped away into a hollow, where there nestled a small wood surrounded by a drystone wall. I raised my nose and picked up the unmistakable scent of humans and bottles and fag-packets but, most of all, the same smell as the golf club carpet.

I looked back at Noddy, nodded at him and quickened my pace to the wall. The overhanging trees had sheltered the top of the wall, so there was no snow to dislodge. I hopped over and almost fell on top of the ten whiffy cushions full of loot that were stashed just on the other side.

I grinned at Noddy, who was looking over the wall. The Pennine Way path went right by the little walled wood, but you had to make a point of looking into it to see the stash.

A good stash; a good plan; but not good enough. All we had to do was wait for them to come back and we had them.

We trotted back to the clubhouse, filled in the local Plod and rang the D.I. As I suspected he wanted obs kept on the stash and the scroats locked up when they came back for it.

The trouble was, it was New Year's Day, a public holiday for which police officers were paid double time, so there were no other dogs on duty. We were it. And it was certainly a dog job, nicking two scroats in the middle of nowhere.

Despite the fact we'd been on all day in the freezing cold, we'd have to stay. Smiddy and Slade would take over at six in the morning. Noddy had one more phone call to make. One that dog handlers made when they could, but wives didn't expect.

'Hello Pet, I'll not be home for a while. We've got some obs to do. Okay, love you. See you when I see you – maybe in the morning.'

The long-suffering-ness of dog handlers' wives was legendary. Call-outs at the ring of a telephone and shifts frequently extended for hours meant that their husbands were simply unreliable. Even days off could be changed or worked. Wives couldn't plan anything for certain

168

and had to have the self-reliance and resilience to run the house and children with a complete lack of support. Add to that the higher than usual bloke-levels of inebriation and philandering and it was a surprise that any of them had wives at all.

This time Noddy was lucky; he'd been able to get word to Pet that he wasn't coming home (again). At least this time she knew it was an official absence and he wasn't lying in a hospital or ditch somewhere. And he was on double time.

Noddy had another cup of tea before we headed back down to the wood. It was properly dark and the temperature was plummeting when we got there. It wasn't a difficult brief; we had to stay concealed in the wood until the scroats placed hands on the stash and then take them into custody. We'd have to walk them back to the clubhouse, where the local Plod would meet us with transport.

We waited in the middle of the wood, Noddy concealing himself by blending in with a tree; an easy job for someone who already looked like one.

He was dressed for the cold in wellies with extra socks, waterproof over-trousers, padded waistcoat and jacket, gloves and topped off with a woolly hat. If they did see him they'd take him for a discarded scarecrow.

I melted in with the darkness at the bottom of the tree, curling into a ball and covering my face with my tail, leaving my nose peeping out. The wind was from the east but the clouds covered the sky, blocking out the moon and starlight, so I would scent them long before we saw them.

And so we waited. And waited. Midnight came and went. Noddy froze and had to start stamping his feet and rubbing his hands, gently so as to make as little noise as possible. I didn't move so as to keep the ground I'd warmed beneath me; it's more economical to conserve heat than it is to generate it. I drifted into a light sleep where I dreamed of running across tundra chasing musk oxen, and curling up in a snow-hole.

It's not a dereliction of duty for a dog to sleep because we can sense change and be awake in a flash. We constantly measure the world, even when asleep, and if anything alters we can snap awake. Even asleep I would know they were here before Noddy did.

But Noddy suffered. He kept moving as well as he could, but when I heard the dog van in the distance his face was blue. I stood up and pointed, and he stood still. It was half past six o'clock and the rime sparkled off the crust on top of the snow-cover like a million scattered diamonds.

A few minutes later Smiddy gently called, 'Alright, c'm 'ere then,' to Slade, who had told him we were here and was called back to his side for the last few yards.

''Allo mate, how's it going?' he called softly over the wall, 'Bit parky, eh?'

'You could say that.' The reply was equally understated. Slade raised a lip at me as he cocked his leg against an undeserving tree. I glowered back to show him he didn't scare me, but we both knew a fight wasn't allowed.

Police dogs are all confident and ready for a challenge. It means that sometimes we see challenges where there are none, but when we are working we put aside any differences for the sake of the job.

Dogs are territorial animals, and that's fine for most pets and working dogs. They have their own area they are familiar with and they tramp it regularly, whether it be the dull trek round the local park or a run up a fell-side rounding up sheep. They mark it and defend it.

We too have a territory, our homes and toileting-walk areas. We mark and defend those too. But we're frequently off-territory. Being off our own territory inevitably means we are on some other dog's, and dogs don't like other dogs on their territory.

170

I appreciate it's kind of strange for humans to understand, not being in tune with other animals, but even when a dog isn't there, its essence still is. As soon as we encroach on another dog's patch we feel its presence. The personality of the other dog surrounds and engulfs us, haunting us through time-lapsed scent, pheromones and the emotions that bind us together.

I'm told that humans sometimes experience the feeling that they're being watched; that's the nearest you'll ever get to feeling the ripples in the canine social ether that we experience. That's how we know things at a distance, such as when a loved one passes away, or is coming home even before they arrive.

For police dogs this is both a blessing and a curse. We feel the other dogs, but we also feel their challenges to our trespass on their ground. A heavily marked territory is a massive challenge that we can't just ignore. We wouldn't be the dogs we are if we backed away from a challenge, so we have to mark it ourselves.

Cocking your leg and leaving a deposit says, *'I don't care who you are, I am superior,'* because without that self-belief we may as well pack up and go home with our tails between our legs.

The wood held my essence from the long night, so Slade had to mark it when he arrived. Making a deposit raised his self-esteem enough for us to maintain a truce, both holding ourselves equal. If he'd pushed his luck I'd have killed him, but I could grant him one leg-cock for his pride.

We'd been relieved by the day-shift without the scroats coming back. We tramped up to the clubhouse, where Noddy had hidden his van amongst the lawnmowers in the garage, and Smiddy had parked his next to it. It would be daylight in two more hours and a farmer's tractor would be borrowed to lift the stashed gear for fingerprinting before it was returned to the steward.

The D.I. didn't want to commit scarce resources to the obs for

171

another day and night. I would have liked to have stayed to the end just to see the job out, but I don't think Noddy would have made it. He was borderline hypothermic as it was. Humans aren't made to be out in the cold.

Come to think of it, I'm not sure what you are made for, but whatever it is you're not as good as a dog.

As Noddy brought my bowl of scran from the kitchen later than morning I heard the radio as he opened the door, '…and the coldest place in England last night was the Moor, where the temperature dropped to minus fifteen degrees…'.

We were off for two days, which it took Noddy to recover, but learned from Smiddy that the scroats hadn't come back before the gear was lifted. Sometimes it goes like that; you can't win them all. At least we recovered the booze and fags. The scroats had taken the cash from the bandits with them, and we knew they were local, so it wouldn't take long for the town's Plods to work out who was suddenly flush with so much loose change.

We started back on evenings and were sent straight to a stolen car Traffic had followed off the motorway. It was a Ford Capri owned by our detective with the coiffured mullet, big-knotted tie and luxurious Zapata moustache.

He thought it was parked behind the nick, but it was now embedded in a gatepost on the outskirts of town. The two joy-riders who'd nicked it had the misfortune to be spotted by a mate of 'Tache's as they'd sped off down the motorway.

Knowing his colleague was at work, Traffic gave chase, but not surreptitiously enough. They clocked him and sped off the motorway, heading for the scroats' home estate so they could abandon the motor and outrun their pursuers on foot

Sadly they only just got off the motorway when they found out they

172

weren't Nelson Piquet, and pranged the beautiful, polished, cherished Capri 2.8i Mark 3, in venetian red, three years old with only one previous owner, into a five foot tall red sandstone pillar gatepost.

When Traffic pulled up behind both doors were open and the scroats had fled. Portliness dissuading him from taking after them into the fields, Traffic did what he was supposed to do and called a dog.

The weather had improved slightly in our two days off, so it was warm enough to snow, which it had all afternoon, a three-inch layer of it contributing to the Capri's sideways skitter, and it continued to flutter big downy feathers when we arrived ten minutes later.

For the second job in a row we were following footprints in the snow. You wait all year for a snowy-footprint job to arrive, then two turn up at once. Traffic hadn't seen them go, but the tell-tale indentations led into the field beyond the gate.

Without harnessing me up we bailed over the gate. Noddy gave me a, 'Seek!' but it was hardly necessary. You talk too much. An abandoned car with two doors open and a track leading across a field. What did he think I was going to do? Tap-dance? Macramé a tea cosy? There is no joy quite like hunting, and the chase was afoot.

They ran hell for leather for fifty yards into the field, away from the glare of the streetlights and to the point where they could see Traffic wasn't pursuing. Then they turned towards the town and slowed to a walk.

We continued at Noddy's jogging pace – a proper jog, not the monkey-stumble. We had enough reflected light from the distant streetlights to see two sets of prints, sloughing their way through the deepening snow, but that deepening snow was also filling them in.

The feathering became a blizzard, coming at us from the west like a big cold wet blanket. The flakes were huge and as well as covering the tracks it stuck to us too. From the right we were dog and handler, from the left we were snow-dog and snow-man, white from head to toe to tail. I gave up shaking myself to dislodge it as it just slowed me down. The depth of the rolling drifts was making it difficult to trot through; I was jumping in and out to make better progress.

'Major.' When I turned to look Noddy had unslung my tracking harness from his shoulder and he dropped it over my head, fastening it below my chest.

He was right, we could barely see the length of the line in front of us and didn't want to waste time losing each other.

We'd both narrowed our eyes to slits and on top of that we couldn't see the imprints any longer. The snow obliterated everything. I'd been tracking on scent alone for the last field, still heading towards town parallel to the main road, about fifty yards in, head down, shouldering my way into the white-out.

Then Noddy's radio blared out, 'Two bolted across the road in front of me. Gone into undergrowth on the other side.' Traffic had parked up and watched. He was about a hundred yards ahead of us (in his nice warm car, engine on, heater running to, 'Keep the windscreen from misting up').

Noddy had a quick decision to make; if we tracked to the scroats we could say in evidence that we had followed a track that led from the stolen car to the bodies. Not quite bang-to-rights, but a good connection to make. However, we had to catch them to do that and it looked like they were still moving. If Traffic had laid hands on them we would have continued the track to their feet, but he hadn't. The priority was to get hold of the pond-life.

Noddy quickly unclipped the harness, 'C'mon, let's go,' and we ran through the drifting snow. It's hard for a dog to fall over, with a leg at each corner, a low centre of gravity and a tail for balance. Not so for a biped.

Noddy's lumbering foot hit an earth mound he wasn't expecting, under the level snow. This in itself wasn't enough to topple him, but his

174

leg buckled and when his other foot searched for ground all it found under the snow was a hollow. That's when he sprawled full length on his face. Moles have a lot to answer for.

I turned and stared at him.

'This is no time to be playing snow angels.'

He coughed and spluttered in response, before staggering back to his feet, now a real snow-man.

'Into the wood about here,' Traffic showed us where he'd last seen the car thieves when we climbed out of the field.

On the other side of the dual carriageway was a wood. When they'd built the new road into town they'd left the old one which ran the other side of the small wood. The disused bit had been fenced off at both ends and become a long lay-by that was used for fly-tipping and clandestine vehicular activities.

In the days before police national computers could give you the registered owner of a car at the press of a button, cars parked up in lay-bys had to be checked for illegal activities. Many a travelling crook had been locked up as a result of a nocturnal check on a parked-up car.

I remember Noddy knocking on the window of such a car and a female voice coming from inside, 'We're just necking officer...' to which he replied, 'Well put his neck back in his trousers and open the window so I can talk to you.'

There were no cars parked this early in the evening, but the roads made an island of the wood. It was a rough triangle fifty yards wide at the base and a hundred yards long on the other two sides. The scroats had come out of the field and, when they'd seen Traffic parked, bolted straight across the dual carriageway into the wood.

'Have you seen them since?' Noddy wanted to know.

''fraid not.'

We didn't know if they'd shot straight through or were still inside.

'Can you stay on this corner while I take Major down the other side?'

That would give him a view of two sides whilst I checked the third to see if they'd come out or not.

Why not track in from where they'd been last seen? Maybe I've led you astray with a description of the place as a 'wood'. Whilst there were woody elements to it in that lofty trees were dotted about, the majority was a thick mix of blackthorn and hawthorn bushes, fighting each other for a portion of the available light, up to about eight or ten feet high. Note the word 'thorn' twice there.

The ground cover underneath was an even thicker carpet of brambles. It wasn't impenetrable, but you'd have to be desperate to endure the spikes. I don't wear boots or any other form of protective clothing. I'd have been ripped to shreds in five yards.

The old road verge was overgrown with weeds and rubbish, from smashed television sets to bicycle frames and mattresses with very suspicious stains, so I ran down the road, with the benefit of the wind blowing through the wood towards me and sheltering me from the snow.

BANG! The scent of scroat hit me like a scrofulous wall halfway down and I turned in towards it. A ripped sofa lay on its side buried in the wild foliage and underneath, trying to fade into the background, was a scroat. I let rip my best staccato baying inches from his ear and Noddy pounded up the road to us.

'Hello, what are you doing here?' Noddy enquired of the scum, but there was no reply, just a burying of head into his hands. Noddy shone his torch, 'Come on then, out you come,' he tried, and this time the scroat crawled out, as befits an insect life-form.

He was in his late teens, thin as a stick and dressed in tracksuit pants and a tee-shirt. Both were ripped and there were bleeding cuts on his face from where he'd run through the blackthorn. He was shaking from the cold, the fear or the adrenaline, or maybe all three.

176

'Where's your mate?'

'Dunno.'

'What are you doing hiding under a manky sofa?'

'Lookin' fo' me dog.'

'What?' Noddy was incredulous at the stupid reasons given by scroats for their presence at criminal activities.

'Ah've lost me dog an' I wus lookin' fo' it.'

'Right, fine, you're locked up for nicking the Capri,' said Noddy, adding the caution ('You are not obliged to say anything and if you try to run remember that the dog can run faster.')

I stood and bristled, but this arsch-tropft wasn't going to run or kick off. He didn't have it left in him. Noddy walked him to the top corner of the wood, still with a view down the old road should his mate decide to run, and sat him down while he waited for the van.

The van arrived at the same time as Tache, screeching up in a plain CID car. Both scroat and Tache went into the back of the van and after some comedic bangs and a little rocking, Tache came back out again.

'We're looking for Nigel Doyle,' he told us.

Nigel was a son of the well-known Doyle family. He was twenty-two and had been a guest of Her Majesty for the past three years, sent down for a violent burglary investigated by Tache.

Just released, the theft of the Capri was his revenge. He'd made some good contacts in the nick and had a buyer for it. He'd also made some other contacts inside and had come out HIV-positive and with hepatitis B, both viruses spread by contact with infected blood and other body fluids.

'Bennie says he last saw him when they crossed the road into the wood. Where did you find Bennie, Nod?'

'Down the back of a sofa,' Noddy explained, then pointed at Bennie-scroat's erstwhile hiding place, 'I'll check out the rest of the

177

perimeter.'

I found no tracks coming out, nor any obvious scent of Nigel other than where they'd gone in.

'Not to worry,' said Tache when Noddy told him, 'I'll lift him at home sometime now we know who he is. There's no need to hang about in this.'

The blizzard hadn't let up and there was no way we could effectively search the whole interior of the blackthorn patch of two and a half thousand square yards.

'Okay then, cheers,' Noddy acknowledged.

The van containing Bennie, Tache in the CID car and Traffic left. We could have walked back up the road to our van, but we didn't. We walked as far away as we needed to get the best view we could of the wood. We couldn't see all of it, the bottom end was hidden, but we could see most. Noddy crouched down under a holly bush on the roadside and I lay beside him. As the minutes passed we were soon both covered in snow again. This hanging around in the cold was becoming a habit.

After forty minutes a track-suited figure struggled out of the bushes on the dual carriageway side. He'd stopped and hidden almost as soon as he'd gone in! The wind had blown his scent into the middle of the wood where the undergrowth had soaked it up. But now he was out.

He hadn't seen us, but he would as soon as we stood up. We were still seventy-five yards away, with cars moving on the dual carriageway alongside; not as many as usual because of the snowstorm, but enough to hamper a straight chase.

Noddy went for shock and awe (with a little bit of bluff), bursting from cover he yelled, 'Police with a dog! Stop! Stop or I'll send the dog!' and strode towards Nigel with me at heel.

He didn't run because he didn't want to spook Nigel into running and we needed to close the gap before he could safely send me through the traffic.

Nigel looked at us, thrust his hands into his tracky pockets and walked across the first lane to the central reservation, pretending everything was nothing to do with him. He ducked his head and slouched away from us towards town.

Our fast march was catching him and in a gap in the traffic Noddy took us onto the central reservation too. I had a line-of-sight chase without crossing in front of vehicles.

'Police with a dog! Stop! Stop or I'll send the dog!'

Nigel looked back over his shoulder and slowed to a saunter, but didn't stop.

Noddy whispered to me, 'Hold him.' He hadn't tracked through a blizzard, run across four fields and fallen flat-out in the snow to let CID pick the scum up at home later.

Nigel was our prey. We'd hunted him down and now we had him. He could give up or not. He'd been warned twice. It was his choice.

I took off down the middle of the road, cars passing on both sides, the snowy central reservation blurring into tundra under my feet as I aimed to take out the moose in front of me.

And Nigel stood still.

Scheiße. I knew I couldn't bite him. He'd given up. Stand-off then. I threw my brakes on, snow-ploughing to a halt, and was about to go into my barking routine when Nige started walking away again. Slowly at first, then quicker.

I hesitated.

'Hold him!' encouraged Noddy and, as I turned towards him, Nigel stopped again. I ran past and circled my prey. When I was at the point of my circuit nearest Noddy, Nigel walked away again. Noddy was lumbering up, but not quickly. Nigel shuffled through the snow, hands still thrust into pockets.

'Hold him!' again, but as soon as I took off he stood still again.

I couldn't!

This wasn't how it went in the Manual or on the training field!

I knew what to do if he ran and I knew what to do if he stood still, but he wasn't doing either. I circled him again, growling in my confusion. He was making my teeth itch.

Noddy caught us up.

'I'm arresting you on suspicion of theft of a motor vehicle,' He said, all officious in his irritation as he reached for the cuffs hung on his belt.

'You're not,' snarled Nigel. Balled fists came out of his pockets as he stepped towards Noddy, then he grunted as I leapt forwards, grabbed his left wrist, twisted and pulled down.

This is where being quicker to see and react really pays off. Nigel staggered forwards and was helped to earth when Noddy sidestepped and swept his legs from under him with a boot, taking hold of his flailing right arm as he went down. I held my grip and squeezed, feeling my sharp canine teeth puncture his skin and muscle, tasting the warm savoury blood seeping onto my tongue.

Nigel struggled, flexing his body like a hooked fish and thrashing his legs, but Noddy had his arm pinned between his shoulder-blades and his knee in the small of his back. I gave my head a rat-killing shake, ripping deeper into his muscle and tendons, and heard him grunt again.

Full credit to whatever cocktail of drugs he had taken, because he should have been screaming in agony. Or maybe having his face buried in a foot of snow helped mute him.

Noddy cracked the cuff on the arm he held and said, 'Major, would you be good enough to leave hold of his arm?'

I gave an extra squeeze before releasing to remind him of what he would be missing, and Noddy drew the two arms together in a behind-the-back cuffing.

'I think you'll find that if you concentrate really hard you will find that actually I am arresting you after all. You are not obliged to say anything...' He was very official this time, meticulously and slowly reciting each word.

Unfortunately he seemed to have forgotten that Nigel was still face-down in the snow and not able to breathe perhaps as easily as he should as he finished the caution, '...may be given in evidence.'

He rolled Nigel over and paused, 'Hmm, I don't know how to spell 'cough, gasp, splutter' so I'll put that down as 'no reply' Nigel, okay?'

Nigel sat up and spat at Noddy's face, spittle spraying all around in the wind. Noddy ducked back and it was difficult to tell if he'd been hit or if it was the blowing snow that wet him. He laughed, but took hold of the cuffs between Nigel's wrists as he helped him gently to his feet so as to keep behind him.

Noddy had confidently radioed in our arrest as he'd sent me to chase Nigel, so the van was soon pulling up alongside, blue light illuminating the snow-scape beautifully.

'I'll walk him in, he has a nasty spitting habit,' Noddy told the van crew, bending the cuffed arms upwards to make sure Nigel didn't bang his head on the roof whilst climbing in.

Nigel's ineffectual response was to try to spit over his shoulder. Sadly he consequently lost his balance and fell face down on the metal floor.

Back at the nick Noddy stood in front of the charge desk with his prisoner and related the circumstances of the arrest to the Custody Sergeant. Nigel was still spitting, but now it was laced with blood from his split lip.

The Custody Sergeant was a salt of many years' experience. He was a huge man with fists like hams and the resigned expression of one who had seen it all before, whatever it was.

He motioned Nigel towards him as though to whisper in his ear and when Nigel leaned forwards clamped one meaty hand over his mouth and the other behind his head, holding him like a vice.

'Search him,' he told his jailer, who patted Nigel down before turning his pockets out, taking great care to avoid any needles placed within for the very purpose of stabbing unsuspecting Plods.

Not unusually for a scroat on the rob, Nigel had left home with only the screwdriver that was now jammed in the ignition of the Capri. Having checked over Nigel's whole body from arm-pits to butt-cheeks, and flipped off his shoes to check his socks* the verdict was, 'Nothing Sarge,'

'Okay, put him in cell four until he decides to stop his camel impression. Noddy, I need to talk to you about HIV and hepatitis.'

Half an hour later I was drinking a very large bowl of milk. The Custody Sergeant had told Noddy to ring the doctor, who had in turn phoned the vet, had a discussion with her and rang Noddy back again.

'Dogs can't catch HIV or hepatitis B from humans, although they have their own form of canine hepatitis. However, the pathogens remain alive at body temperature so there is some risk that they could be passed on to the next person Major bites if they are still in his mouth. The best advice is to wash his mouth out and avoid him biting you.'

Ever a good judge of what I may or may not allow him to do, Noddy used his discretion and washed my mouth out by giving me two pints of full cream milk. Delicious. And a fitting reward for biting an infected scroat. Noddy wasn't quite so lucky and was booked in for vaccinations the following morning.

Nigel was even less lucky. Being out on licence he was back inside the following day, with a tetanus jab, a course of antibiotics and a

---

* It's an exciting life in the custody suite. Even though they wear gloves they wash their hands a lot. Sometimes it's difficult to wash off a feeling.

suitably bandaged wrist to finish his sentence.

He'd know to stop when challenged by a police dog handler next time.

He'd be spitting mad not to.

🐾🐾🐾🐾

The cold snap broke later than night, when rain carried on the back of the low pressure area washed the snow away.

Weather forecasting is another skill we have that you don't, both long and short range. Scent clings to the ground when the air pressure is high and lifts when it is lower. High pressure compresses the softer ground and when low pressure moves in it releases the trapped scents of decaying detritus. The whole world smells different when the weather changes. Of course rain itself exerts downward pressure, so I'll leave to your imagination how the competing forces cause scent to spatter and bubble – after all, it's all you have.

We can smell those changes on the prevailing wind, which also carries to us the distant sounds of storms, and the screams of the sea-birds as they move inland to avoid them.

Not all dogs are equal of course, and only the best German Shepherds' abilities include hearing higher and much lower pitches than you and other, less fortunate, dogs.

A couple of days later Noddy was filling the van with petrol at the Traffic Unit pump. It was about half-one in the morning and it had been a quiet night so far, the intermittent rain blowing in as good as a dozen coppers any night. Even scroats like to be warm and dry.

'Good morning.'

'Sir!'

Noddy straightened slightly in deference to the uniform of the Traffic Inspector who marched out of the office in his direction. The uniform was immaculate, all shiny and pressed, in stark contrast to Noddy's, which was mud-spattered uniform pants tucked into wellies and scruffy civvy anorak with my lead looped over his shoulder.

'Can you tell me who was driving this vehicle at 5.15pm yesterday afternoon?'

Noddy looked puzzled as he returned the nozzle to the pump and screwed the filler-cap back on. It wasn't that the question was difficult, just that he wasn't expecting it. It was past the Inspector's finishing time, and not far off ours and Noddy was refuelling the van in preparation for tomorrow's day shift.

'Yes, sir.' We'd been training at HQ and late coming back to hand over the van to Arthur, belting up the motorway to make up time, 'That would be me.'

'Were you attending an emergency?'

'Depends how you define it sir, but we'd not been sent to a job if that's what you mean.'

'No, you weren't, because I checked with the control room.' He paused, smugly congratulating himself on springing his elaborately planned trap.

'So can you explain to me why you were doing ninety miles an hour on the motorway when you overtook me just after the northbound services?!'

I could smell the triumphant flourish in his voice from inside the van. This was where his plan of supervising from his own private car was paying dividends. He'd caught one of those dog handler oiks speeding. Now he was looking forward to tearing him off a strip.

Noddy smiled innocently at him. They both knew that prosecution wasn't in the offing, but they also both knew how much the Traffic Inspector was looking forward to administering the lambasting. But he wasn't the only one who could have some fun.

'Of course sir. You see it's fairly flat there and she'll only do just

184

over ninety on the flat. But don't worry, a couple of miles on, where it dips down towards the junction, I had her well over a ton.'

The Traffic Inspector's face turned purple and he started to splutter when Noddy's radio crackled a series of short commands sending three Pandas to the edges of the Woodlands estate, ending, 'Householder at 26 Aurelius Avenue has just seen someone hanging around in the back gardens of Cohort Crescent.'

'Sorry boss,' completely straight-faced now, 'it's been nice to chat but I've got some dog handling to do,' as Noddy jumped into the van, revving away to the top of each gear as he left. Only I heard the muttered, 'Tosser.'

The Woodlands estate was a new garden village development tagged onto the end of the Shambles to try to improve the area. They'd given the road names a Roman theme in an attempt at gentrification.

What they'd neglected to consider was that they'd built houses for posh people, who had money, a short hop from houses for poor people, who hadn't.

The inhabitants of the Shambles probably didn't know that entropy is a basic law of the universe, but they played their part in its effect by trying to level out the peaks and troughs in the distribution of wealth, removing it from the Woodland's residents and passing it on to bookies, publicans and drug dealers.

But this could be more than just a normal prowler. Cohort Crescent backed onto the railway yard. The yard was past its prime and although the main line still ran through the middle, most of it lay abandoned, waiting for a developer to make the investment in Veni Vidi Vici Way, or some such Roman-esque boulevard.

The open wasteland, dotted with low scrub, was ideal Walking Man territory; lots of access to decent houses and many escape routes.

'Everybody stand off. Give us time to come in from the far side and

185

cross the main line. Control, can you tell BTP?'

Noddy wanted to come at him from behind, but to do that we had to cross the main railway line joining England to Scotland. The British Transport Police held sway on railway property and would place an alert on the line to warn train drivers we would be crossing, but the trains wouldn't stop. Luckily we'd be across it in two seconds.

He killed the lights on the van and coasted the last fifty yards, pulling on the handbrake so the brake-lights didn't show, and we both bailed out at the old entrance to the yard. Now it was fenced off and heavily festooned with barbed wire in an attempt to discourage youths from playing on railway lines, so we went in the same way they did, through the loose panel behind the ash tree growing to the side.

Inside the old roads were breaking up, and most of the yard was a staple of railway yards everywhere, compressed cinder, that cracked under Noddy's boots as he tried to creep noiselessly towards the distant back gardens. The whole area was dark, but anyone moving, including us, was silhouetted by street lights on the perimeter.

We had a hundred yards to go to the backs of Cohort Crescent, Noddy bent double and quietly crunching, with me padding silently alongside.

Because the old gateway wasn't directly opposite we were angling our way across, and were still a good way off when I saw him run. It was just after we'd seen a torchlight appear, waved about by an over-eager Plod in the back garden of 26 Aurelius Avenue.

We'd hoped to be closer when he made his break, but the shadow in the gloom cleared the fence and took off like the hounds of hell were on his heels, away from us down the back of Cohort Crescent. He wasn't far wrong.

'Police with a dog stop! Stop or I'll send the dog! Hold 'im.'

The last was said to me and I didn't need telling twice. I shot off, cinders scattering in my wake.

In six strides I was over thirty miles an hour and still accelerating; in ten I'd reached maximum speed of almost forty, covering over ten feet with each stride. I was in the zone, every fibre focussed only on running down my prey. Endorphins filled me with euphoria, heightened my perception of the running scroat in front of me, and shut down pain receptors and extraneous senses. I didn't need touch, scent and sound, just sight and speed.

I'm not sure how I heard the desperate yell from behind me, but it was so small it was easy to ignore.

'down!'

I didn't break pace, despite registering the frantic tone. Surely he didn't mean me? I was locked on, a Major-to-scroat missile.

'D O W N !'

Louder, and even more urgent. I hesitated in mid-stride and out of the corned of my eye saw, thundering obliquely towards me, the oh-one-forty-six sleeper to London Euston. Twisting in mid-air, I threw myself to the side, exploding through a small willow tree and tumbling over and over as the train trundled past, slower than usual because the driver was keeping watch for a police dog handler near the line.

I don't know what saved my life that day. Was it the train travelling a little slower than usual? Was it Noddy alerting me - just? Or was it my superbly honed fitness and awareness of the world around me? It certainly wasn't the dummkopf driver's eyesight.

I stood squarely, tongue dangling and panting from the adrenaline rush of escaping danger, as the carriages rattled past, passengers inside asleep oblivious to the drama outside.

How big a bump does a train rolling over a dog make? Would they have woken up? Probably not. When the last carriage passed I stared at the back of Cohort Crescent. Gone. Not a sign of our fleeing pond-life. I set off across the line at a trot.

'Stay,' I paused as Noddy crunched up breathlessly behind me,

'Are you alright?'

What did he want me to say? I thought hard at him, *'No, you schwanz, I've just had the living scheiße frightened out of me by a hundred tons of steel trying to turn me into sliced salami. But the scum's on the run, so get your act together and let's go!'*

He looked both ways along the line, like he was in the Tufty Club*, before stepping across. I sighed and trotted after him.

At the back of Cohort Crescent I smelled Walking Man, that mix of the camo jacket, cotton shirt and jeans, trainers and paperwork. There was no mistaking him. This time there was a touch of panic in him, a dread not normally there brought out in his fear-fuelled dash.

He was easy to follow out of the railway yard at the next cut between the houses where the local kids had bent another hole in the fence, then left and right down cuts at the end of cul-de-sacs so the Pandas couldn't spot him.

Panda drivers cruise past the end of culdies and are easy to hear coming. All you have to do is hang back in the shadows until they pass and then zip through to the next one.

We crossed the main drag into the end of yet another culdy and then, *'Bike,'* I stared hard at Noddy. The unmistakable scent of rubber tyre and metal frame mingled with the Walking Man's smell.

Walking Man had just become Cycling Man. I could have still followed him for a while, but he was pedalling faster than I could track and we'd eventually lose him. Might as well cock a leg on it now.

But the bike wasn't his; there was another human's scent on it, and I knew whose it was. *'He's knicked a Plod's bike. It's that esel Colin Dimmock the RBO off Woodlands.'*

'Seek on...'

---

* Road safety advice provided for young humans by an animated squirrel in the 1960s. A squirrel. Do you know how much road sense a squirrel has? Splat! It's things like this that make me sure I'll never understand humans.

'Don't be daft, he's on a bike.' I drilled at him as hard as I could, staring intently into his eyes.

'Come on Major, seek him...' a pleading tone wheedled into his voice. I turned around and walked back the way we'd come. This was as close as I'd come to the Walking Man, and I'd lost him.

Noddy radioed in, 'I've lost the track in the culdy between thirty four and thirty six Legionary Lane. I'll have a root about, but Major says he's gone.'

I wandered around disconsolately marking the odd gatepost to let the locals know a proper dog had been past whilst they were snuggled under the duvet, but there was disappointment in the odour of my urine that night.

The bike turned up in an alleyway in the town centre later that morning, giving no clues as to the Walking Man's ultimate destination. But not until after Donkey Dimmock was hauled over the coals by his Sergeant.

Of course he'd had to report the loss at six when he'd gone in to clock off. It seems he'd thought he'd have better luck with the Walking Man if he was on foot, so had left his bike hidden in a bush in the culdy and sneaked off in entirely the wrong direction.

We'd learnt something else about the Walking Man though. He wasn't your run of the mill scroat who ran for home at the earliest escape. Although he'd been disturbed before he'd got in, and the only incriminating possession he would have would be the awl, which we presume would be concealed inside his clothing to avoid the Plod 'pocket turn-out', he'd purposely headed into town rather than give us a clue as to where he lived.

And he knew he needed a getaway because the hounds of hell were right behind him.

He was right.

He'd been in bed an hour when the phone by the bedside woke Noddy, and I heard him sleepily acknowledge the caller and clatter out of bed. The Controller knew they were talking to a half-awake person and didn't give many details – they could come later over the radio once he was on his way.

I was waiting impatiently at the gate for him, his face freshly splashed with water after he'd thrown on the half-uniform he kept by the bed for the purpose of speed-dressing. Even his boots were pull-ons to slip into for speed, and help with the frequent changes into wellies. He'd thought this through. Three minutes after the phone rang we were in the van and moving.

In the age of the acronym, where other forces were changing their dog handling sections into 'K9 Units' our handlers had voted to call themselves Fast Action Response Teams, but it had been vetoed by the Inspector. Shame, I thought it was apt; they arrived with just a whiff of a smell and they were gone.

We headed to a farm on the fringes of town. There'd been a spate of diesel thefts and rather than pay for proper security the tight farmers had taken to ringing in every time they saw something suspicious. You'd think they didn't have their own shotguns.

Anyway, Old MacDonald had been up exercising his bladder when he'd seen lights in the fields behind the farmhouse. So far so mundane, but when he'd got back into bed he thought he'd heard a shotgun blast.

Only 'thought'.

We had a force armed response capability, but it was one double-crewed traffic car and they were at the other end of the county. They were on their way, but could we have a look first?

Noddy killed his lights on the main road and we were walking up the lane towards the farmhouse when we saw a piercing beam light up the field in a circular motion, and then die. The signature give-away of poachers 'lamping'.

Yet another scroatal activity, lamping was wandering the countryside in the hours of darkness, when cute, fluffy and above all tasty animals like deer, hares and rabbits came out to play.

The scum would crudely attach a car battery to a single headlamp. The battery would be supported in a bag slung over the shoulder and the whole thing made a very effective spotlight to dazzle nocturnal creatures. Caught unawares in the beam they would literally be transfixed in the headlight whilst dogs were set on them, bringing them down and ripping the throats out of deer, or tearing the smaller fluffies apart.

Extremely effective; extremely illegal. On a poor night, rather than go home empty handed, they'd take a sheep as a consolation prize.

We'd seen the beam flashed around the field, which meant they hadn't sighted any wildlife and would move into the next field. If they were any good at all they would be working into the wind, so we knew where they were heading.

Any kills were quickly stashed and not collected until they were on their way home, so the time they were in possession was minimal. It was unusual to take a shotgun with them for the same reason. If they were caught without any game they were, 'Just walking the dogs officer,' but shotguns don't need to be walked.

You can't talk your way out of carrying a shotgun.

I didn't need to track them. We could both hear them chatting as they walked, carried on the wind, as I leapt and Noddy climbed over the gate into the meadow.

We were still a field apart when the beam swept in a full circle and picked out my eyes, moved on, then did a double-take back, stopping abruptly pointing straight at me.

Dog eyes aren't like human eyes. Of course ours are much better. We don't see colours like you do, but there again who needs to? Our motion detection is far superior to yours, as is our low-light vision. This is in part due to our tapetum lucidum, which you don't even have.

Light entering the eye has to hit a photoreceptor to be registered as an image in the brain, but some light misses. The tapetum lucidum is a reflective surface right behind our retinas that bounces the missed photons back for a second chance, collecting all the available light. We are brilliant aren't we?

It also makes our eyes appear to shine when light is reflected from them. Like our coat colour differs between dogs, our eyes shine in different colours too. Mine are dark yellow.

The headlamp beam wasn't enough to illuminate us as we were both wearing black against the dark hedge, and human eyes don't shine, so all the small gang of scroats saw was a pair of gleaming yellow eyes across the field.

'Bluddiell,'s a fox! 's a fox Colin! Sic t' dogs on it!'

'Satan, Killa, Wendy - sic 'im!'

I could see the huddle, just as well as Satan, Killa and Wendy (seriously, 'Wendy'?) could see Noddy and me, and I saw the leads slipped and three dogs set off.

Colin and his two partners in slaughter thought they'd sighted the dogs on a yellow-eyed fox in the distance. But the dogs saw a human and a big black dog waiting for them.

They shot off like champagne corks, but after the first twenty yards fizzled out dramatically. It takes a special kind of dog with exceptional training to attack a human on command, and these weren't it.

They were lurchers. Not the noble first generation cross of a greyhound or whippet with a collie, adding speed to brains, but a mongrelised mix of lurcher with lurcher, with a bit of bull terrier thrown in somewhere for bulk.

Satan and Killa were both dark brindle and stood just under two feet at the shoulder. Wendy was taller, black as a Beauceron's bum hole, and weighed about seventy-five pounds. Long limbed and roach

192

backed, they were all built for speed and muscled-up, but when the brains were handed out they were still in the queue for extra-long muzzles. They radiated confusion.

All three loped towards us, wary of the man they'd been sent to chase. They weren't trained for this. They weren't trained at all. They were allowed off the lead to chase creatures that ran whilst they ripped and tore at them. If they caught them, they tried to gorge them down as quickly as they could before Colin and his rustling scum-mates grabbed the spoils from them.

They practised by ripping up stolen cats and small dogs thrown to them. Often the bait-dogs had their jaws taped shut so they couldn't defend themselves. Bets were placed on how long they'd last.

These three were scarred about the head, chest and forelegs; evidence of previous fights with animals that fought back. Could have been foxes, badgers or dogs - or particularly tenacious rabbits. I've no real time for lesser animals, but that's not 'sport'.

I stood up squarely and faced them down, enquiring a hard, *'Yes?'*

Wendy smelled of testosterone and mange, with a hint of the distemper he'd recovered from as a puppy. The other two were less prominent, less masculine, less showy.

Noddy saw them as shadows, but heard them panting as they pulled up just short of us, and left them to me. Scroats running towards us was a novelty he didn't want to upset by showing our hand too soon.

I addressed them all, *'You guys have made a mistake. A big one. Don't make it any worse.'*

'We've been sent to kill you.' Wendy walked threateningly towards me, flanked by Satan and Killa.

'The arsch-tropft thought I was a fox. I'm not. I'm your worst nightmare. I see your scars. I have no scars. I have no scars because I win easily.'

'We've been sent to kill you. Wendy's a good dog. Good boy

193

Wendy,' he half snarled, half whined, head on one side radiating insanity.

Wendy faced me head on while Satan and Killa took up positions on each of my flanks, but hanging back slightly. They moved side to side, looking for an opening, waiting to follow Wendy's lead.

I drew myself up high and looked down upon them with disdain. They smelled more feral than pets should do; pariahs, circling just outside range. I could easily take two, but wasn't sure about three at once. I rumbled a warning growl and tensed for the first move, sure it would come from Wendy as he lowered his head for the lunge.

The gutter-snipes were running to catch up and at the point where their beam illuminated Noddy it snapped off. 'Oh shit! Old Bill!' The-One-Who-Wasn't-Colin had been watching too much television, but the penny had dropped.

'Bug'r, it's Mad-Dog!' joined Colin.

Noddy's beam flashed on, lighting up the three amoebas as they ran for the hedge-line. 'Now then boys, don't rush off, I'd like a word.'

His torch wasn't as powerful as theirs and barely picked them out as they reached the hedge, and realised there was no way through the eight foot tangle of distressed hawthorn.

There was scuffling and mumbling, then they turned and shuffled towards us with heads lowered in that, 'caught bang to rights but ain't done nuffin' wrong,' pose known to every parent, and genetically imprinted into scroats from birth. I knew their bottom lips would be drooping long before I could make out their faces.

The cowardly lurchers had turned to run with their masters, Wendy last to leave with long loping strides, sinews stretching over bunched muscles. I gently exhaled my relief, not aware I'd been holding my breath until then, but it wasn't over yet. We walked up the hedge-line to meet them.

'I know I'm going to regret it,' Noddy was almost apologetic, 'but I have to ask the question boys. So, what are you doing here?'

The-One-Who-Wasn't-Colin was spokesman, 'Just walking the dogs Mr Mad-Dog, sir.'

'Okay, you win the prize for most obvious answer of the year. Do you have explicit permission to be on this land?'

'Eh?'

'Do you have a piece of paper signed by the farmer giving you permission to be on his land?' Not technically required, but Noddy knew it was the quickest way to get the answer he needed to move on.

'Err... No. Didn't know we needed one?'

'You have a lamp and lurcher dogs. You are trespassing in pursuit of game. Have you killed any?'

'No Mr Mad-Dog sir, just taking the dogs a walk,' said Colin.

'Haven't seen you since you fell off your bike Colin. I'll give Hamish your regards – who are you two?'

'Colin' was Colin Doyle, general scroat and dabbler in every illegal activity, and the other two were his cousins. Noddy took their details, checked with Control that their addresses came back as recorded and patted them down.

'I'm reporting you for poaching and seizing the lamp. Where is it?'

'Err... I'll get it sir, we left it in the grass back there.' The One-That-Wasn't-The-One-That-Wasn't-Colin nearly broke his back turning to gallop there and back. The lamp was handed over.

'Couple of things before you go boys. What's with the 'Mad-Dog'?'

'It's what the Firm are calling you since the Boxing Day match Mr Mad-Dog sir.' Colin wasn't a Firm regular, but he knew those who were.

'Okay. And, I get 'Satan' and 'Killa', but why 'Wendy'?'

Colin had all three dogs on bits of string fashioned into nooses around their necks, 'Cos yer dogs 'ave to be 'ard see? An' if a 'ard dog's called Wendy, he REALLY 'as to be 'ard.'

The One-That-Wasn't-The-One-That-Wasn't-Colin rolled his eyes,

''E's a Johnny Cash fan sir.'

'Okay boys, you've got off lightly tonight because I haven't caught you in possession of any game. When you get a summons in the post, plead guilty. Now get off and don't come back.'

'Yessir, nosir, yessir, yessir.'

Of course the one thing we all knew with absolute certainty was that they would definitely be back.

As they turned to go I eyeballed Wendy, *'Big dog when you've got back-up Wendy. Hope for your sake I don't catch you alone one day.'*

He walked away just a little bit too quickly, tail held just low enough to show the jibe had hit home. We stood and watched them go, heading back towards the road. Without the lamp they were done poaching for the night and if any sheep were reported missing they knew we'd be baa-a-ack.

'Okay Major, where's the gun?'

Noddy had purposely not mentioned the shotgun blast to the pond life, but he knew that if they'd had a gun they'd have stashed it at the last minute. Even these three arsch-fällt weren't stupid enough to walk up to a Plod with a shotgun; that's serious prison time. And they'd been too polite, too nice, too helpful.

I trotted away up the hedge-line and soon clocked the smell of warm metal and burnt cordite enveloped in sacking and grubby human. I stood over it and looked at Noddy. We didn't need telepathy for him to understand me this time.

'Good lad; easy eh?'

He picked up the bundle and a cloth bag of cartridges alongside it. They hadn't had much time and had just shoved the gun in its hessian sack into the bottom of the hedge, intending to come back for it later. They'd left the lamp with it and that's why The One-That-Wasn't-The-One-That-Wasn't-Colin had raced back to offer it up. Better to give away your lamp than to be caught with a shotgun. But they'd lost it

196

now. We didn't bother waking the farmer on our way out.

The gun had been stolen weeks before at a country-house break by one of Colin's 'uncles'* and had been stashed under the floorboards at an empty safe-house when Colin had decided to borrow it for some fun. He reckoned he'd have a go with it and put it back before anyone knew and that his cheeky grin would get him away with using a couple of cartridges when he coughed borrowing it. He'd fired it for the same reason that Wendy had tried to face me down; to show his mates he was top dog.

Now he had to rely on his cousins not grassing him up to keep his youthful looks unsullied. If his uncle found out he'd lost the shotgun he'd shove his teeth so far down his throat he'd be taking his underpants off to clean them.

And he would find out because there were prints on the gun and cartridges. The Crime Squad would be paying Colin and his uncle a visit as a result of us finding the gun. They were going to have some difficult questions to answer, starting with, 'Have you ever seen this gun before?' and ending with, 'Would you like to trade some of your prison time for the names of your accomplices?'

And I'd marked Wendy's card.

🐾 🐾 🐾 🐾

Training days were always great fun, in one way or another. Dogs and handlers from around the county would gather at Headquarters to practice our skills on each other under the supervision and direction of the greatest humans ever to walk the planet, Dog Handling Instructors.

I've already mentioned the superhuman qualities of a proper

---

* There were women in the Doyle clan who could say, 'Meet my father, my brother and my husband,' and there would only be one man standing in front of you.

Instructor, but their aura of accomplishment, finesse and ultimate control astounded me every time we met. Of course, others were complete schafsköpfe as well.

Peter was one of the latter.

We were supposed to have six continuation training days a year, on top of a two-week refresher course, to provide the Home Office required sixteen days annually. Licensing hadn't yet been invented, but we had a 'Police Dogs Training and Care Manual' that outlined the exercises we were supposed to be able to perform to the required standard. I say 'supposed' because most dogs were better at some than others.

When it was first published in 1963 you could buy a copy of the Manual from Her Majesty's Stationery Office if you had seventeen shillings and sixpence to spare, but now there are heavily redacted versions available online. Don't bother looking for it though; it was and still is badly written by people who may have once seen a dog, but who obviously have no idea how one functions.

You won't be surprised to learn that I was pretty good at everything, a real all-rounder who could often be persuaded to leave the sleeve after a bite exercise, eventually. But some dogs weren't as adept and if their handlers thought they could avoid the bother of training they would try to find a job to go to instead. Operational requirements always took precedence over training, so finding an urgent job was a good excuse.

Amazingly the Instructors were able to spot when handlers regularly found imaginary jobs rather than training and, when they thought it necessary, called them in for extra days.

The day we'd been unofficially clocked speeding by the Traffic Inspector we'd been on a training day with Nuffer & Ava, Jamesy & 'Arry and, because he was behind on his number of days, Smiddy & Slade.

Unless we went somewhere special, such as a disused school or warehouse to practice person-searching, the Instructors tried to fit every exercise into a packed day. This usually meant starting the morning with a track, and this day had been no exception.

The Instructor would go out before we arrived and lay a track for each of us. Tracklaying was a skill in itself. Tracks were made by walking them out, leaving the combination of human scent mingling with the odour of the crushed earth and whatever foliage was there, but they had to be remembered in great detail so that the Instructor could tell if or where a dog made a mistake. Some dogs would inadvertently drift away down-wind and lose the scent, or be distracted by other scents.

If an instructor laid four tracks that would be about three miles over which they had to remember where they'd placed every footprint. Adding intricacies like acute turns and dead-end legs where the track turned back on itself meant that if they lost the pattern by a foot near the start they could be wrong by fifty yards come the finish. Some Instructors made notes, but the good ones held it all in their heads.

Knowledge of how scent operates helped them devise challenging tracks for each dog and handler. Walking upwind along the edge of a wood would push the scent into the trees; hollows collected scent and exposed hilltops blew it away; the wind against a drystone wall could pick the scent up and drop it yards away from where the track was laid.

Articles such as we might be expected to find on a real track were used both to test us and keep motivation up when a dog might flag a little. Finding a watch or screwdriver on the track gave you a little boost, and they were judiciously placed to do just that. A big friendly article, often the dog's own tug-toy or ball, signalled the finish.

Because handlers had to learn the art as well, to help their own and each other's dogs, Instructors taking S-S courses came up with a cunning plan to ensure they remembered their tracks. They had them place their own fifty-pence coins down as articles.

Most learned quickly, but occasionally the day would end with the prospective handler wandering round a field with a torch, muttering, 'Turned right by the telegraph pole, lined up the red farmhouse door in the distance with the rock on the wall that looks like Napoleon's hat and walked towards the left hand gate stoop. Or was it the right hand gate stoop...?'

Pete wasn't well. That's another detailed skill we dogs have that you don't. We can smell illness. When I say 'smell', it involves investigating the whole, not just sniffing up the nose, but even humans can detect some tell-tale odours such as acetone on the breath, a sign of concern for diabetes sufferers.

We can smell tumours, detect the early signs of tuberculosis, seizure or blackout, and a host of other conditions. It is difficult to explain because it's a feeling you can't experience, but it's an awareness of 'wellness'; how everything about a person fits together.

Medical Detection Dogs are especially trained to seek out cancers, but we all have the ability. We just don't always alert you.

It's not something we tend to focus on, otherwise it could take over your life. We know when and how you're unwell, but if I was to tell Noddy that his heart wasn't always in rhythm and it would probably get worse as he aged, would it help him? He'd probably just worry unnecessarily. So we don't tend to make a fuss about illnesses.

It has been suggested in some quarters that we developed it as a way of assessing which prey animal would be most likely to succumb after a short chase; which would be the easiest meal. I don't think that's the case. I think we all are born with the ability but you useless humans lost it because you're self-obsessed. You've just lost the habit of paying attention to others.

However, even the humans on our training day could tell Pete wasn't well because he stank of beer and looked like he'd spent the whole night wrestling with several bears. And lost. He was hung-over so far he was dangling down the other side.

Not one to let a minor hangover knock him back, and concerned that taking a day sick would mean he had his lovely wife in his ear instead, Pete thought a bracing walk in the countryside would see off what he assured everyone was an awful head-cold and gippy tummy.

Consequently he'd had been out early and laid tracks across the moorland for us. When we got there they were almost two hours old, but heather and bracken hold their scent well and we bombed round them. I say, 'we', but mean Ava, Slade and me. 'Arry wasn't quite so successful.

Each track was a continuation of the previous one, starting at the fell gate with Slade. Smiddy harnessed him up and he tracked whilst the rest of us followed, scenting his way along, sometimes overshooting a turn and casting about until he picked it up again.

Smiddy, holding the end of the tracking line, offered encouragement but was otherwise not much use. In just less than a mile Slade came to a cats-eye left by Pete to mark the end of his section and was released from his harness for a short game.

It would normally have been our own rubber ball (on a rope for added throwing distance) at the end, but Pete had set off before we arrived and so improvised. The rubber cats-eyes dug out from the middle of the road when it was repaired were usually discarded, but made great chew-toys for dogs. A nice reward to chomp on at the end of a track.

Ava then took over the next leg, twisting and veering about the fell-side, crossing becks, through stands of trees, into fields and back again until she too collected her cats-eye.

We were nearly two miles across the fell-side and still heading away as 'Arry took over. Mine would be the last leg in a huge loop that would take us towards the parked vans again, and we were all following a discrete distance behind 'Arry and Jamesy.

We didn't want to cramp 'Arry's performance by being too close. If he'd overshot any acute turns thrown in by Pete to challenge his skills he would have to work back to pick up the scent again. He wouldn't want to find us standing in the way.

Really good Instructors laid tracks that would challenge the team, but not defeat them. There'd be switch-backs, false legs walked straight out and back again, circles, walking on top of drystone walls, up becks, in the lee of woods where the wind played with the scent; but always with the intention of the dog and handler being able to work it out successfully. Laid well, these advanced tracks were great fun. Laid badly, they were soul-destroying as you lurched from mistake to mistake. Even Pete had a go at laying them from time to time. Occasionally he got it right.

Slade and Ava ran fairly easy tracks, nothing too challenging and well within their capabilities. Pete clearly wasn't taking any chances of being accused of trying to trip them up. 'Arry set off well too. A straightforward couple of turns and he was merrily pushing his way through the tall heather and bracken. Breasting the two-foot tall foliage kept him slow, but as an added bonus it really gave his undercarriage a good scrubbing.

Good Instructors hang off the shoulder of the tracking handler, there to give advice or encouragement if needed, pointing out where they'd done well or could improve. Pete had decided that 'Arry was doing fine and had dropped back into the following group where he was regaling Smiddy, Noddy and Nuffer with tales about the tough life he lived as an Instructor on day shifts at Headquarters.

'Arry was plodding away when he came to a stretch of moor that had been burnt off the previous autumn. Burning off the heather took out the older woody stems and provided fresh new succulent growth for the grouse and sheep, and it reduced the foliage that was holding 'Arry back. Now that his undercarriage was no longer being sandpapered he could speed up a bit. And so he did. He shot off with Jamesy loping after him, arm outstretched holding the line, over the brow of a small gulley, and dropped out of sight. The gulley was made by a stream coming off the fell top and cut through the surrounding sparse birch woodland on its way to the river.

We all held back from following him as it was an interesting place that may have involved a change of direction.

When Pete casually said, 'S'okay, he'll pop up the other side in a mo. Just give him a sec to work it out,' we expected him to quickly show up on the far side, and Pete resumed his anecdote about reports becoming trapped in Headquarters Time.

Headquarters Time is a reduction in the passage of time only normally found when travelling at near light-speed, because everything there is taken too seriously. The dense mass of seriousness generates a temporal black-hole which slows down time for anyone or thing entering its field of influence. That's why when information is sent into headquarters it takes ages for a decision to come out. Birds fly overhead and wonder where their life went. The event horizon, the point at which nothing can escape, currently surrounds only the senior officer's rooms, but is expanding. It will eventually encompass the whole of the HQ buildings and will only halt when it reaches the Dog Section, where ridicule is regularly deployed to puncture seriousness. The formula is $S10/N + G > c < R$, where S = seriousness, N = number of people, G = Newton's gravitational constant, c = the speed of light in a vacuum and R = Ridicule. Ridicule is the reason that days pass really quickly when police dog training, and will ultimately save the universe.

But Jamesy and 'Arry didn't pop up the others side. Pete droned on and it wasn't until eventually Nuffer said, 'Hadn't we better see where they are?' that he decided to look over the edge.

'Blu-ddy 'ell! Jamesy!'

He yelled the name again, 'Jamesy!' and started running downhill, following the ridge. We all jogged to the edge.

'Is he wrong?' asked Noddy.

Jamesy was a speck in the distance towards the bottom of the hill and 'Arry was going like a train down the side of the beck.

''e's ruddy miles wrong. 'e should be up 'ere!' Pete flung over his shoulder, repeatedly muttering, 'shit, shit, shit,' under his breath like a potty-mouthed white rabbit, as he bolted into the hole after the disappearing Jamesy & 'Arry, punctuating it with yells of, 'Jamesy!'

But he was too far away, and 'Arry looked like he was on a mission.

'If it doesn't go that way, where's he going?' Nuffer asked no one in particular.

We stood and watched as Jamesy & 'Arry sped purposefully down the hill, followed by Pete, bounding along bellowing, 'Jamesy! Stand still!'

Quarter of a mile later, at the bottom of the fell, Jamesy hit the road and stopped. I thought I'd wait here in case I was wrong,' he told a gasping Pete, who was doubled up and losing both his breakfast coffee and the remnants of last night's ale from the exertion.

The long slow walk of shame back to the edge of the ridge wasn't edifying for any of them.

Pete showed Jamesy the other side of the gulley, 'You should've gone straight over.'

Back on track, 'Arry snuffled around and then took off, this time in the right direction. A quick left turn and he came to his cats-eye. He'd been less than thirty yards from his finish.

I sidled past him as I headed for my own start and asked, *'What went wrong?'*

'Deer.'

'What?'

'Deer. I think I'm addicted. I thought I could handle it, but maybe I've got a problem.'

Lots of dogs like to chase things and will follow game scents when they are out on their walk. Many pets get their fix from tracking rabbits and squirrels. But 'Arry's right, there's something about the scent of deer that dogs find hard to resist. It's the primeval call of the wild.

Rabbits and squirrels are alright, but deer bring out our inner wolf.

'I wasn't thinking, I was just coasting along the easy track and when we dropped into the gulley bottom I was hit by the gorgeous musky savoury odour and... something just clicked in my brain. Every fibre of my being told me to hunt the deer. I couldn't not do it... and when I did it felt like the best buzz ever. I want to do it again.'

'You stay away from deer 'Arry. You're a deer-oholic. You know one's never enough. You'll have to go cold turkey.'

'That's all very well for you to say, you've got willpower. Anyway, where am I going to find a turkey round here!?'

I left him to ponder and, harnessed-up so I didn't lose Noddy, buzzed round my track, ending up almost back at where we'd started the morning. Yes, I came across deer tracks and had a quick snort of them, but no, I didn't follow them.

I can handle it.

Next up was a property search each. Pete had basically walked along the road throwing articles into the verge. 'Article' encompasses all the items or objects used for training police dogs to find things. In the bad old days they consisted of bits of wood doweling or squares of carpet, until some bright spark had the idea of using things that we would actually be expected to find.

Nowadays articles are much more realistic, like screwdrivers, mobile phones, fake jewellery, shotgun cartridges and purses. They were kept in an aptly named 'article bag' in the Skylark and regularly changed as they became more and more manky through use.

There were six articles for each dog to find in an area of verge about fifty yards long. Kick-marks in the grass at the edge of the verge showed where each area started and finished.

The verge was very overgrown, with trees, bushes and dense foliage, including brambles with their tendrils of spiky thorns ready to wrap around and gouge through hair and skin. Because we had a search-area each we were not in each other's way (and because he'd lost half the morning chasing after 'Arry, snorting after deer), so Pete set us off all at once.

I've never really been into searching for property. I know some dogs get a thrill out of it, but I'm not one. Tracking, yes; searching for people, yes; but where's the chance of a bite in property searching?

The trick to it is not to try too hard. If you rush round concentrating on searching for and sourcing human scent you'll waste effort by picking up every footprint or hand-odour on a tree he's leant on. If you clear your mind and just allow the background to wash over you, you get a feel for what should be there and what shouldn't. And that's what you want; the incongruous – the thing that shouldn't be there.

Instructors regularly contaminate the search area with as much human scent as they can, tramping and wiping their hands about the place. This isn't unfair, as many operational crime scenes are heavily contaminated too. So, as human scent should be part of the background everywhere, I don't search for it to give me a clue to articles.

On a fell-side road verge, if you can merge all the vehicle, human, foliage and wildlife scents into one composite 'verge-odour'. Anything that shouldn't be there sticks out like a sore schwanz.

On the first pass I quickly got the old perfume and fabric scent of the purse, stashed behind a tree. The plastic of the broken pager in the bush was next, followed by the acrid powder from the shotgun cartridge sneakily tucked under a clump of grass right by the road (cheeky Pete!). The oily metal of the screwdriver stuck halfway up the drystone wall and the leather of the old watch-strap in the bracken followed, and all were fetched back and dropped into Noddy's hand.

I'd missed one though. I wasn't displeased, five out of six on the first pass was pretty good, and it wasn't unusual to have to go back over the ground. In fact it was good practice to check if anything had been missed. I went over it again; still nothing. And again. The others were still working too, but I was getting bored with not finding the last article.

I came back and stood in front of Noddy, staring, *'That's it mate. If there's another one, I can't find it.'*

'Get on son, go find,' he said.

I wandered off disconsolately, my heart really not in it. When I was a little way in front and not looking Noddy dropped the purse in the grass beside him and called me back.

He didn't usually speak during a search; we had an arrangement where if he moved I moved in the same direction. When he went forwards, I went forwards; when he moved to one side, I paralleled him; if he walked backwards I moved towards him. It was an easy enough system for him to pick up, and saved a lot of shouting. So I knew what he had done when he called, and trotted back to pick up the purse.

'Yay! Finished!'

The praise was heartfelt enough, but came across a bit faint. It's not difficult to work out that the last purse was the same one as earlier on. But I humoured him by wagging my tail and bouncing a bit. He'd done his best.

'Just got five, Pete, and he was flagging a bit so I've dropped one in and finished on that.'

'What have you got?'

Noddy listed our successes.

'Yep, that's all there was.'

'Sorry, I thought you said six?'

'Oh, I did. I just wanted to see if you had enough confidence in your dog to trust him.'

Noddy's voice was ripe with exasperation, 'You soft bug'r.'

'Ah, always expect the unexpected Noddy. Always expect the unexpected,' Pete grinned.

'Guys!' Noddy shouted at the top of his voice, 'There's only five out. Pete's playing silly bug'rs.'

The other teams wandered back to their vans, parked on the roadside, throwing their five articles each into the bag in the Skylark as they passed, and various comments of derision and looks of contempt at Pete.

'Always expect the unexpected,' he replied, rather less assuredly now.

We drove back to the kennels where the handlers lunched and we chilled in the vans.

The afternoon was DTF, and started with a little light heelwork. We lined up in a mini-formation of four dog and handler teams and marched to Pete's command up and down the football pitch. Left, right and about turns; halts in the stand, sit and down, then the same again off the lead with the addition of being left in the three positions and either collected on the next pass or recalled to heel. On the last pass we were left fifty yards away and the handlers turned and faced us, halted in a line.

Each handler gave his dog commands to stand, down and sit several times over, on the whispered instructions of Pete in his ear. The wind was towards us, so of course we could all hear Pete and consequently seemed really quick to respond. At the end we were recalled to sit in front and on the final command round to heel.

Unfortunately when Nuffer called Ava, 'Arry was chatting with Slade about deer rather than paying attention and he thought the call was for all of us, and set off back with her at the gallop. That caused Jamesy to bellow, 'NO!' at him, which caused Ava to hesitate, which caused Nuffer to bridle and call her on, which caused 'Arry to keep coming...

Jamesy set off up the field towards him and 'Arry stopped. Ava growled at him, raising a lip as she passed. 'Arry spun around and trotted back to the line, turned and sat in exactly the place he'd mistakenly left.

'Give 'im a bollockin',' shouted Pete to Jamesy in the distance.

'What for? He's where he should be!'

'For leavin' in the first place!'

'But he's back now. I can't bollock 'im for being in the right place!'

''e'll know what it's for.'

'Right, you're the Instructor.' Jamesy looked 'Arry straight in the eye and in the sweetest voice said, 'Now, I know you are a GOOD BOY now, but you were a bad dog when you got up and left. So don't do it again and be a GOOD BOY!' and marched back to his place in the line.

'Arry smiled back at him, acknowledging he had had, or not had, a bollocking, depending upon which human viewed it.

We finished the obedience exercises with a retrieve; the dumbbell thrown in front then picked up and returned to hand on command.

Ava had a party trick for when we performed at public displays. Nuffer had a huge iron spanner that weighed about four pounds and he threw it out so it made a loud thud on the grass. Ava sometimes struggled to pick it up, but she'd mastered balancing it, which was most of the effort, and, tottering a bit for effect, returned to sit with it in her mouth in front of him. The crowd would cheer, particularly as she was the smallest dog there.

She followed that with an egg. Nuffer would take a raw egg and balance it on the neck of a milk bottle ten yards in front of her, then come back to her side and send her out. Gingerly she'd pluck the egg off the bottle without knocking it over and return it to Nuffer's hand.

Nuffer, hamming it up, would theatrically break the egg one-handed into a bowl for her to eat. The crowd always went wild. Seriously. It was picking up a wrench and an egg. How patronising can you get?

'Ooo, isn't she clever, she can pick up a spanner and an egg, and she's only a dog'.

Nuffer had already done that when he'd brought them from the van. Nobody found it necessary to applaud him. Dogs can do many miraculous things that you can't, but picking up tools and eggs hardly qualifies for a Dickin' Medal.

Anyway, she was welcome to it. It's not enough payment for the scrape and jarring of that metal spanner on your teeth. She'll be sucking Chappie through a straw before she's nine.

But obedience is a side-show. The reason police dogs were invited to public displays was what we were about to practice next: criminal work. Did I mention I love training days?

There were four main criminal-work exercises: the Straight Chase (now called the Chase & Detain following the big re-write of the Manual), the Stand-off, the Stick, and the Gun. They, together with Crowd Control, fall within Use of Force deployments, as opposed to disciplines such as searching for suspects and vulnerable people, which are (supposedly) Non-use of Force deployments.

Often included in criminal work was the Emergency Stop or Emergency Recall, where the handler either dropped us on the way to a Straight Chase, or recalled us from it before we bit. In theory forces could choose to train either, but in practice those with Instructors and handlers who could teach dogs would always choose the Stop because the dog was in a position to take up the chase again if the suspect ran off. You only trained the Recall if you couldn't teach a dog to drop (usually by attaching a long line tied to something solid and giving a command to come back just before the dog reached the end of it, then dragging it back in whilst it was still stunned). We used the Stop.

As we didn't have a crowd we weren't practising Crowd Control, so that left us with three 'bite' exercises and the Stand-off, and they all broke down into similar components.

The first rule was, 'Don't go until you're told.' This could be a bit of a tough one because everything that went before was designed to arouse us into biting good and hard.

As soon as we were DTF we knew the fun was in the offing, so we'd start to wind ourselves up like a rubber-band-powered toy aeroplane before we began.

We'd smell the padded sleeves in the Skylark and when we saw them come out the tension went up a couple of twists. Sometimes the lighter biters were kept out to watch us more, shall we say, competent stoppers, to give them confidence and encourage them to wade in. No one DTF that day needed that kind of help, so we went one at a time, while the others stayed in the van waiting our turns.

The handlers would park the vans for best effect, with as little view of the action as possible for those dogs with a tendency to overkill, but if they thought that would keep us calm...

Almost everything that could possibly be done to maximise our arousal for the bite had taken place. It was in total contrast to how we were expected to perform on duty, where chases came out of the blue.

One minute you'd be quietly searching for a scroat and the next he'd be pounding away over a hedge or down an alleyway. No arousal, no forewarning, just sent cold. Whilst I could cope with it, some of the quieter dogs just couldn't translate the training into reality.

It was the difference between two cage fighters baiting each other before a grudge match, standing nose to nose and spouting bile, then going through their pre-match routine, building up their aggression until they burst into the cage roaring, and alternatively being kicked in the pflaumensack from behind whilst shopping in Waitrose by a child who runs away afterwards.

So we marched onto the field with all that pent-up aggression, making small darts forward on the lead in anticipation. Then we would halt whilst the lead was removed and we could be asked to not-go, in increasing levels of difficulty, whilst sitting, standing, or on the march, whilst all the time the runner, clearly visible and padded-up, would make feinting dashes away, trying to dislodge us from our handlers' heels.

I'd learned my lesson early. It took huge self-control, but if you stayed until told to go, you got to go sooner. Other dogs weren't so bright or didn't have the will-power to resist. If they broke away the criminal would stand still and take the sleeve to the other side of their body, and their handler would bellow and fume until they got the message and slunk back.

Sometimes a dog would break and go all the way, forcing the criminal to present the arm to take the bite or be bitten anyway, such was their desperation.

The secret of course was not to over-arouse dogs to the point where they couldn't cope with it any longer, so you weren't punishing them for wanting to do what you'd wanted them to want to do, but Pete wasn't the sharpest nail on the paw.

A dog would never be that aroused before being sent in reality, so it was only an issue in training. But we went through this pantomime every training day. They wound us up to exploding point and, when some of us exploded, danced their angry-man war dance. If only they'd had half a brain between them.

Schafsköpfe, the lot of them.

Randomly drawn at the behest of our mighty Instructor, Ava went first. I watched from the cage in my van, with a view through the front windscreen.

She did well enough. Smiddy ran criminal for her and made a fairly good job of it. Good Instructors run for the dogs to get the feel for how

212

we are performing. The take on the sleeve, the strength of the bite, how quickly we respond to the 'leave' command. Pete didn't.

The padded sleeves came in a variety of shapes and sizes to suit the dog; big heavy leather with hessian wrapped around to give our teeth better purchase, right down to thin jute puppy-sleeves. Yet, even the heaviest of them was no protection from the pressure of the bite.

This of course is once again something in which we dogs massively outperform you humans. An adult human's jaw can exert a pressure of about 120 pounds per square inch; a German Shepherd Dog's jaw comes in at 250 to 300psi. That's the equivalent of Kylie Minogue walking on you in six-inch stiletto heels. Well, it might not be, but I have your attention now, don't I?

Anyway, handlers would wrap bandages around their arms under the sleeves, not to mop up the blood as was commonly thought, but to prevent their skin being nipped tight under the pressure. They still came away from a good day's training with bruises all over their forearms.

With Nuffer yelling, 'Police with a dog, stop! Stop or I'll send the dog!' over and over, Ava stayed at heel as he marched twenty yards in two about-turns, as Smiddy appeared from behind a six-feet tall solid scale jump fifty yards across the field and walked away.

On Nuffer's whispered command of, 'Hold him,' she took off like a coiled spring, flying after the now galloping Smiddy at over thirty mph. As she neared him, he held out the sleeve invitingly just below shoulder height. Of course in reality scroats didn't do that, but the point was for her to hit him on the sleeve, not just anywhere, so naturally he fed it.

And... *whuump!* Sixty-five pounds of dog hit the sleeve at twenty-five mph (slowing down to aim), grabbed it and held on for all she was worth.

Smiddy grunted at the sheer force of the hit as Ava's weight and momentum took his arm forwards and down, swinging them both in a half-circle as he expertly rode the bite. It can be hard to keep your feet

213

when hit by a dog, but with practice handlers learn to go with the energy-flow and stay upright.

Ava was on the second rule now: 'Take hold and keep hold no matter what happens'. Smiddy fought with her, pulling the sleeve back and forth and raising a foot to (gently) kick her ribs.

Scroats fought back. If we weren't used to being kicked at there was a chance some dogs might let go in real life. And we can't be having that can we? So we practiced being kicked at.

For the bleeding heart liberal bunny-hugging animal lovers out there, trust me, of the two of them Smiddy was in a lot more pain. Every time his foot raised she clamped down harder and shook her head like a crocodile.

Smiddy started to relax as Nuffer pounded up behind him, and was not resisting at all by the time he bellowed, 'Stand still! Ava, leave!'

Rule three: 'Leave on one command'. Ava thought about it, gave one final shake and suddenly released her grip, in one fluid movement spinning round to Nuffer's heel five yards away.

'Prisoner, hands on your head!' Smiddy lifted the sleeve high and held it on top of his head with his other hand.

'Forwards march! Left wheel!' Nuffer marched Smiddy, still red-faced and panting from the exertion, back to Pete.

'That'll do thanks, pop her back on the lead for the stick.'

Jamesy had padded up and armed himself with three feet of half-inch bamboo cane. It wasn't in itself terribly formidable, but it represented any kind of striking weapon that might be used to attack us.

Appearing from behind the scale jump he wailed his battle cry as he advanced on her, striding purposefully and brandishing his weapon.

'Aaaaaaaarrrrggghhh!'

Nobody could accuse him of being imaginative.

Nuffer countered with the scripted challenge, 'Police! Put the stick down or I'll send the dog!'

'Come on then! Send the dog! I don't care! I'll kill it!' Jamesy was going for realism. Suicidal realism.

'This is your last chance,' quieter now as the gap closed, 'Put the stick down or I'll send the dog.' Nuffer paused to give the acting nut-job one last opportunity to consider, then flicked the chain from Ava's head, 'Hold him'.

Jamesy was three bounds away and Ava already on her back legs. He was still brandishing his stick above his head as though to bring down on her as she steadied herself and aimed for the sleeve held across his body.

Again, there's an art in being stick-criminal. Take the stick away at the last minute and let the dog in to the sleeve, then step sideways and ride the bite so the arm is taken past you when we hit it, rather than being flattened backwards.

We're not stupid either. We know it's a game and we won't get hurt. But we also know that there are real criminals out there and we signed up to stop them. Sometimes they are violent and it would be stupid not to practise taking them down. Proprioception is a powerful tool that can take over for us when the going gets tough.

When you hear gunshots and the screams, see the fists flying, the thugs, the demonstrators, the hooligans, the nut-case with a knife; when you see people running away from danger, you'll see the police run towards it. We are the ones just in front of the police. And we meet violence with violence. We don't start it, but we do finish it.

And what happens to them if they injure us? Are they charged with assault? No. Criminal damage. We are property in the eyes of the law. At best, our protection comes from the Animal Welfare legislation – cruelty to animals.

I don't know why we bother.

Sorry about that, rant over. I do know why we bother. Because

215

biting people's brilliant fun. Biting people legally, and even being encouraged to do it, is the most fun anyone can ever have. All working dogs love their work (ask a collie) but when a police dog's biting people it's just fantastisch!

Jamesy duly waved the stick in Ava's face and lightly stroked down her back and flanks enough to make her growl her anger and thrash her head. Nuffer was standing back admiring her work and grinning.

Jamesy relaxed the stick and whined, 'That'll do won't it? It bluddy hurts!'

'Put the stick down you wuss!' Nuffer commanded, adding slightly to the script this time, and Jamesy, relieved, threw it to one side.

Nuffer strode over on his short officious legs and picked it up, tucking it under his arm like a swagger-stick, then stepped backwards again.

He was entitled to keep himself safe and out of reach of the criminal, but it also gave Ava time to calm down a little. These little 'assistances' to the dog could mean the difference between pass and fail. Leaving on one command was mandatory, not optional, and a few seconds to calm down from the rage would help.

'Ava!' Pause... two... three, 'Le-e-e-a-a-a-v-ve-ah!' Ground out with as much feeling as Nuffer could instil into one word.

Jamesy was bent double, holding the sleeve out in front of him at Ava's head-height, trying to offer as little resistance as possible.

Ava looked deeply into his eyes, slowly squeezed her jaws together and then unlocked, whipping round to Nuffer's side.

Off on one use of the word 'leave', although in reality Nuffer had given at least six commands: her name, the pause, and the four syllable word, 'Lee-err-ver-ah'. But, hey, could you come down from full-on all-out red-eyed traffic-warden-punching-rage in that time?

I thought not.

Noddy stepped out from behind the scale, 12 bore shotgun cradled

216

in the crook of his padded sleeve, screwed up his eyes and drawled, 'I know what you're thinking. "Did he fire six shots or only five?" Well to tell you the truth in all this excitement I kinda lost track myself. But being this is a err... dirty big shotgun, the most powerful err... dirty big shotgun... in the world and would blow your head clean off, you've gotta ask yourself one question: "Do I feel lucky?" Well, do ya, punk?'

'Police! Put the gun down or I'll send the dog!' This of course was not an attempt at simulating the kind of situation in which a dog would be sent, because we'd be hiding behind something solid, but for the sake of ensuring that we would indeed take out a scroat with a firearm, it gave us practice.

'Go ahead, make my day,' said Noddy in the same drawl, but quickly switching films, then blasted the first blank into the turf six feet in front of him, the boom echoing around the field and bouncing off the woods, and the wadding kicking up clumps of earth.

Nuffer slipped Ava. She didn't need or get a command this time, she was expected to attack on the sound of the shot, and she did.

When she was halfway there Noddy blasted the second round into the air above her head. She tore through the smoke and knocked Noddy staggering under the impact. If this was real life he'd have been on his back screaming in agony. As it was the hardened leather of the sleeve took the brunt of her anger.

Nuffer let her fury subside again as he meandered up. Noddy held the shotgun up in his free hand, gripping the barrels just below the balance point.

'Put the gun down!' Noddy placed it carefully on the floor and allowed himself to be dragged away from it by Ava, tugging backwards on the sleeve.

'Stand still!'

Another helpful little tip. Nuffer was entitled to give a moving or struggling prisoner directions. It was also an indication to Ava of what

217

was to come next. Another extra command. It's like giving your child a five minute warning to put down their tablet. If you've had a warning, it doesn't seem quite so bad. The idea of giving it up is planted in your head and you're a bit more ready to do it.

'Ava!' Pause... two... three, 'Le-e-e-a-a-a-v-ve-ah!'

Straight out this time, and back to heel.

'Pete's running.'

Noddy could see behind Nuffer, Pete was legging it across the field, and nodded in his direction. Nuffer passed him the gun back, 'Look after this for me?' and turned around with Ava.

'Police with a dog, stop! Stop or I'll send the dog!' he repeated the challenge as prescribed and Ava took off when he sent her. She flew lightly across the grass, ears pinned back and tail streaming behind.

She wasn't daft, she'd done Straight Case, Stick and Gun, so this was going to be the Stand-off, but there was just a chance that it would turn into a bite... There's always a chance.

No, as suspected, when she was twenty yards away from him and approaching the point of no backing down, he turned and faced her, and, sleeve in the protective box position across his gentleman's euphemism area, stood stock still, ramrod straight, eyes on the horizon.

Ava threw on her brakes and dug in, snow-ploughing clods of earth with her front paws, at the same time staccato barking in annoyance at being denied the bite. Pete didn't blink an eye and she bounced in front of him, rapid-fire barking all the while, just far enough away that he couldn't kick out and connect, until Nuffer pounded up.

'Ava, come.' She whipped round to his heel on his nodded command and lay down, still eye-balling Pete. Nuffer stepped away from her and made a triangle, each side ten yards.

'Why didn't you stand still when I told you?'

'Que?'

'Why didn't you stand still?'

'So sorry Meester Fawlty, I run for bus? Hi ham from Barthelona.' These comedic impressions were getting out of hand*. Nuffer was supposed to interrogate Pete whilst Ava kept him under surveillance. Pete would give a reasonable explanation and be allowed to leave, whilst Nuffer and Ava went the other way, thus demonstrating the perfect control of the police dog.

'Aye, alright then, go get your bus.' Nuffer turned, called Ava and walked back towards the van with her, leaving Manuel standing there.

'Didn't see me take off though, did you?'

'No eyes in the back of my head, Pete, so hard to see how I could've.'

'Ahh, always expect the unexpected Nuffer, always expect the unexpected,' said Pete. Nuffer just sighed.

'Arry and I both went through our criminal work without any hitches. I decked Jamesy on my Straight Chase, hitting him hard at the elbow and dragging him to the floor; Pete leapt out from behind the scale and attacked with the stick as 'Arry was still escorting Smiddy back from his Straight Chase, but by then we were already expecting the unexpected, so he still nailed him.

Then came Slade. You've probably already gathered that Slade had a bit of an attitude problem, and none of us could figure why Pete had left him 'til last. But he'd certainly been working himself into a frenzy in the van listening to our fun and games.

I've never pretended not to thoroughly enjoy biting, and sometimes I've overstepped the mark with it a bit, but with Slade the mark was so far behind him he'd lost sight of it. It was like to he went to a place in his head where demonic cats prodded him with fiery tridents. He came on to the field with his hackles raised, scanning for trouble.

---

* Manuel, the Spanish waiter from the late 70's TV sitcom 'Fawlty Towers'. I know, the people who heard it barely recognised it either.

219

Pete was at Smiddy's shoulder, 'In the sit, lead off and ten paces forward, challenging, about turn, ten paces, about turn and send him'. That was the same as the rest of us.

Smiddy sat Slade, threw the lead over his shoulder and with a harsh, 'Heel!' stepped off smartly.

'Police with a dog...' Slade bolted as soon as Jamesy appeared.

'Heel! Slade! Come! Basta'd! Come. Here. Now!'

'Better go and get 'im,' Pete advised.

Smiddy ran up the field. Jamesy had already stood still and held the sleeve tight into his body, covering his euphemisms, but Slade didn't care. He'd been sitting in the van waiting for his bite for what seemed like an eternity and he was having it now.

He slowed as he approached Jamesy, lulling him into a false sense of security, then walked up to him, grabbed a jaw-full of sleeve and tugged.

'Don't let him have the sleeve!' yelled Pete.

It was all Jamesy could do to stand up, let alone take control of the sleeve back.

Slade saw Smiddy arriving out of the corner of his eye and dived sideways, returning some of Jamesy's self-respect.

'Heel!' Smiddy growled and when he turned back to his start-point Slade trotted just behind his left leg, out of range of everything but the vitriol steaming from Smiddy's ears.

They set up and started again.

'Don't let him break this time,' was Pete's helpful advice.

'Police with a dog...' Slade bolted again, followed by Smiddy's lead, which had been held in preparation over his shoulder. Whirling with the accuracy of a Gaucho's bolas the combined lead and chain wrapped themselves around Slade's hind legs, hobbling his progress. He looked back at his fuming handler, and voluntarily returned to his heel,

Smiddy picked up the lead and slung it over his shoulder, making

220

Slade flinch at the 'clink' it made.

'Police with a dog...' No bolting this time as Slade respected Smiddy's power at a distance. Smiddy stalked the two about-turns and sent Slade.

Jamesy, already sporting mud on his knees from being decked by me, held the sleeve out invitingly, almost at right-angles, hoping to stay upright.

You know that thing that happens, when you're concentrating so hard on one thing that you forget something else?

Slade hit the sleeve at full tilt and kept going, ripping the sleeve out of Jamesy's grasp and off his arm. He hit the ground still running, sleeve held limply in his grasp, then turned, glared at Jamesy and spat it out.

'Nooooo! Leave 'im! Dooooowwwwnn!'

Smiddy had already been running towards the pair, but managed to find extra speed in his desperation. Jamesy, meanwhile, shrank. Every part of him, including his demeanour, became smaller; his life- force itself, said, 'Don't mind me, I'm not really here'.

Inside, he was trying to assess which part of his anatomy would volunteer to take one for the team, which limb could be sacrificed, but all he could hear in his head was, 'shit-shit-shit-shit-shit-shit-shit,' over and over.

'Aaaaaaaarrrrggghhh!!!!!'

Nuffer ran from behind the scale, 'Come and get it you bastaaaa - aaaad!' brandishing the stick over his head.

Slade didn't need telling twice; he turned away from Jamesy to face the new threat. This was his lucky day. It was Jamesy's too.

Nuffer rode the bite, but threw down the stick immediately. Slade didn't need any 'tickling' to encourage him to stay on the sleeve. Smiddy was up with him in no time.

'You okay?'

'Yep, well padded and bandaged. He's got my full arm so the pressure's even.'

'I'll leave him on for a bit, let him wind down then.'

'No probs.'

'Get him off! Now!' Pete was furious, 'He's not getting his reward for that!'

''ang on Pete, he's not done anything wrong, Jamesy just lost the sleeve and Nuffer came at 'im.' Smiddy played for time.

'Get 'im off!'

Smiddy paused, walked towards Slade, still locked-on to a grinning Nuffer, who was bent double and riding the tugging on the sleeve, and took hold of the lead hanging threateningly over his shoulder, causing it to rattle loudly.

'Slade!' rattle, 'Slade, Le-e-e-a-a-a-v-ve-ah!' RATTLE.

Slade looked out of the corner of his eye at Smiddy and slowly opened his jaws, quivering with the effort. Nuffer stood up just as slowly, still holding the sleeve in front in case Slade changed his mind.

'Right, get back 'ere, 'e's not getting a gun after that der-bacle, I'll do the Stand-off,' Pete walked to the van as Smiddy and Slade went back to the start point.

We all knew what the chances of Slade not biting on a Stand-off were on a good day. And this wasn't one of those.

'Errrr, maybe I could do the first one, without a sleeve?' Smiddy offered.

He knew that without the sleeve to tempt Slade, he wouldn't bite him. All handlers practised stand-offs on themselves, without a sleeve, but with a ball as a reward to encouraged them to chase and stand out, barking. I'd got Noddy to pass the ball around his back to give me something interesting to look at as I circled him.

'No, I've got a plan. I know how to keep him out.' Pete came out of the van with a light sleeve and... a fire extinguisher. Everyone looked at him.

'This'll stop him.'

Druggies had used guard dogs for a while. They stopped the Drug Squad bursting in unexpectedly, or at least held them up while the stash was flushed or swallowed. In the law enforcement arms race Drug Squads started taking dog handlers along with them, believing they had mystical powers that could prevent them being bitten. They didn't, but it helped prevent Drug Squad officers being bitten. A dog can't bite you with its mouth full of dog handler.

Helpfully the dogs were used to all kinds of scroats turning up at all hours, it's what happens at druggies' houses, so mostly they were pussies, but occasionally one would be less than happy at the intrusion of the Plod.

Dog handlers turned the balance in their favour by the use of CO_2 fire extinguishers. When lightly blasted the dog's face froze temporarily, rendering them incapable of biting and frightening the living scheiße out of them, but without any lasting damage. Even if they didn't come close enough, the whooshing propellant was like a space-rocket launch in their living room.

Pete was going to use one to keep Slade out. The assembled handlers grinned and shook their heads.

'What?' said Pete, 'Has anyone seen a dog go through one of these?'

Nobody had.

'I don't expect he will either. And when he stays out, I'll reward him early with the ball.'

Smiddy set Slade up, lead over the shoulder, and Pete lumbered away up the field, massive red fire extinguisher tucked under his arm.

He needed two hands to operate it, one to hold and one to point the nozzle, so he wore a light hessian sleeve loose enough for his hand to poke out of the end. The sleeve was worn to simulate a standard

Stand-off, but wasn't enough protection for a bite from Slade. But Pete didn't expect to be bitten.

'Police with a dog...' Slade stayed with Smiddy, glancing up at the lead until the whispered, 'Hold 'im'.

Pete stood still almost immediately, facing the onrushing Slade, heavy extinguisher in his left hand down by his side, tucked behind his leg, trying to make it unobtrusive, but with the nozzle in his right, sleeved, hand. He'd already pulled the safety pin and was ready with the lever.

The handlers, including Smiddy, looked on. Maybe he wouldn't need to use it. Maybe Slade would stand out anyway. Maybe the world would stop and we'd all get off. Slade didn't break stride. Pete raised the nozzle.

Racing towards Pete, Slade suspected a trick. Pete seemed to be holding a new kind of weapon. He knew sticks and he knew shotguns, and he knew they would be deployed just as he came within range, and he would battle through them, so he didn't let up.

Then the air in front of him exploded into a white cloud and Slade baulked as his face tingled with the cold. But he'd never refused a bite in his life and he wasn't going to start now. He couldn't go through it like he did through the acrid gun-smoke, but he could go round it, like the stick.

Furiously embarrassed that he'd allowed it to slow him, Slade dodged sideways and darted forward towards the sleeve. Pete turned and blasted the frost beam at him. Slade dodged sideways. Pete turned and blasted. Slade dodged faster; Pete turned faster.

Slade was now performing a perfect stand-off; circling at a distance of five yards, running and barking, centred on Pete, who was spinning on the spot continually blasting a freezing cloud of CO_2. He looked like he was trying to take off with a faulty jet-pack.

It it hadn't been for my impeccable house-training I'd have wet myself in the van. Noddy, Nuffer and Jamesy were supporting each other to prevent them falling over laughing, tears rolling down their cheeks. Smiddy giggled.

The grass around Pete was frozen; he was rotating inside an arctic circle. Round and round and round... Slade looking for that extra bit of speed that would let him in to the sleeve; Pete denying him it, whirling like a fireman-dervish.

Global warming took a hit that day.

And then *pft-pft*, the extinguisher coughed, *pft-pft*.

Like a dying Catherine wheel, Pete continued to spin, but his power was waning.

Pft-pft, pft and then the extinguisher... extinguished.

Slade made one more circuit to be sure.

'Goodboy!' squeaked Pete hopefully and, dropping his CO_2 cannon, threw a rubber ball towards Slade.

Slade, however, was not done. Dodging the ball as though it was another missile, he lunged at Pete and grabbed the sleeve. If dogs indulged in maniacal laughter, this would have been such a time. The sleeve was soft and he crunched down on it.

Pete grimaced, trying not to show his pain, but failed badly.

Smiddy had been standing, waiting to see how it would end, and strolled up, hands in pockets.

'Alright Pete?'

'No, get the bug'r off,' came the reply through clenched teeth.

'You've wound him up a bit. Can I leave him on to bring him down?'

The clenched teeth were in danger of collapsing under the pressure.

'Please... Just... Get... Him... Off.'

'Slade!' rattle, rattle, rattle, 'Slade, Le-e-e-e-a-a-a-a-v-v-ve-arrh!' RATTLE-RATTLE. Slade looked out of the corner of his eye, with a *'Must I?'* expression, and then s-l-o-w-l-y chattered his jaws apart.

Pete and he just stood, looking at each other, chests heaving, tongues panting, exhausted.

'That didn't go as well as I'd hoped,' understated Pete, rubbing life back into his crushed arm.

'Ah, well,' Smiddy kept a dead-pan face, 'Always expect the unexpected Pete. Always expect the unexpected... Slade, heel,' and with that they both ambled to their van, jumped in and drove off.

So, had Noddy wished to have given the Traffic Inspector an honest answer as to why he was speeding up the motorway, he should have told him that he was running late to drop the van off because it had taken him an hour before he could safely drive without dissolving into fits of incapacitating giggles.

🐾🐾🐾🐾

The other dogs were having no more success with the Walking Man than we were. Beddo had tracked him across a school field after he'd been disturbed actually in a bedroom. He'd been going through her jewellery box in the same room they were sleeping in when the wife had woken up and mistaken him for her husband in the dark.

She'd said, 'What are you doing Harry? Come back to bed,' then turned over and found Harry was lying next to her. When she'd looked back the Walking Man had disappeared, and when she woke Harry he thought she'd been dreaming until he sat up to look at the time and saw his watch was gone.

So was the Walking Man by the time they'd called 999 and Arthur had raced to the estate.

Dog handlers sometimes don't drive straight to the crime-scene for the very reason that scroats tend not to hang around once disturbed, and if we can work out which way they are going we can head them off. If there's a chance they are still around we coast as close as we can, as quietly as we can, then dump the van in favour of the silent approach on foot.

Arthur knew the house backed onto the school field and left his van at the far side before walking across in the darker shadow of the hedge, but seeing the house lit up like Oxford Street in December, he and Beddo realised the Walking Man would have scarpered.

Casting in the school field by the back fence, Beddo quickly picked up the track, followed it through the grounds and out onto the road. He could follow it on the road, but not fast enough to catch up before it petered out.

That's one of the problems with hard surface tracking. Sometimes we have to go so slow to pick out the track that the scroat is always going to beat us just by continuing to walk away.

The four of us Town dogs all tracked the Walking Man at various times that winter, but none of us caught him, and when you traced out all the tracks on a map it looked like a spider had wandered through an ink-blot test. None of them converged to give us a clue as to where he lived, or where he'd strike next.

It was Big Ernie who went in to see the Detective Inspector and hatched the nearest thing to a plan they could manage. It was pointless putting Plods in cars out to catch him. He used the ginnels, the railway tracks and the dark spaces, like the school field. You'd never collar him from a car.

Besides, they'd tried that already and the Plods had so little confidence in their ability to come across him they preferred to scupper their own chances along with his.

Big Ernie had been called out into the country to a crashed and burned car, but there was nothing for him as the scroats had made off in another motor. On his way back in he'd seen a blue light revolving and drove towards it to see if it was anything he could help with, but it had flicked off before he got close. He parked and walked in with

227

Gerald towards the engine sound.

He found the Panda with Donkey Dimmock sitting in it. He'd been assigned covert obs for the Walking Man on his patch, but he knew he couldn't find him and that if there were any break-ins whilst he was on special obs duty he would be for the high jump. It was not uncommon for Plods to be dragged out of bed and hauled in front of the Chief Super to explain themselves if there had been breaks on their bladdy patch that they should have found or prevented. So throughout the night Donkey had regularly flicked the blue light on to keep the Walking Man away.

Schafskopf. Inventive, but still a schafskopf.

He was dozing with the heater on full when Ernie crawled up and hammered on the Panda door, Gerald simultaneously standing up and staring at him through the driver's window. Apparently years later, when the Panda was sold at auction, they still hadn't removed the stains from the driver's seat.

As we headed into spring and the new financial year neared, the unused overtime was a ticking finance-bomb. Headquarters allocated the Divisions a fixed overtime budget, to be used as they wished for the twelve-month period. Chewing furiously on his pencil-stub, the Chief Super worked out what they would need to cover bank holidays, football matches and other generally fixed costs, then divided it up amongst the departments, keeping back a 'contingency fund' in case there was a big murder investigation or CID invented another new way of fiddling the system. Any that wasn't spent was not only raked back, but also knocked off next year's provision, as they could obviously manage on less.

Bosses, terrified firstly that they wouldn't have enough to last the year, held on to it like it would have to be prised from their cold dead fingers for the first ten months, then, terrified that they wouldn't spend it all, handed it out like treats from a nervous vet in the last two. If you thought 'accountant' was a risk-averse occupation, meet 'police-accountant'.

Fortuitously, it meant that Big Ernie, without dropping Donkey Dimmock in the sticky-stuff (there'd been enough of that already), was able to persuade the D.I. that dog handlers could catch the Walking Man if only they were paid extra to sit and wait for him.

Of course it wasn't all overtime, we'd have to contribute some ordinary duty time to it as well, so it meant switching the shift patterns a bit, and more night-work, but I didn't mind that. Three dogs could cover the routine work and one would be allocated just to the obs; plotted up in the dark, waiting for just one scum-bag burglar.

Big Ernie took the first week, and chose the railway yard where I'd chased and lost him. He walked in at ten o'clock with flask and sandwiches, and back out at five, cold, damp and morose.

Meanwhile we waded through the usual dross.

It was six o'clock on a midweek evening and there'd been a day-time break on the end of London Road that had an estate behind it; the Town end where the houses were cheaper.

The young couple had come home from work to find the back door kicked in and all the electrical and valuable stuff gone. Big telly, little telly, microwave oven, video recorder, stereo music system with double cassette player and record deck with a rack for LPs, radios, ghetto-blaster, radio-alarm clock, hoover, jewellery boxes, ornaments, big whisky jar half-full of small change, the lot.

These weren't rich people, but they'd worked and were enjoying the fruits of their labour. The operative word being 'were', but not anymore, because two scum of the earth had helped themselves to it.

I knew it was Paul and Colin Doyle from the smell as soon as I got out of the van, but obviously couldn't communicate it to Noddy, no matter how hard I concentrated.

'Blimey, they'd need a van to move that lot,' the Plod filling in the crime report told Noddy, 'There's a ruddy big hole in the back hedge, but I haven't been near it.'

He had. I could tell he was lying (his blood pressure and pulse increased, his breathing was more rapid, his sweating increased and contained more adrenaline and cortisol), but at least he hadn't been through it.

Paul and Colin had been through it though, many times. Their stink hung in the air, making it easy to follow them. Everybody, me included, expected the track to go straight across the back garden of the house behind, down the side and out onto the road, into a van; a fifty yard track to nowhere.

Noddy harnessed me up for appearances sake and I hopped through the hedge. There had already been a small gap, no more than a thinning of the privet, but the Doyle boys' to-ing and fro-ing had battered a hole big enough to get their mother through, and Big Claire Doyle was designed for kick-starting Jumbo jets. They didn't make 'em like her any more. They couldn't afford the materials.

Noddy followed me through and sure enough the scent took us to the back of the house on the back-to-back street. The erstwhile well-off young couple hadn't been quite affluent enough to afford a detached home on the outer reaches of the Town, but had instead settled for a semi on admittedly a nice part of the road, but that backed onto the scummier estate. It was like sticking feathers to yourself, sitting in a field going 'coo', and waiting for the pigeon season to start. You were sure to get picked-off sooner or later.

The house behind was empty, waiting refurbishment. What that meant was that the last tenant had trashed it and either been chucked out or left, and the council couldn't afford to do it up (because they'd spent all their money for the financial year last April, doing up the houses wrecked the year before).

230

But instead of the track continuing down the side and onto the front road, Paul and Colin had turned along the back of the house, and stepped over the low fence into the next garden along. I say, 'garden' because that's what it had been before the estate had gone down the pan*; now it was overgrown with couch grass and weeds, dotted with broken bicycles, mangles and the occasional ripped sofa.

Then they'd gone through the back door, which was now closed and locked. I hesitated then continued past it a few steps to make sure, but no, that's where the track went. I came back to the door and stood up against it, staring at Noddy and sending, *'Inside.'*

'Really?'

'No, just kidding, a helicopter came down and air-lifted them away with the loot. Of course, Really!'

I pushed against the door to emphasise it to him.

He tried the handle gently. It turned but the door didn't give. He peered through the window into the kitchen.

'It's empty, unoccupied.'

I was still standing with my front feet against the door, looking at him expectantly. This is one area where we lose to you. We're no good at locked doors.

'You're sure?'

'How many times do you need telling?' I stared as intently as I could, then looked back at the door, dropping to my feet to make room for him.

Noddy turned the handle to free the latch then put his shoulder to the door. It didn't give until the third shoulder-barge, when the keeper popped off the inside of the frame. That's the good thing about derelict council houses: very poor security.

Noddy tumbled inside, sprawling on the floor.

---

* Sorry, I mean, 'Tragically fallen upon hard times and tumbled into despair; the inhabitants, through no fault of their own, being failed by society'.

You probably know the philosophical thought experiment that goes, 'If a tree falls in a forest and there's no one to hear it, does it make a sound?' A similar conundrum goes, 'If a dog handler falls into a heap on the floor but there's only his dog there to see it, does it make him a prat?' The answer of course is, 'Yes, but we can't share it with his mates, so he gets away with it.' But he knew I knew he knew. And he had the good grace to go red.

But we were in. I did a quick scent scan and realised we were on our own with regard to people (or Doyles) but not with regard to property. The whole loot was stacked up in the hallway, like it was waiting for the removal men, which, in a sense, it was. They must have been too afraid to be seen shifting it in daylight and had stashed it here to come back for later.

And if they were coming back later, we'd be waiting for them. Noddy was about to radio it in when we heard a key in the front door.

He whispered, 'Heel,' and dived back into the dining room. I knew it was the dining room because the previous inhabitants had left takeaway trays and chip wrappers mouldering in the floor. But there was no furniture for cover, so we ducked to one side of the doorway as we heard the front door open.

'Ah just want t' ga through t' jew'l'ry for any decen' stuff 'fore Kev gets 'ere wi' t' van. Y' kna wot 'e's like, 'e'll want t' lot an' gie us nowt for it.'

'Aye, we dun t' 'ard wuk, luggin' it back 'ere.'

Kevin Doyle was one of the family fences. He had connections that could spirit away stolen property, but the boys would see only a fraction of either the true value, or even the reduced price uncle Kev got. They would make more hawking any decent bling around the pubs.

We heard them picking their way through the stash looking for the jewellery boxes and then, 'In 'ere, there's more light.' We were about to be busted. They were bringing the jewellery into the dining room to take

232

advantage of the streetlight glow streaming through the grimy window.

Noddy and I stepped into stepped into the doorway, shoulder to knee.

'Police with a dog, boys, stay where you are,' he growled.

I just growled.

Colin visibly slumped inside his skin, 'Mad Dog,' he sighed.

Paul stepped behind his brother and shoved him at us, using the ensuing scramble to bolt for the back door. I used it to bite Colin on the thigh; four deep fang gashes, shake and release. He screamed in pain and dropped to the floor in shock, gibbering and crying.

'Hold 'im,' Noddy inclined his head towards the now open back door, through which Paul was scarpering. Built like a cross between a weasel and a whippet (a weaspet... or a whippel?), he weighed seven stone wet through and had a turn of speed and agility honed by years of evading store detectives. I took after him as Noddy grabbed Colin by the collar and propelled him through the door.

Paul had turned right and gone back over the garden fence, hurdling it like a steeplechase champion. I didn't have to chase him, we knew who he was, but there's reputation at stake in these matters and we can't allow scum to think that they can beat us or they'll never learn not to run.

Noddy didn't have his cuffs with him, as was often the case they were lying in the van foot-well with his baton, so he shoved Colin, who was limping in an over-dramatic fashion, after us. I leaped the hedge, landing lightly on the other side to see the back of Paul clearing the next one. The back garden hurdles were on.

Still heaving the hapless Colin, Noddy radioed to the Plod at the scene to come into the garden and as he passed he threw the sobbing scroat at the hole in the hedge he'd been so keen to make a few hours earlier.

'Kevin Doyle's going to be in the front street with his van any minute now to collect the stolen gear from the derelict house behind me with the open back door. I'm chasing Paul. You keep Colin. He's bleeding from the right thigh. First Aid him. POLICE WITH A DOG STOP!'

The last was shouted not so much for the benefit of Paul, who already knew we were coming, but for any witnesses who would later back up our claim that he was fairly warned.

The Plod looked bemused but fielded Colin whilst his brain caught up with the rapidly fired information. It was fine to bite scroats when we had to, but we also had an obligation to look after them once they were our prisoners. Colin could go into shock and he was bleeding heavily from his leg. Personally I'd have used a tourniquet around his neck to stem the blood, but Noddy was often more sympathetic.

Meanwhile I was three gardens down and making ground on Paul. I was touching down as he was a stride away from the next hedge. Timing was becoming important. His technique was good. He had four strides between hedges to my two and a half, so the distance suited his flow better than mine, as I had to check halfway across each time.

His luck ran out when he tripped over a rusty bicycle half-hidden in the long grass and stumbled. He lost momentum and had to stop at the foot of the next hedge, which was neatly top-trimmed, with a four-foot lattice fence on the other side of it.

He hopped up and as he placed his foot on top of the fence I hit him from behind, crashing open-jawed into the most prominent and accessible part of him, his left buttock. He howled as we both tumbled over the fence into the freshly manured vegetable patch on the other side, his trailing foot taking out three cloches with a clash of breaking glass on the way.

I'd closed my teeth reflexively but opened again when we both hit the clart. As luck favours the just, he landed face down in it and I landed on top of him. I could smell the blood oozing from his left ankle where it had crashed through the cloches on his way down, and from

234

the fang marks on his arsch. He was lying groaning as I lightly skipped off him onto the grass path surrounding the soil-bed. This was a well-kept vegetable garden. I stood head-on in front of him, waiting for him to make his next move, every hair on my body tingling with adrenaline-charged electricity.

Noddy, running three gardens behind us, caught up to the last fence and looked over at the devastation, newly illuminated as the back kitchen light flicked on and the door opened. A corpulent bald man in a string vest and trousers held up by braces stood framed in the doorway. He had tattoos of anchors on his Popeye-like forearms and smelled of old beer, fags, and lard.

'What t' bluddy 'ell's ga-an on?' he bellowed.

''s alright mate, police. We've just detained a burglar,' Noddy informed him.

Lard-man took in the scene, 'Aye, an' flattened my bluddy leeks!' His ire was evident in the red-ness of his head decorated with purple throbbing veins starting at each temple and snaking their way over the top in an impression of the world's most convoluted subway map.

'They're ruddy championship stock they are! ...were,' he corrected himself.

Leek-growing was a highly competitive sport in working men's clubs, where large cash sums could be won by the growers of the heaviest, tallest or most perfect, and to stand a chance they had to be started early, under glass. Lard-arsch clearly had had ambitions.

Everyone looked to where his quivering finger pointed and we could just make out lines of straw-thin baby leeks, bent at right-angles where they'd been squashed by the glass frames that had been protecting their tender progress, until now.

'Championship stock!' it was more a sob now.

'Errr... sorry?' Noddy, a bit lost for words in the onslaught of emotion, fell back on the standard English response as he hopped over the fence.

'Aye, like, sorry Uncle Lee,' Paul raised his face from the ordure.

'Yore gunna pay for this.' Lard-arsch's cheeks were past flushing and heading towards a good stiff thrusting with the bog-brush as his anger built.

'Well, I can put in a request for compensation for you…' started Noddy.

'Ah'm not bluddy talkin' to youse,' came the swift reply.

'Ooooohhhhhh,' groaned Paul.

It had not been a good night. And it was getting worse as Uncle Lee Doyle stepped out in his carpet slippers, horny blackened nails poking through the tartan toe-ends, and grabbed Paul by the throat, lifting him onto his toes with his left hand until he was nose to nose.

'Help mister! I demand police protection!' squeaked Paul.

'This appears to be a family dispute, in which I am loath to interfere,' replied Noddy, as Lee drew back his fist, 'and as I haven't yet arrested you, I can't protect you as a prisoner either.'

'But I dun it! I dun the thievin' from t' posh 'owse! Y' 'ave t' arrest me!'

'I'm not sure that's serious enough to warrant an arrest,' said Noddy, as Lee's fist poised menacingly, 'I could just report you for summons. Have you done anything else?'

'Aye, yeah, I've dun loads o' stuff. I dun Mum's meter an' the phone box at t' end of t' road, an kicked-in t' Co-op winder last week.'

'Hardly the stuff of legends, is it?'

'I'll tell yer anythin', ask me anythin' an' I'll tell yer.' Paul dangled helplessly, held almost off the ground by Lee's throttling grip on his throat.

'Okay then, if the majority of the world's religions are monotheistic in nature, how can they square the dualistic belief in a struggle between good and evil? Surely the only explanation is that, if only one God

236

exists, then he must be evil?'

'Eh?' said Paul.

'Oh, I see,' replied Noddy, 'Not ANYTHING, then.'

'Ah can tell yer where 'e nicked 'is championship leeks from though.'

The air resounded with a smack like a wet fish being dropped onto a blancmange from a large height as Uncle Lee opened his hand and applied it with some force to the side of his errant nephew's head.

'Shut yer munn, man!' Uncle Lee's face was confusing rage with embarrassment. It knew it had to be red, but not quite what for.

'Whoa!' Noddy hastily intervened, stepping towards Lee, 'That'll do for now.'

'Oo sez?'

'I do. Now put Paul down gently and we'll say no more about it.'

'D' ya think I'm frit of you filth? I've boxed fo' t' Navy.'

Never one to miss an opportunity, Noddy smiled as he went with, 'You're a big man, but you're in bad shape. With me it's a full time job. Now behave yourself,' although his Michael Caine cockney twang was lost on Uncle Lee, who thought perhaps his chewing gum had got stuck.

Lee was still pondering his options when Noddy stepped around Paul, whispering, 'Watch 'im,' out of the corner of his mouth to me, as he took hold of Lee's right wrist, twisted and jerked him forwards.

Although not officially in the Manual, 'watch him' is used by handlers to warn us when something is about to kick off (like we don't know). It covers everything from 'keep an eye on him' to 'bite if he so much as blinks'. Commands are designed to be aide-memoires for witnesses, which is why they are always non-violent: 'hold him' rather than 'rip the scum-sucker's arm off'. Witnesses remember and relate, 'The policeman told his dog to watch him, so he must have done something bad to be bitten.' Perception is reality.

237

A second later Paul was back in full contact with the ground, coughing and rubbing life back into his throat, and Lee was on his tip-toes, Noddy raising him up from behind with the intertwined arm-lock. I was standing in front of Lee's gentleman jewellery showing him my best snarl.

Noddy whispered into Lee's crumpled ear, 'Haven't boxed for a bit though, have you? Now this could go two ways, and I'd like to think you'll choose the sensible option. Up to now, there's been a little misunderstanding, which I'm prepared to overlook. And I'm willing to bet there isn't even a crime report for the theft of some baby leeks, championship or otherwise, so no one has anything to worry about on that score. So, when I put you down, you're going to go back inside and I'm going to take Paul here with me. Okay?'

Noddy increased the tension on the arm-lock so that Lee had to reach even higher on his toes to stop his shoulder dislocating, but still found the bottle to ask, 'What's the other way?'

'Ah, I'm glad you asked. The other way is the one where you take a swing at me and my dog rips your bollocks off before I can stop him.' I increased the pitch of my growl from 'distant thunder' to 'jet-fighter' for effect.

'Fair 'nough, just wanted to kna'. I think t' fust yan'll be alreet.'

I backed away as Noddy released the big klumpen, gave him a little shove and stepped backwards. I spun round to heel, both of us facing Paul and Uncle Lee, whose turn it was to massage pain relief, this time into his shoulder.

'Paul, you going to be any more bother?' Noddy asked the dazed, heavily bleeding, half throttled youth, who, head still performing its own campanology extravaganza, shook it imperceptibly in reply to save the effort of speaking.

'Okay, let's go.' Noddy indicated the fence, 'Major, hup!' I hopped over and waited on the other side as Paul clambered back, considerably less gracefully than he had over the previous fences. Each time I went first and Noddy followed Paul, until we walked through the gap into the back garden of the burglary. Two – nil to us.

Kev did drive to the front of the house the gear was in and waited for a bit, but obviously Paul and Col weren't there to greet him. As he drove away again he was pulled by the waiting Panda, but he had nothing on him and nothing to connect him to the job, so he was left to go on his thieving way again. It's not like the whole world didn't know that he was fencing stolen gear anyway. He would come again.

Noddy had been right – there was no crime report for the stolen leeks, but he had a word with Big Ernie nevertheless. Big Ernie had a word with a bloke on the allotments, just passing the time of day, asking if anyone had lost any leeks, and what do you know? Soon Lee's horticultural heist became common knowledge. Everyone in the Leek Club knew what he'd done, but no one was quite sure where the knowledge had originated; fittingly, it had just sort of grown organically.

Before the spring had turned to summer, Lee's back garden was visited by an unusual nocturnal weather phenomenon, a very localised heavy shower of rock-salt, like you get in bins for gritting icy roads in winter. Doubly unusual was that it seemed to have dug itself in, rendering the soil completely useless for growing anything for years to come.

Maybe Noddy's right: if there is just one god, he must be evil.

🐾 🐾 🐾 🐾

Dogs aren't religious creatures; like most other animals, we have more sense than that. Some people like to think that we worship our humans, and there's some truth in that, but only in the way we recognise that there's a little of a god inside everything. Everything has worth and we acknowledge that in our connection with the world; but we also

239

acknowledge that the universe will expand anyway, regardless of what we do; a thing humans sometimes forget.

Call it karma, fate, kismet, wyrd, destiny, whatever. It's not predestination because what we do has effects, but it doesn't revolve around us, or our gods. It's not organised, it just happens. What all dogs are trying to do is to make the best of the kacke going on around us.

We can ask our gods for help, like asking the god of scents to send us a favourable wind, or our human to hurry up and open the tin of meaty lumps*, but we don't expect them to respond every time. We know they don't always hear us because they are capricious, but we keep asking because sometimes they understand and answer. In this way we all control our own destinies, up to a point.

We keep the right side of the gods, ask their help when we need it, and receive our just deserts. If you're a, 'Ba-a-ad Do-o-og,' you'll be treated badly by the universe, but if you're a, 'Good Dog!' you'll be treated well.

If you're a street dog in Mumbai that means there'll be some offal to scavenge some days and not too many fleas biting you. If you're a German Shepherd Police Dog you will be well fed, well cared for by a human with at least half a brain, and be allowed to straighten the path of other, errant, pond-scum-sucking low-life, humans. In fact, you have won the lottery of life.

Big Ernie's gods didn't favour him for the week he sat in the railway yard. He didn't get a whiff of the Walking Man, but the scroat hit three houses that backed onto a riverbank on the opposite side of Town. We all knew we were in this for the long haul, but you always hope for a quick result. Except me. We weren't scheduled onto the obs until the

---

* Manufacturing dog food in this is of course a diabolical conspiracy to prevent dogs from taking over the world. If we could use a tin-opener…

240

third week, so I didn't want him caught before then.

Day shifts can be a bit boring as much of the time is spent mopping up breaks and other crimes where the scroats are long gone, and catching them at it isn't an option.

The night Arthur & Beddo took over the obs we were on the dayshift. A couple of meter-jobs, where the honest and upright householders had reported a break-in where nothing had gone but the contents of the electric meter – yeah, right, of course. I could smell their guilt whilst I padded round the patch of mud that passed for garden, looking for the 'point of entry' that wasn't there.

I stood in the muck and looked hard at Noddy, *'What are we doing this for? We both know they're lying.'*

'Yes, I know mate, there's nothing here, but we go through the motions anyway. Come on, we'll go for a ratch.'*

Mid-morning found us in the grounds of an abandoned factory-shop on the edge of the Riverbank estate.

When scroats thieve they often discard the unwanted parts of their proceeds in out-of-the-way places where no one looks. Except us. Over the years we've found safes, cashboxes, jewellery boxes, handbags, all with and without their contents. They are all evidence and at the very least worth collecting for SOCOs to examine. An identified print lifted off the inside of a cashbox is a reason for CID to lift the print's owner.

We were ratching through the overgrown shrubbery when I came across a familiar smell. Pungently threatening, testosterone with an overlay of sly, devious and shifty. It was the mange and hint of distemper that finally gave it away. Wendy.

I stiffened and inhaled the air. Yes and wherever Wendy went, Satan and Killa weren't far away. The reek of Ba-a-a-d Do-o-o-g-g

---

* Ratch - to search or rummage about. Most dogs are permanently on the ratch, we just don't always know what for.

permeated the rough garden like lavender in an old people's home. My nose wrinkled in disgust just as Satan hit me behind the right shoulder.

The shoulder barge is a good move that can knock a dog off his feet and Satan had exploded from the undergrowth behind and to my right. Although I wasn't ready for it he didn't have the weight to topple me and I rode the blow by skipping to my left as he glanced past.

I recognised his scent signature and knew he wouldn't have the courage to try me on his own. Noddy was twenty yards behind me, pushing his way through the brambles and overgrown bushes.

Killa came fast from my left, teeth burying into my ruff, and I knew I had to move before Satan was able to turn. The ruff-bite is a killer if you've hold of a smaller animal, but Killa didn't have the jaws to harm me and as I sprang forwards I reached under him and grabbed his leg, pulling it with me and wrenching hard. I heard the tendons in his shoulder twang and he screamed.

'Major!' Noddy had heard Killa's agony and plunged into the undergrowth towards us, but I was on my own. Humans are useless in a dog-fight.

Then Wendy played his hand, coming at me hard, low and head-on, trying for a throat-bite. I was taller than he was and it was an obvious move, so I parried with my shoulder and we collided like stags.

'You smell like a puppy on heat.' He taunted me with what he thought passed for insults.

'Come on you powder-puff-Pomeranian, let's finish this,' I goaded him, 'I can't stand your freshly-bathed smell much longer.'

Dogs like things to smell natural. Changing smells by using soap and shampoo is an anathema to us. Baths are disgusting. Calling a dog 'freshly bathed' is like telling a human they stink.

As we circled each other, looking for an opportunity to strike, Satan grabbed me from behind. The hock-bite is a disabler. He was trying to rip out my tendons   my hamstring in particular   to put me on three

242

legs, but I felt his charge and tucked under as he hit me. He caught a mouthful of hair from my right thigh, and took a gouge out of me with a top canine tooth.

I spun around to confront him and Wendy lunged at my tail. As I looked to protect my back, Satan lunged for a throat bite. I stepped to my right and bit down on the back of his neck. I bore down with all the strength I had, reared up onto my back legs, lifting him off the ground, and I shook him like the rat he was.

It would have killed a smaller dog by snapping its spine, and I had no right to expect it to work on such a large beast, but the frenzied whiplash stunned Satan's tiny brain and he landed heavily on his back as I threw him to the side. Wendy looked at me aghast, and fled.

I took after him as he ducked and dived through and under the bushes. This was not finished. The grounds were surrounded by a chain-link fence, which, like so many others, was broken down.

Wendy knew where the gaps were and flew under one without breaking stride. I came upon it a second later and leapt over the top. I didn't know it right away, but Wendy was heading for the safety of home, which was only forty yards away.

The Riverbank estate, as you would expect, was on the bank of a river. But the bank was a tall one and the river a long way down; it looped away, forming a great water-meadow. The effect was of a huge amphitheatre that could be seen from the back gardens of the houses and beyond them the school playground, along the top of the ridge.

Wendy had a bolt-hole in the back garden fence, but running from me along the top of the ridge meant he would have to slow down to cut in at right angles. And if he slowed down I would be on him.

By all the gods, he was fast though. I was bigger and heavier, with a longer stride and the strength to use it, but although lighter than me, he had the build of a sprinter – deep elliptical chest housing massive lungs, a roached back for leg extension and muscular thighs for propulsion.

I coursed him like he was a hare. He shot past his back garden and along the ridge, with me two strides behind him. Noddy was watching from behind the fence he hadn't bothered to climb. He had metaphorically removed his helmet* and was merely another spectator.

I say 'another' spectator because I was aware of an increasing number of people coming to the edge of their gardens to watch. By the time we'd run the half-mile length of the ridge to where the field hedge barred our way, most of the estate and children from the school were watching and cheering one or other of us on. Wendy turned downhill towards the river,

He had the home support of course, but there were those (who had probably suffered at his jaws in the past) who were shouting for Mad Dog. Always keen to take advantage of an opportunity for free entertainment, neighbours were placing wagers with each other on the likelihood of Wendy making it.

I registered all this, but only vaguely, like you'd register the wallpaper when you are chasing a burglar from your house. It's there. You know it's there. But you are too intent on the job in hand.

I was mad. I'd been set up by Wendy and his gang. There was no doubting it had been a trap. Probably a hastily assembled, but a trap nonetheless. Satan and Killa had paid their price. They'd never bother me again. But Wendy still had to pay. My temporary insanity was a red mist that descended and blocked out all else but the dire-wolf inside me. When I caught him I'd kill him; no quarter; cry 'havoc'…

But catching him was proving problematic. He made ground on me on the turn as my weight pushed me wider than the line he took. As we started on the downhill stretch I'd dropped three paces on him, but

---

* Police training school advice for the times when they are at a complete loss and have no idea what to do is 'Take your helmet off and mingle with the crowd'.

244

weight is an advantage running downhill.

The crowd roared as I closed the gap. I was almost touching his tail as he veered right along the river bank. It was either that or jump the river, and even he wasn't that stupid. The turn lost me ground again, but now we had an even surface in a straight line it was about muscle power, and I had more.

He streaked across the top of the short and sandy turf that was regularly washed by the river over-spilling, and I pounded hard in his wake. I wasn't panting, I was grabbing huge lung-fuls of air. Each stride stretched my body, pulling my diaphragm like bellows, dragging air deep inside me, only to be expelled again when I contracted. I was an engine fuelled by anger.

The problem of course was that Wendy too had fuel. Yes, he was lighter on his feet; yes, he was built for speed; but more than that he was running for his life. And that's what was giving him the edge; fear. I was as mad as a kicked wasps' nest and would kill him if I could. And he knew it.

Running for your life is always more motivating than any other reason. It's why prey escapes from even the most impressive predators. Wolf packs on average only kill on one out of every five hunts. Four prey escape with their lives for every one that loses theirs.

I was running hard because I wanted the arsch-tropft dead. I was running for pride, for anger, for justice. Wendy was running harder because he didn't want to die. If he wanted to live this was his last chance. Win the race or die. Your own life is a prize worth putting in the extra effort for.

We were both tiring by the time we came level with Wendy's home high on the banking above us. I knew what he was doing. He would make the last right turn that would take him straight up the hill so he could slip through the hole on the fence into his own garden and safety.

He had to hit it square on so that he didn't need to slow down and

245

risk me catching him at the death.

In anticipation I changed my heading so I was on the inside track. He could see me in his peripheral vision* outside his right flank and he knew that I'd out-thought him. When he made his move he would have to turn across my path.

But whilst I had the brains, he had the adrenaline, and when he banked right he put on a spurt that took him in front of me. I snapped at his backside as he went past, but he'd tucked it under and I missed, my momentum taking me past him. I lost valuable speed and time veering round as he took off up the hill.

The crowd were going wild, cheering and stamping as we sprinted towards them and I closed the gap to four strides, muscles burning with one final effort, then three, then two, then...

The world went black. Wendy lithely skimmed under the gap one pace ahead of me and I hit his home fence like a ton of bricks. Like a ton of bricks fired from a cannon at point blank range.

I lay there groaning, vaguely aware of about a hundred people cheering, as the world spun around and slowly came back into focus. As I stood up and looked at the hole under the fence, I was seething, but knew Wendy would be long gone and any further attempt at pursuit would be pointless.

'Major,' Noddy's voice wasn't unkind as he grinned, leaning over the fence I'd chased Wendy through a lifetime ago, although in reality only seconds had passed.

'C'mon mate, time to go.'

I padded over, slightly dazed, and he kindly lifted the chain-link to ease my way under.

'Time to take your helmet off.'

I ached for a week afterwards, but you can't let it show. The next

---

* About 250° of vision compared to your puny human 120°. Yet again we win.

246

evening we were in the old part of town, just off the centre, where the streets were still cobbled and the houses terraced. After every fourth house a ginnel gave access round the back and whilst some had individual back yards others were open-plan grassed areas that afforded more space for the kiddly-winks to play, and much less security.

We were met by a Panda-Plod who told us the end-terrace had been done in the last five minutes and the elderly lady had seen the poisonous scum leg it out of the back door. Teenaged boy, jeans, trainers, blue jacket and United hat. He'd sneaked in through the unlocked back door, taken her purse and legged it when she came into the kitchen. She only saw his back as he left.

'Probably out the ginnel onto the street, but you never know, so we asked for you,' the Plod told Noddy as I jumped out of the van.

I wandered over to the Panda and cocked my leg on the wheel. As I walked back past the Plod I caught a familiar whiff from the crotch area. I didn't know she knew Smiddy that well.

'Has anybody been in the back since?' asked Noddy.

'Na, I've looked out the back door but that's all. It's open lawn through to the end of the block.'

The chances were indeed that the kid had gone straight back onto the street down the ginnel, but all evidence is useful, so Noddy knocked on the door and asked the lady if we could come through.

Starting from where the scum had last been seen gave us the best chance. There are often lots of tracks to choose from when they fasten you in a harness and say, 'Seek', and whilst sometimes the fearful smell of the perpetrator comes though like a beacon telling me which one to follow, in a place where there are a lot of scum there could be many perpetrator's tracks. After all, everyone is guilty of something.

I once went to a sneak-theft at a garage and followed a guilty-smelling track from the scene only to find myself at the door of a man who'd forgotten his wife's birthday and was making it up to her with filling-station-flowers. Luckily we arrived just in time to save her from committing his murder. Sometimes destiny just works.

'Now then love,' Noddy said to the elderly lady, 'Did he take your kettle?'

'No son, I was coming into the kitchen to fill it when I saw the little bug'r.'

'Good-oh, is that it I can hear whistling?'

'No, but I can soon put it on.'

'Lovely m' dear. Milk and one sugar please, I'll be back when Major and I have had a look round.'

The request for tea wasn't so much because Noddy wanted a cup, but it would keep the lady in the house and out of the way whilst we worked.

Afterwards Noddy could sit down with her and chat about this and that. This and that being: who was betting or drinking more heavily than usual, which local kid had a new skateboard, or whose wife was suddenly flush enough to buy new clothes, and did she know of any bloke who liked to go for long walks in the evenings? Walking-Man was never far from our thoughts.

I picked up the track inside the back door but waited whilst Noddy harnessed me up before setting off into the garden. I checked back to the left. Yes, he'd come in over the wall, but he'd gone right towards the ginnel. The track looped as he'd run out of the door then swung away down the grass. It was easy to follow, but although it had a faint familiarity about it, it wasn't anyone I knew. Probably a Doyle connection, but there were so many half and quarter cousins, and back-crosses to parents and siblings.

The track went straight down the back gardens. Each garden was marked only by its proximity to the house, with no hedges between making it easier for the council to cut the grass. Washing lines were

248

strung from the house wall to the back fence at regular intervals, but Noddy ducked under each one as we trotted to the end.

I looked at Noddy and back at the end wall, '*Over here, by the bins.*'

He'd used the dustbin to give himself a leg-up over the wall. We walked round through the ginnel and back onto the street to where he'd dropped down again. I picked him up and followed more slowly as he'd crossed the street, the hard surface not retaining as much scent and the disturbance confusing it slightly. He'd gone straight across and over the wall into the next block along.

'*Straight over again.*' I told Noddy.

'Let's go over this one mate,' he replied, so I scaled the six-foot brick wall and as I perched on the top could smell the purse below me. I dropped down and swung round, staring at the bin. Noddy landed heavily beside me and lifted the lid. The smell of the old lady wafted out, and he picked up the purse, dropped it into an evidence bag and thrust it in his pocket.

The scum had lingered here to empty the purse of cash and the track was stronger. I took off again and Noddy paid the rope out, setting off as his hand reached the end of it. The track went out over the far wall again and I barely paused as I hopped over, crossed the street and over into the next set of gardens, Noddy keeping pace all the way. We were gaining on the pond-life. I picked up speed and loped across the next lawn, Noddy running to keep up.

Which is probably why he didn't see the washing line strung across his path. At neck height. The tension on my line increased momentarily then ceased altogether as he gave a strangled gasp, was first propelled horizontal as the momentum of his legs took them high into the air, hovered for a split second, and then fell like he was poleaxed as gravity claimed him.

The washing line twanged back into place.

The dull thud as he hit the deck reverberated around the close and brought the family to the back door as Noddy sat up, embarrassment fighting the pain for dominance. Mother was first in the doorway, built like a brick out-house with a curly perm and lipstick, her flowery apron stained with what was hopefully gravy.

'Wha' d' you want?' Mum asked past the fag-end hanging from the corner of lips painted in the shape of a cherub's bow, below a half-decent moustache.

'...air...' wheezed Noddy.

I stood where I'd stopped, which was incidentally the end of the track. What wind there was in the sheltered back gardens was behind us, and I'd overshot the turn. I lifted my nose and picked up the scent again, turning right towards the door in which Mum was still framed and Dad was pushing past her. He was one of those weedy men that marry big women, wearing the obligatory off-duty slacker uniform of trousers and tucked-in vest, both of which had been made for someone several sizes larger. The Oxfam shop had a lot to answer for.

'Are you awreet lad? Yer look a funny colour.'

Noddy was still doing an inventory of his body parts to make sure they were all in the right places after the unexpected pounding.

'Aye... Just got taken out... By your washing line... I'm police... Have you seen a teenager... Wearing jeans, trainers, a blue jacket... And a United hat... Come through here...?'

A gawky youth wearing jeans, trainers, a blue jacket and a United hat appeared in the doorway behind Mum and as one we turned to stare at him. He had his father's build and his mother's moustache.

'Stuart! You little bastud! What 'ave I tole you about not shittin on your own doorstep?' his doting mother yelled, turning to cuff him around the head with a shovel-like hand.

Stuart did what every self-respecting little scroat did when identified in the presence of his parents: he ran. Ducking under his Mum's flapping hinge-wing he bolted for the ginnel.

250

'Police-th-dog. Stop-r-I-send-dog,' croaked Noddy, and nodded at me. Still wearing the harness and with the line trailing behind me I took off after him.

I didn't see which way he went at the street end of the ginnel and his scent was just a huge puddle of fear with no obvious direction, so I had to pause to look. He had gone right and was pounding straight down the street in blind panic, arms and legs pumping like pistons.

I sped after him, neither of us looking as we crossed the first road, and then the second as I neared my take-off for the bite. One more stride and I'd have his arm, but for him glancing over his scrawny shoulder and leaping for the lamppost straight in front of him. He swarmed up the pole like a monkey as my impetus took me flying past underneath, braking desperately and reaching ineffectually up for his leg.

By the time I'd turned he'd scampered to the top and was clinging on with his arms and legs like a novelty pencil-eraser. I bayed at him to come down. I'd earned this bite. I'd tracked from... well, from about here... and chased him all the way back. I deserved a bite! I barked louder in frustration.

Our little old lady victim opened the front door of her house, outside which we'd exactly ended our chase, to see what the commotion was. She took in the scene without much comprehension, looking first at me, bouncing and barking, then up at the lamp-post.

'Stuart, what are you doing up there?'

'Sorry auntie Barbara,' wailed Stuart.

'Auntie... Barbara?' Noddy was still having breathing difficulty, not helped by his dash down the road after us, 'Do you know... This little f... Fellow?'

'Yes, o' course, Stuart's my nephew's son. Lives up the street.'

Weedy and Outhouse had joined us and I gave up when Noddy told me to, 'heel'. I knew I'd recognised the scent when I'd left the back door, but it wasn't a vague familiarity with a Doyle, it was a familiarity twice removed with the victim! He was her great nephew and I'd spotted the distant scent-resemblance, but not twigged it.

Thieving. Nothing like keeping it in the family is there?

🐾🐾🐾🐾

Obs are boring. Everybody thinks that waiting to catch bad guys is exciting, until they actually do it. They only think of the burst of action when the Sweeney swoop on the blaggers, all yelling, running and punching, and not the seemingly endless hours of waiting, not daring to move or make a sound in case the targets are just about to arrive.

Over the years I've done loads of obs. If CID get a tip-off they always think it's a guaranteed job, but often waiting for it to happen takes place after the pubs are open, and no self-respecting detective will tie himself up on obs when the pubs are open; too many 'informants' to liaise with. So we dogs get the job. And who better to catch the septic-sores on the backsides of humanity if they run?

On occasions the premises to be hit are licensed, a pub or a club, and on those jobs CID have been known to lend a hand. I've done obs where Noddy has had to pour the sleeping detective into the car that came to collect him in the morning, having lost the capacity for independent movement in direct correlation to the consumption of the whisky left out for him by the landlord, 'to keep the cold out'. If that's what whisky does, he should have been aflame by the time we'd finished.

Usually though there are long hours of waiting in varying degrees of discomfort, often concealed in undergrowth to cut off escape routes, sometimes inside the premises to pounce on them red-handed and other times parked up round the corner in the van, to bear down on them with the wrath of the righteous.

More than half the time they don't show. There could be many reasons for a no-show, from the original info having been falsely fed to the CID for a laugh, to the scroats bottling it, getting lost on the way to the job, or getting locked up for something else.

One job was called off when we were waiting inside a bank for scroats to come through the wall in a JCB. We later found they couldn't get the JCB started so they'd given up and gone home.

Another was a drug hand-over that never took place because the courier was locked up for shoplifting a chocolate bar at motorway services. The Traffic-Plod who pulled his car later searched it and found two carrier bags crammed with kilo blocks of cannabis. Truly a case of the munchies getting the better of a dope-head.

The public tend to view criminals as masters of their trade (I blame television) but they're mostly not. They're thugs, many without two brain cells to rub together. But the Walking Man was a cut above.

He'd done at least thirty breaks since last summer and not been caught. He'd been close a couple of times, but he didn't panic. He only ever took what would go in his pocket, and nothing identifiable had ever been fenced. When he took identifiable jewellery it hadn't shown in the local dealers so far as we could find. All he carried was a hand-awl and a pair of gloves. There was no discernible pattern to his breaks, in location, days of the week, or frequency. SOCO had lifted fibres from his clothing at points of entry, but fibre-recognition wasn't yet an art that could identify him, until we had his clothes to match them to.

I knew him by scent. I had him down as an office worker, because all I could smell of his job was paper. He was never drunk on any job I tracked him from, and his food varied. He wasn't ill.

I'd even seen him at the Boxing Day match, but that didn't help.

Noddy had decided, after talking it through with the other handlers, that the best place for our week would be the school field. We could have done a day here and another there, but without a pattern to the breaks we were as likely to miss or hit him anywhere. Picking one spot and sticking to it just seemed more organised than chopping and changing.

It was a good hide though. The school field split into two, between infants and juniors, and was divided by a short metal fence and ditch. The ditch was a remnant of when it had been a farmer's field, but the improved drainage meant it was always dry now. Slap bang in the middle of the field the fence had been broken down by the kiddiewinks and that's where we made our den.

We had direct line-of-sight on all four sides; the school on one and the gardens of the houses that backed onto the other three. Because of the pleasant aspect to the rear, most houses had a low fence separating them from the school field and we were within about seventy-five yards of all of them.

Walking Man had broken into three of the houses at various times, although it's possible he'd hit others and not taken anything if they had no cash or portables he was interested in. With nothing missing and no obvious entry, many householders didn't know they'd been burgled.

Noddy got a Plod to drop us at the school, and we hopped the school fence to get in. Nobody from the school knew we were there; they didn't need to.

Noddy carried his bait, flask, tracking harness, torch and lead. He wore full waterproofs and wellies because even if it didn't rain the ground would be wet by the morning dew. That made him clumpy and clumsy, but he wasn't going to need to move fast. That's what I was for.

One of the few things we knew was that Walking Man always worked in the early hours, so we went into the ditch each night at eleven and walked back out of the estate to be picked up on the main road at five, when the early-shift factory workers started moving about.

Walking out of the estate involved passing the bakery just as the day's first batch of pies came out of the oven. There were always two mis-shapen or broken that the baker couldn't possibly have sold, and

254

he was happy to have our company for the few minutes it took us to eat them; two seconds in my case.

Dogs can eat quickly because we only need to chomp and swallow. The necessity for humans to chew food for much longer is the price you pay for the ability to speak. The same evolutionary process that resulted in the human larynx moving down your throat so you can make a wide range of noises means you cannot breath and swallow at the same time or you choke, because your pharynx serves as a conduit for air going to and from the lungs and for fluids going to the stomach. Other mammals can breathe and swallow easily without choking because the oesophagus (to the stomach) and trachea (to the lungs) separate much higher up, but we can't speak. Fair trade I think. Speaking is way over-rated.

You see many things when you are on obs, especially looking onto back bedrooms. Things that shouldn't be seen; traumatic things that sear themselves onto your memory, despite attempts to expunge them from your recollection.

People, hear this plea. Even if you think that no one can see into your bedroom, please have a thought for the poor police dog on obs, and draw the curtains. And switch the light off. That applies to the back kitchen as well. And I hope you're going to wipe that table down before you use it for food preparation again. Properly, with disinfectant.

I was just glad the weather was still cold enough to prevent any al-fresco shenanigans. Many's the time I've heard and homed-in on rustling noises in the bushes, only to find amorous couples (and sometimes more than couples) locked in passionate embrace.

I remember the first time not knowing what the heaving beast with two backs was up to, and sniffed at the white buttocks in front of me as they rose to meet my cold nose, bringing a terrified shriek from their owner and a satisfied moan from his girlfriend, as he instinctively flinched away from me. You can't un-see things like that. I always hope it is a hedgehog rustling in the undergrowth now.

The first nights were damp and drizzly; not bucketing it down but with enough rain to make it unpleasant to lie out, and there was little movement anywhere. It was a long week.

By the last night the mundanity of the routine had crept in, but at least the weather had improved. There was enough of a covering of light cloud to shield the crescent moon, but no rain. The only light we had was the dirty yellow sheen of the sodium streetlamps, but we were used to it. There'd been no Walking Man breaks reported at all during the week, but that's not to say he hadn't been about, just that no one had noticed.

At two o'clock I heard the barely audible flick of the window latch. I'd been watching and there was no way he'd come through the field, so I sat up and looked towards the noise, confident that my silhouette was broken by the longer grass and weeds growing up the fence. He must have walked down the side from the street.

I picked up the slight scuffling of him climbing through the window and the faintest 'tap' as he closed it behind him, but saw no movement.

'He's here,' I told Noddy with a low growl.

He rolled onto his front and peered over the rim of the ditch in the same direction, picking up my excitement. It's uncanny how animal-like humans can sometimes be, when they're not too busy being human.

Then he blew it again by asking, 'Where is he?'

I knew he only said it to conceal his anxiety that we may have lost him already, but really? 'Where is he?'

'He's in a house and we're waiting for him to come out with the nicked stuff so we can rip his arm off. That's where he is.' I tried to convey the gist of the sentiment with a look, but I'm fairly sure it was lost on him.

Tick.. tock.. it is said dogs have no concept of time, which is true up to a point because we don't care what the numbers on your clocks say,

256

but we're very good at waiting. We spend our lives waiting for humans to do something or other.

I strained every fibre of hearing and sight for the movement I knew would eventually come. My nose checked, but we were too far away for scent to play a part. I narrowed the sound down to two possible houses directly opposite our position halfway across the field. I knew it was the Walking Man. I don't know how I knew, but I knew. Even Noddy knew and he often doesn't know which way up he is.

If he came out the back he had seventy-five yards to go in any direction before he got out of the field, unless he went back the way he came when he clocked me. I had seventy-five yards to cover to make sure of catching him.

If he left by the front door we'd be stuffed. With luck we'd hear it snick closed, but then we'd both need to leg it across the field, trying to get sight of him before he disappeared. Or it'd be a track; a slow track on hard surface with residual disturbance from the day's road traffic.

These are the times that dogs pray; *'Please, let him come out the back. Please.'* We were both quivering with the tension, and Noddy was worried we may lose him out the front. So was I.

Noddy spoke quietly into his radio, sending Pandas to the edge of the estate, but not too close. The sound of an engine approaching might have spooked him, and the sight of a Panda would definitely have had him legging it. Softly softly catchy scroaty as they say.*

We could have done with being closer as he came out, but I knew

---

* The Concise Oxford Dictionary of Proverbs notes that more correct (but probably less politically correct) form of the saying, 'Softly softly catchee monkey' was the motto of the Lancashire Constabulary Training School and the inspiration for the name of the popular 1966 BBC TV Z-Cars spin-off 'Softly Softly', which featured Police Dog Inky with his handler PC Snow. Inky must have demanded too many smarties in his dressing room because he was killed off after one series (heroically shot dead on duty) and replaced by Radar. Inky's death caused such a furore of grief that the dog that played him appeared on Blue Peter to assure children that he still lived.

that standing up would take our silhouettes above the fence line and Noddy would stand out like a sore thumb. Even more than usual.

Then came the sound I'd been longing to hear, the soft click of the back door as it closed behind him. My heart soared. He was coming out the back, not the front.

'*Thank you gods!*' It's only polite to acknowledge the favour.

I saw the movement as he climbed into our field and heard the fence creak in protest. I licked my lips and opened my mouth to pant slightly as Noddy elbowed forwards and slipped his cold but sweaty hand through my collar.

He started the whispered mystical chant into my ear, 'Police with a dog! Stop! Stop or I'll send the dog! Police with a dog! Stop! Stop or I'll send the dog!' over and over. He thought he was doing it to prime me, but I didn't need priming this time. I'd waited there a week. I'd tracked him, and I'd seen him. I'd even started a chase after him. I was having him this time.

The yellow light was murky and at that distance I couldn't make out detail, but I saw him start away from the fence to cut the diagonal towards the back of the school. No lights had come on at the house, so they didn't yet know they'd been done over. The Walking Man would have cash and hopefully jewellery on him; something identifiable to tie him to the break.

Still the whispered chant, 'Police with a dog! Stop! Stop or I'll send the dog!' Noddy could see the distant figure as well, walking smartly away from the house and towards his destiny, in which I was about to feature in my own modest way.

I pulled into my collar against Noddy's hand and risked looking away from my prey to glance at him imploringly.

'*Now! I'm ready! Come on!*'

Noddy lumbered out of the ditch. He was stiff from lying still for so long but managed to burst upright and stagger forwards, trying to find his balance on numb legs.

He was still stumbling when he whispered, 'Hold him, son!' into my ear and slipped his hand from my collar. I didn't need to be told twice. I didn't need to be told at all, but I'm sure it helped to make him feel a part of the team. He was only a minor player at that stage, but it keeps his morale up if he thinks he has helped.

My nails dug in to the soft earth as I made the first short strides to power me to full stretch, and time stood still. The Walking Man was reduced to slow motion and I was a blur. Legs pounding, hardly touching down before taking off again, eyes narrowed, ears flat back against my head, tail streaming out behind for balance over the uneven ground.

I don't know if he sensed me or saw the dark shape of Noddy lumbering towards him, but when I was halfway there the Walking Man looked up. It didn't matter. He couldn't make it back to the fence before I hit him. Noddy saw him look and let rip at the top of his voice.

'POLICE WITH A DOG! STOP! STOP OR I'LL SEND THE DOG!'

The prey paused aghast for a fraction of a second then turned towards the fence. I smiled inwardly because I'd been running diagonally towards his left hand side. There was no easy bite from that angle and I might have had to take a leg just to put him down. But by turning away he'd presented his back to me.

I made one last half-stride to maximise power and launched from five yards. I timed my bite in the air and hit his right arm, clamping down just below his elbow on my way down. My weight spun him around and down to the ground, throwing him onto his back, but I held on tightly. A text-book take-down.

It's a serious thing to ask a dog to do, to take down a man. Dogs are almost automatically subservient to humans; our evolutionary survival has depended upon us being useful, cute, no trouble. Historically the dogs that survived to reproduce weren't the aggressive ones. They were the ones who backed off, who didn't challenge people. Those genes for deference take some overcoming.

Sure, dogs do attack people, but it's only usually when they have been pushed so far they've snapped. They've lost the plot and gone berserk. But people always have the last say and they often kill the dog. Sure, they phrase it nicely, 'put to sleep'. But the dog dies, along with its genes.

It takes a lot of training, and a lot of bottle, to overcome our natural reticence. It takes a certain mind-set to get your head around it being the right thing to do. It's easy when the guy is an intruder, coming into your territory, when your back is against the wall and defence is all you have left. If he keeps coming the choice to bite is an easy one, but even then we warn him by barking first.

To chase a man down when he's running away, not on your home territory, when he's not offering any threat, you have to think of him as prey. There are natural prey animals, like rabbits and deer, that only have to run to be tempting, but a man is not one of them. The dog was the first animal to be domesticated, not by force, not captured and subdued, but by voluntarily coming to the hearth. Ten thousand years of domestication is a lot to go up against.

I manage it quite well. There's always an extra edge, a slight fear, not of the conflict, but of having done something wrong. I overcome my natural reticence by doing it to the best of my ability.

The wind went out of the Walking Man as he hit the floor and his arm twisted in my mouth. I went down onto my shoulder, but was back up on my feet in a flash, and thrashed my head side to side like a terrier with a rat to stop him from moving. As I stood over him I could see the fear in his eyes, and the pain.

He was on his back looking up at a big black dog that was sporting a ridge of erect hair down its neck and back, holding his arm in a grip like a vice, teeth penetrating down to the bone, snarling bloody phlegm

260

at him. By all the gods, I'm good.

Noddy thundered up behind us and smiled, 'Good lad.'

'Keep still,' he fiercely told the Recumbent Man, then, softly to me, 'Major, leave.'

My teeth chattered as I forced my jaws apart. It wasn't easy. I'd won it. It was mine. Letting go wasn't the natural thing to do. Then the training took over and Noddy called me to heel, where I lay down, daring the prey to move, to run again. No chance, he was as quiet as a sleeping Saluki.

Noddy cuffed him, checked his wounds were sufficiently impressive and, before he walked him through the school to Section Van, checked his pockets. The bulge in his jeans pocket was a roll of fivers and tenners; undoubtedly stolen, but hard to prove. In the right flap of his camo-jacket was a small hand awl and in the back poacher's pocket was a handful of watches, necklaces and other jewellery.

Identifiable.

Bang to rights.

🐾🐾🐾🐾

Then I recognised him. The Walking Man, or as I prefer to call him, the Bleeding Man, was the Council Caretaker. But of course you knew that already didn't you? In any mystery where the dog is the hero, narrative determinism insists that it has to be the caretaker wot done it.

Some narratives are so strong that they force a path into the story, so you know that if a little girl takes a shortcut through the woods on her way to visit Grandma, a wolf will not be far behind, or if a young person is forced into drudgery in the cinders (or an under-stairs cupboard, or on a forsaken planet) you just know they will one day get their prince (or wand, or light-sabre).

I really don't know how the Caretaker resisted the urge to say, 'I would have gotten away with it if it hadn't been for you pesky kids!' but he somehow managed. Sadly, neither did he have a fairground clown, or any other kind of mask.

Except in a way he did, because he had no previous criminal form, not even a parking ticket, and everyone was astounded that the law-abiding, polite chap in the council offices, who thought that saying 'blimey' was a bit strong, was a dedicated burglar.

In interview he said he didn't know why he'd done it, but it was obviously for the thrill. He remembered every single job and, when CID took him on a drive around, his arm heavily bandaged, he pointed out a dozen more that had no idea he'd been in their bedrooms whilst they were asleep.

When TF turned over his mother's house, where he (naturally) still lived, they found his bedroom was an Aladdin's cave of bling. He'd spent the cash (wisely, of course) but had no idea what to do with the jewellery. He'd taken it, but didn't know any fences or what else to do with it, so he'd kept it all, each piece a trophy, a memento of his daring.

But this tale was never meant to be a who-dunnit, or even a how-or-why-he-dunnit; it was always a how-a-police-dog-does-it.

Would he ever have been caught in any other way? No form, no trace of the stolen goods, not obviously carrying anything, no vehicle to stop, no one to suspect him. Sneaking out of sight in the dark spaces; riverbanks, railways and fields where Plods rarely venture. He could have been nabbed in the act by an irate householder, but they were always going to be half-asleep, and he took the precaution of opening a door to escape through as soon as he broke in.

No, the chances were that without our intervention he would have continued to blight people's lives for years, but he'd been taken down by the long canine teeth of the law, and now he was banged up, sharing a cell with a big bearded biker who liked to call him 'Shirley'.

We may provide a service, but I definitely joined a Police Force.

So, if you're thinking of a career in crime, remember this:

I can predict the weather and sense if you're ill, I can see faster and further and hear more clearly, I react quicker and am alert even when I'm asleep, I know where you've been and how long ago, I can trace your movements in space and time, I can run faster and further, and withstand the cold and the wet, I can communicate without words, and I know when you are lying and when you are guilty. I can take you down.

Mind how you go now.

Lightning Source UK Ltd.
Milton Keynes UK
UKHW02f1501250218
318458UK00017B/370/P